The Final Alibi

The Lawson Chronicles
Book 1

Simon King

D1739205

First Printing: 2019

For George,

my brother.
You saved my life when I was 9 years old.
I've never forgotten.

The Final Alibi

The Lawson Chronicles
Book 1

Contents

Chapter 1: The Time Before

1.

"You'll get used to it, kid. Trust me." It was my partner Warren, sounding almost academic, as I tried to steady myself, one hand firmly gripping the doorframe for balance. The smell had overwhelmed me with such speed that my breakfast had already fallen at my feet before I had a chance to try and stop it. Warren had been a great mentor, showing me the ins and outs of the job with youthful enthusiasm, himself now almost 20 years in uniform. He understood that it was hard when you first started and I had only been in Cider Hill a little over a year. The killer's victims had numbered 9 then, a large number already, but no-one was really prepared for just how long the monster would elude us. I fought my stomach back under control and wiped my mouth with a handkerchief. Warren gave me a pat on the back and resumed searching the room for evidence.

Victim 14, as we would come to know her, had been suspended by her wrists from a rope thrown over one of her living-room ceiling beams, her hands bound with a thick cord. She was naked except for her shoes, black leather T-straps. I approached the body, careful not to interfere with anything around the room and looked at her face. Both of her index fingers had been chewed off at the base and forced into her eye sockets, both eye-balls still oozing gelatinous remnants down her cheeks. We were guessing that it was some sick signature which he had adopted, to let us know it was him. The eye-balls and the fact most of her right thigh had been chewed off, confirmed our worst fears. Lucifer, as the locals had dubbed him, had killed again.

2.

Susan Heidenberg had lived alone in the house on Pickets Lane for almost two months, having moved from Melbourne earlier in the year to take up a teaching position at the prestigious Cider Hill School for Girls. She was 24, single and a pretty blonde. Her father had walked out on the family when she was 9 and her mother had passed this previous year from cancer. No other known family existed as far as we could tell. Our subsequent questioning of friends and colleagues revealed no known suitors, instead, we had found her to be a loner who favoured books to people. There were no alcohol or cigarettes found in the home and a bible sitting on her bedside table confirmed one person's information that she only ever really ventured out to attend one of the local churches. Other than that, we had nothing. We had a young girl bound, gagged and then half eaten while suspended in her living room. The medical examiner would confirm later that, like the other victims, Miss Heidenberg had been conscious throughout the ordeal and had passed out due to blood loss and shock.

I shudder every time I think of her, and the rest that died under such horrific circumstances. We had 14 victims, all young women, ages ranging from 17 to 29, all living in the Daylesford/ Cider Hill areas and all cannibalized by a monster. A monster that not only enjoyed dining on his victims but one who also left that gruesome eye socket signature. The newspapers were in a frenzy over the story of the Daylesford Devil, had even coined the name within the first two weeks, after 3 victims had been discovered within mere days of each other. That had been back in 32, three long years before the nightmare finally ended.

3.

The problem we were having (and by we, I mean the 4 police officers from Daylesford, two (including me) from Cider Hill, and the seven officers from Melbourne), was that the killer severed any links to the crime scenes as soon as he was finished, erasing any possible evidence that could connect him to the deed. If there ever was any to begin with. Not a single clue was found that we could use to help us identify him. Even the teeth marks, of which we had many from the various victims, were perfect. It was as if he had pristine teeth with no distinguishable features. No gaps, no misalignments, no visible cavities, just perfect impressions. We had plenty of false leads too, ones we would initially get excited over, only to discover in a short amount of time, that they led to nothing more than dead ends. On one particular occasion we had discovered a used condom in the bathroom of victim 7, Nadine Johnstone, the youngest of the victims.

Subsequent interviews had led us to a boyfriend, one Thomas Wright, 19, kept hidden from the victim's family because of the overbearing and protective nature of her father. Mr. Wright had visited the victim earlier in the evening and the couple had engaged in some activities of a "private" nature. Witnesses had confirmed his alibi, that he had left the victim around 8 that evening, and her parents had discovered the young lady suspended from the shower rail some two hours later. After all the leads had been followed up and all the questions had been asked, we still had nothing.

There was nothing left at the scenes, not a single fingerprint left out of place. According to eyewitnesses, there weren't any trophies removed from the victims. Valuables such as money and jewellery were always left intact, a fact we believed as a sign the perpetrator was well off. Another interesting note worth mentioning was that none of the victims appeared to have been sexually interfered with.

As far as we could tell, money nor sexual gratification had been a motivation for the murders. It was as if he had a genuine thirst for blood, and that appeared to be his only motive. To feed. But, as the old saying goes, luck doesn't last forever. And if that was how the Daylesford Devil had been eluding us for so long, through luck, then he was about to run out.

4.

Our big break came just two weeks after the Heidenberg woman had been killed. It was a Thursday evening and Warren and I had just returned to the station after a day of door knocking and patrols. Alyce, our resident switchboard operator and receptionist, took a phone call from old Mrs. Weaver who lived out on Drummond lane, which ran off the Daylesford- Cider Hill Road. She said she had seen a man loitering around the Kennedy house, which she could see from her kitchen window. Joe Kennedy ran a butcher shop in town and Mrs. Weaver knew that he worked late on a Thursday. His 17-year-old daughter, Tami, would be home alone, the girl's mum having died two years before from pneumonia. Since her death, it had been just the two of them. Mrs. Weaver said the man had been sitting in a thick clump of bushes, appearing to be watching the house and that someone should make sure the girl was OK. We agreed to pop out and check on her.

The funny thing about fate is that you can never guess how it will shape the future. I still believe to this day, that if the events of that evening had played out any other way, then Lucifer would have escaped again. But one Simple Twist of Fate had sealed his.

5.

The day that would come to be known as "Lucifer's Last Day" was January 24th, 1935. What I believe to be the intervention of fate, was nothing more than a mere oversight by my partner, Warren, who had driven us all over town that day. He had forgotten to keep his eye on one very important aspect when driving a motor vehicle. Our car ran out of fuel two miles from the Kennedy house. If we hadn't run out, and ended up driving our patrol car to the farmhouse, the killer would have surely heard our approach and been alerted, thus allowing him to escape. Instead, he never knew we were coming.

The sun had disappeared over the far horizon as we drove out of town, and by the time the car coughed and spluttered, it had grown almost dark.

"Fuckin piece of crap," Warren cried as he pulled the car over to the side of the road. He smacked his hand down hard on the steering wheel a couple of times in disgust, then got out and slammed his door shut.

"Ah damn it. Come on. Nice night for a walk." I nodded in agreement and we walked along the edge of the road, Drummond lane only ten minutes further along. It was only two days after the full moon had peaked and the large shiny disc was already sitting high in the sky, illuminating our way like a huge lamp post.

"Those lights over there," I said as we turned onto Drummond Lane, pointing across the paddock to our left, "is that it?" Warren looked and nodded.

"Yup. That's it," he said, and then suddenly turned and cut across the ditch, grabbed hold of the fence that flanked the road and swung his leg over. He stood there, straddling the wires and beckoned me to climb over.

"Cross country?" I asked and swung my leg over, then the other in a small hop. My pants temporarily caught on the barb wire that topped the fence, threatening to tear a hole in them, but Warren lowered the fence a little more and they popped free. I turned and held the fence down for him in return, once I was safely over. We continued heading towards the lights, a few hundred yards across the freshly harvested paddock. January was always a great time for farmers with harvesting dominating this time of year. The smell of freshly cut grain hung thick in the air. It looked to be a wheat field, and the stubble reached knee height. Warren walked ahead of me a little and I followed, steadily increasing my pace, eager to ensure the girl's safety.

6.

We heard a very faint crying as we neared the tree line that skirted one side of the Kennedy's yard. The main house looked to have a single light burning in the kitchen, the rest of the house appearing dark and ominous. There was also a light burning in the main shed which sat about a hundred yards off to our right. Warren had put his finger to his lips as we neared the trees to ensure my silence, and just as he was about to whisper something there was a small scream followed by ghostly silence. The scream had sounded more like an exhausted protest, but the silence that now followed was what panicked me most. The echo from that scream had played havoc with our sense of direction and for a moment we weren't sure which building it had come from.

"You go to the house. I'll take the shed," Warren said, and then as an afterthought, "Be quiet, Jim." He began to turn, then pointed at my belt. "And take your pistol out," he said pointing at my still holstered weapon. I hadn't seen him draw his, but he now held it with two hands in front of his chest, barrel pointed toward the ground. I nodded, drew my pistol and turned towards the house.

13

"Hello?" I whispered with a wavering voice as I peered in through the fly screen door. The main door was open and I could see the kitchen deserted, the only sound, some crickets chirping somewhere out in the darkness. I felt for the handle, pulled it down gradually, then slowly pulled the door open, my pistol pointed straight ahead of me. My senses felt like they were on a knife edge, my bladder suddenly feeling full and tender. The door let out a slight creak, and I nearly dropped my weapon as I flinched. My skin broke out in gooseflesh, my nerves on edge. I had never been in this type of situation before, especially knowing there could be a serial killer looming inside.

I stepped in through the doorway and made my way into the kitchen. I still remember the faint smell of lavender and saw some, freshly picked sitting in a vase on the dining table. The floor creaked loudly beneath my foot and I jumped again.

"Anybody here? It's the police." I whispered, afraid of a reply. There was no answer, the house silent. I remember feeling relief when I realised the house had electric lights. If something had forced me to search the house by torchlight, I think I would have turned and ran. I moved to the living room, felt for the light switch and snapped it on, again, nothing but silence greeting me. The rest of the house proved the same, quiet and deserted. Fear crept into my middle at the realization that the scream had come from the shed. I ran back through the house, barged the door open with one outstretched hand and bounded down the front steps, two at a time. I could see the light burning brightly in the shed, but now saw the front door wide open. I ran, blindly sprinting toward the open door, then struck something hard and blunt with my shin, sending me sprawling into the dirt, the gun falling somewhere in front of me. My shin screamed in pain, feeling as if it was on fire. I could feel something warm on my leg, as I fumbled around in the dark, desperate to find my revolver. After what seemed like an eternity, my fingers felt the familiar cold touch of steel and I grasped it tightly. The wooden handle of my revolver slipped back into the palm of my hand as my lungs sighed with relief. I struggled to my feet, trying to stifle the pain flaring up my leg. I hobbled toward the shed again, the silence becoming more pronounced with every painful step. As I neared the door, I stopped, peeked inside and noticed a shadow slowly pendulating back and forth along the side wall. My fingers were cramping as I gripped the weapon with all my might, the fear now pulsing in my temples. I held it out in front of me, pointing it at the door and slowly crept forward.

There was a faint sobbing coming from somewhere further inside the building as I stepped through the doorway. But just as I was about to call out, to reassure the sobbing girl, my heart stopped as my panic boiled over. I finally saw what was creating the swinging shadow. Warren was dangling from a rope that was wound around his neck, hangman style. His arms hung lazily by his sides, his back towards me. There was no movement coming from him and I ran forward, calling his name. When I reached him, I grabbed one arm and swung him around with all my strength. He spun, the horror passing my face, then disappeared as he faced way from me again. He began to slowly turn back again, the rope creaking like a door straight out of a matinee horror flick. I meant to yell at him, to help me get him down and stop being stupid, but then his eyes met mine and I realized that Warren would never wake up again. There was a knife protruding from his chest, the brown wooden handle protruding out next to his policeman's star. The blade was completely embedded to the hilt. There was a patch of blood around the handle, but it was nothing compared to the gush of blood that was still pouring from his sliced throat. His eyes hung open, staring blankly at me, the tip of his tongue jutting slightly from between his lips.

I don't remember screaming, but Joe Kennedy would later tell me different. He came running into the shed at that moment, and I whirled around so fast, that I very nearly blew his head off. The explosion from my pistol sounded like a canon, the deafening crash reverberating around the shed like tidal waves.

"Where's Tami?" he screamed at me, tears and snot running down his face. "Where's my little girl?" It took me a moment to understand him, the ringing in my ears slowly abating.

"I haven't found her yet," I answered, then paused when the faint crying resumed from somewhere behind us. Joe looked over my shoulder, then pushed past me, running to the back of the shed, past a small tractor parked against the far wall. I called for him to wait but there was no stopping him. I followed him closely, my pistol never dropping an inch, ready to shoot anything that moved. As Joe rounded the corner and saw what was hiding behind the dividing wall, he screamed his daughter's name.

8.

She was hanging from a rope, although not by her neck, but by her hands, both bound at the wrist and then suspended from the rafters. She was naked except for the pillowcase tied over her head. Joe was trying to cut her down with his pocket knife as I ran up behind him. I could see blood pouring down her arm. The index finger on her right hand was missing, a stump of raw raggedy flesh poking out from the bloody fountain. I removed my jacket and put it over the girl's shoulders then helped Joe support her as the rope finally let go. He removed the pillowcase from her head and I saw that the girl was mostly all right except for a small bruise blooming next to her right eye and her missing finger.

9.

The girl lost consciousness as we laid her down on a pile of hay that sat to one side. I was about to suggest that we carry her into the house, but suddenly heard a revving engine break the silence. I stood, turned and peered towards the sound.

"MY CAR," Joe suddenly yelled, and I ran as fast as I could toward the door with one thought screaming at me, 'He was out there, the Devil was out there'. The person at the wheel of that car was the killer that had been eluding us for 14 victims and I was the only one that could stop him.

16

I saw the headlights drive past the door as I reached it, the silhouette of a single person in the driver's seat of the car. He looked to be hunched over the steering wheel, gripping it with both arms. He looked at me as he passed and our eyes met for the first time. It was what I didn't see that sowed the seeds of doubt in my mind. I didn't see anger in those eyes, or rage, or evil. I couldn't even say it was panic. What I saw was fear.

The car now passed me completely, turned in an arc and headed for the driveway. If he made it to the end of it, he would be out on the open road, with every chance to disappear. Without thinking, I aimed my pistol, held my breath, then made it roar as I unleashed the remaining bullets in a furious hail of hope and fear. The back window blew inward in a shower of glass and the right rear tyre exploded in an eruption of flying rubber. There were two metallic pops as the bullets struck the car body and then the vehicle lurched to one side, rolled through a fence, then into the ditch with a final thud. The driver's side door opened and a dark figure rolled out into the night, staggered a little, then turned towards the distant line of trees. I was after him in an instant, desperately trying to reload my pistol with each step, the pain in my shin now a distant haze, blocked out by the adrenaline-fueled charge I was making.

"STOP," I screamed, so loud that it felt like my vocal cords had torn, my throat burning like I had swallowed hot coal. The figure didn't hesitate, only continued running, the desperation evident in the leaps and bounds he was taking across the field like a spooked jackrabbit. My legs felt like they were running on pure adrenalin, some strange propulsion that was moving me with such an incredible speed that the countryside felt like it was passing me in a blur. I was gaining on him and he knew it, each nervous glimpse followed by a groan of desperation and a quickening of his legs. He must have had the dawning realisation that his freedom was nearly at an end. I could just make out the sounds if his panting when a louder more piercing noise came rushing over the far hill. My eyes darted in that direction and I felt instant relief wash over me as I saw the accompanying flashing red lights that were now blazing through the trees in licks and splashes, first one patrol car and then another. I pulled out my flashlight and shone it towards the headlights that were now driving along the road, desperate to get their attention. I watched with relief as they slowed, turned a little, then stopped, their headlights illuminating the field before me. I pointed my pistol at the running figure one final time, barely 50 yards behind him now, then shot once, aiming above his head.

"STOP! STOP OR I'LL SHOOT YOU," I screamed again. This time the figure came to a halt and held his hands skyward. The sobbing was what I heard first, then the pleading voice.

"Please, I did nothing, it was Loui," he cried at me. There were two other officers now running toward us, both brandishing their own weapons, Lester Redding and Col Thomson. Lester was in the lead and screamed at the man to get on the ground. The man dropped to his knees, his hands pressed together in front him, as if in prayer. None of us even registered the fear that was on the man's face.

"Please. I was just walking past. I did nothing." His words meant nothing to us as we closed in, pounced on him then handcuffed his hands tightly behind him. When he was finally cuffed, Lester gave him a swift boot to the middle of his face.

"Take that you cunt," he snarled in his thick Irish accent. I can still hear the crunch of his nose to this day. We all just stood there, silent, looking down at the now sobbing, pathetic figure lying at our feet. A small skinny man, not much older than me, scared and trembling. All of us knew we had the man responsible for the murder and torture of 14 women as well as one police officer, and that now, hopefully, the nightmare had finally come to an end.

10.

The man we had arrested was Harry Edward Lightman, of Mitcham Road, Daylesford, aged 30. He worked at the timber mill out on Jackson Street, had never been in trouble with the police and had no wife or children. The press noted his initials and immediately jumped on the fact that the Daylesford Devil had the initials of H.E.L. Close enough to Hell as far as they were concerned and the headlines that followed were straight from a Hollywood movie.

"TAKEDOWN" one flashed across its front page, the line beneath it reading "The fall of the Devil". "CAPTURED" read another, "THE END OF THE HORROR" another still.

He denied it all, no one doubting that he wouldn't admit to any of it. He claimed to have been walking past when he heard a commotion coming from the barn and had freaked out when he saw the dead cop swinging from a rope, stealing the Kennedy's car in a panic. We conducted our investigation and although we couldn't find a single piece of evidence on him, we knew the lack of alibis for any of the murders would not be enough to convict him on. Most of the other evidence was circumstantial, such as his perfect teeth, a witness spotting him leaving one of the murder locations around the time of one, carrying a coil of rope. He also had blood on his shirt sleeve when we arrested him that was Warren's but he claimed to have touched the officer whilst checking on him, getting it on his sleeve in the process. What ultimately convicted him though, was Tami's eyewitness evidence, the only person to have ever survived the devil.

11.

He fronted court for the final time in April 1935. The death penalty was requested and although almost granted, the judge determined that there wasn't a 100% airtight case against Lightman. He said that the overwhelming amount of circumstantial evidence, combined with Tami's testimony satisfied him of Lightman's guilt, but only as far as a life sentence, not one of death. Lightman screamed his innocence when he was sentenced just like they all did, then was led from the courtroom in chains and taken straight up to Crab Apple Hill, which sat less than 10 minutes' drive from the courtroom. He could have been taken to Pentridge Prison in Melbourne but Crab Apple Hill was already home to the state's worst killers and Harry had overtaken them all. On Monday, April 22nd, 1935, Harry Lightman began the first day of his sentence at Crab Apple Hill Prison.

Warren Smythe was buried next to his mother and father in Melbourne Cemetery with very little fanfare and almost no recognition from Victoria Police. A number of officers from Cider

Hill and Daylesford were granted leave for the day, including me, and we had hired a bus to take us there. In the days before and also after the funeral, I approached Chief Rademeyer on several occasions to request Officer Smythe be nominated for the Victoria Police Star, which I had heard was the appropriate medal for an officer killed the way he was. And each time, I was ignored. A couple of other officers also put my name forward but I didn't want anything. I had performed my duties the way I had been trained and for what I was being paid for. Warren, however, gave his life. He deserved it. To me, it felt as if the hierarchy weren't interested in medals or awards, as if they wanted the whole matter finished with so they could go back to the way things were before. Before a man went on a killing spree, killing 14 innocent victims, and a police force that had failed to protect them.

Whatever their reasons, I didn't care. The officers of the two police stations involved, had done a remarkable job in ending the carnage. Had gone above and beyond to ensure the public could walk the streets again without fear. Just as they always had. To hell with the Rademeyers in this world.

I was never 100% sure that he was Lucifer, also known as the Daylesford Devil. I was never absolutely positive because I didn't actually see him do anything. All I ever remembered were those frightened eyes that passed me in the car on that fateful night. I had put my faith in the system and allowed it to decide for me. The nightmares that followed, the ones that would play out in my mind where Lucifer would continue his crime spree, the ones where I would wake in a cold sweat, sure I had made a mistake, continued for a long time. As the years passed, and the memories withdrew into the darkest recesses of my mind, the nightmares gradually disappeared. Once they had completely vanished from my mind, the nightmares never returned, never causing me to doubt the final result. Not until June 1st, 1954.

Chapter 2: The Return of the Devil

1.

"Dr. Lawson?" the young Constable asked as I opened the door. She was wearing her police uniform, her hat held in one hand. The dark hair was tied back in a bun revealing a face far too young for the horror she would see in the coming weeks. She held a hand out for me to shake.

"Yes?" I asked, hesitating a little.

"I'm Stephanie Connor. We spoke on the phone yesterday?" I shook her hand, remembering the brief conversation we had held the previous day and invited her in.

"I'm sorry, Constable. I haven't been a police officer in many years. There was a reason why I left the force." I could see the frown on her face as I repeated what I had told her the previous day.

"I think you may change your mind after you see what I've brought with me," she said, following me down the hallway.

"I won't change my mind; I have no interest in catching criminals anymore. Those days are long behind me." I ushered her through into the sitting room, bare except for two sofa chairs, a table and a single floor lamp. The chairs faced the window, and I used them, or rather one of them, for when I was in the mood to read. The paddock that flanked my house was one of the main reasons I had purchased the home in the first place, serving as a wonderfully peaceful foreground.

"I understand Sir, but-" I held my hand up, cutting her off.

"First, I have to ask you not to call me Sir. I much prefer Jim. And Mr. Lawson was my father, a title I was never too fond of either." I was hoping I didn't sound insincere and her smile confirmed it.

"I'm sorry. Jim. And please, while we're on the subject, I am a constable but definitely prefer Steph. Constable is just way too formal for me." She reached forward with her hand once more and we shook a second time, resetting ourselves back to the beginning. I liked Steph immensely from the moment we met.

"Mr, sorry, Jim, I really need your help." She sounded genuine, and I felt almost ashamed of my own brutal honesty.

"I understand, Steph. It's just that I haven't been involved-"

"He's back." Now it was her turn to cut me off, and her words were enough for me to shut my mouth with a snap, the curiosity and shock on my face confirming to her that she finally had my attention.

"Who?" I asked dumbly, knowing perfectly well who she meant.

"Lucifer." The word hung in the air like a bad smell, neither of us wanting to touch it. The silence was almost overwhelming as her eyes questioned mine.

"That's impossible. Lightman is up in-"

"Yes, he is," she said, not needing me to finish my sentence, although sounding a little annoyed, her annoyance not aimed at me, "I can definitely confirm that. I called the Governor yesterday morning and after having one of his guards double check for me, confirmed that Harry Lightman was reading a book in his cell."

"Well, there you have it then," I said, still unsure of why she had bothered to drive all the way to my house when she could have just told me as much on the phone. She opened her handbag, reached in and pulled out an envelope. She handed it to me, and when I didn't reach for it, leant forward and dropped it in my lap. I took it, my curiosity peaking, my stomach feeling a dread I hadn't felt in almost twenty years.

2.

The envelope contained half a dozen photos, black and white and not ones you would see published in any newspaper. They were all of the same person, a young woman, maybe mid-20s and definitely deceased. She appeared to be lying on a table, probably in some morgue and was covered in a white sheet, blood spotting it in several places. In one photo, her right arm was exposed, and it appeared that something had chewed most of the muscle tissue from her wrist to shoulder. Bits of flesh hung askew from the end of her elbow and it looked like whatever had gnawed on her, had not taken its time. The next photo showed her left leg; or rather what remained of it, half the muscle tissue missing. I had flicked passed the third, then stopped and looked at Steph.

"This proves nothing, Steph. A copycat maybe. There hadn't been one in-"

"Look at the last one, Jim." Her voice now sounded almost scared, wavering a little. Her gaze told me I should just shut up and do as she asked. I looked down and as soon as I saw the picture, the pit of my stomach felt as if it had been hacked into with a bone saw, the unwanted truth finally slapping me in the face.

The picture was of her face, looking pale and young, almost innocent. Her mouth was closed and if the rest of her face had not been visible, could have sworn she was grinning. But it was her eyes that dropped the anvil into the pit of my stomach, the sinewy stumps of fingers protruding out from her sockets with shiny ooze still decorating her cheeks. On the outside, I began to sweat; on the inside, I screamed.

3.

The horror that came flooding back in that instant, the dread, the doubt I had been trying to run from for twenty years, came flooding back into my mind in a hurricane of images and flashbacks.

The silence in the room felt numb, my arms tingling with gooseflesh as I lost track of just how long neither of us spoke. Steph gave me the time I needed to comprehend the gravity of the situation and I was grateful for it.

I stood, walked to the window and just stared out at the countryside. There was a crow sitting on a barbed wire fence some way off in the distance and I could see it eyeing off a dead rabbit, probably chased down by a fox the previous night. It sat and stared, looked across the field to a couple of other crows nosing around in some grass, then re-fixed its focus on what would make a fine breakfast. Finally, it dropped to the ground, bobbed toward the rabbit and began to peck.

"Are you OK, Jim?" Steph finally asked. I turned back toward her, opened my lips to speak but found no words to say. I was gob smacked in every sense of the word. I closed my mouth again, walked back to my chair and plopped down into it.

"Do you think it's him?" I finally asked her. Now it was her turn to look puzzled.

"What do you mean?"

"I mean, forget the photos, the evidence. Do *you* believe Harry Lightman committed this murder? I mean a good cop looks at all the facts." She sat forward a little, considered the question for a long time, then turned to me.

"No, I don't think it was Harry, but if it was, he'd have one rock-solid alibi," she finally said. "Chief Rademeyer told me to tell you that Harry was back and to see if it would convince you to help us." Her voice sounded almost apologetic.

"Frank Rademeyer? You know he was my chief when I was a cop? That prick has been in charge of that cop shop for almost 30 years." I made sure there was no apologetic tone in *my* voice. Frank Rademeyer and I had a history and he was not someone I had sent Christmas cards to on a regular basis.

"Will you help, Jim? Will you help *me*?" she asked quietly.

"Why you, Steph? I'm sorry for answering your questions with more questions but I have so many as I'm sure you'd understand. Why did Rademeyer send *you* here? I mean, he must have officers that are far more qualified for this? No offence intended. How long have you been on the force?"

"None taken. And I have been out of the academy exactly 2 years, my first 18 months served in Carlton, before transferring here to Cider Hill. And as for why Rademeyer selected me to come out here and ask you to help? I believe his exact words were 'you have what they call breasts. I suggest you use them.' He -" But I drowned the rest of her words out with my roaring laughter, which now filled the room, rolling off the walls in great waves. Steph looked at me with some bewilderment at first, then her own smile broke through, followed by tiny controlled giggles, sounding as if she was trying to hold back but really wanting to free them. I had actual tears rolling down my cheeks and when she saw them, Steph went from controlled giggling to a full-on belly laugh in a second. Hearing her laughter set me off a second time.

It took a good minute for us to regain our composure, and by the time we had ourselves back under relative control, my sides were physically hurting.

"That arsehole always had a way with words, no doubt about it." I stood, tucked my shirt back into my pants then held out my hand to her for a third time. "I am more than happy to help you, Steph." I could see actual relief wash over her as she shook my hand, although inside, I still wasn't sure I wanted to help. I'm not certain why I agreed to help, other than to get in the face of Rademeyer again. I had a feeling that we would work on this for a few days, find the copycat, then watch as that prick took all the glory, just as he always had.

"Could you give me a moment to pack some necessities?" I figured this wouldn't be a simple overnight trip. My schedule was already fairly slim, thanks to me wanting some time to myself, so I had kept my diary free for the past few weeks. A few more would not hurt me too much, especially not in the financial department.

"So, where do we go first?" Steph asked as I came back into the sitting room, one suitcase in hand. I considered for a moment, trying to think of the right answer. Visiting Harry was the obvious choice, but I didn't have the details of anything yet. I would ask one question and then that would be it. What I needed, was information.

"Can we go to where the young lady was found? Is that OK?"

"Sure," she said and headed for the door. I followed, grabbed my keys and hat, then followed her out the door.

She must have driven the three hours to my home in almost complete darkness, to reach it by 8 that morning. I respected her eagerness and felt compelled to help her. The drive back to Cider Hill, one I hadn't undertaken personally in well over ten years, was pleasant, even if the day was a dreary one.

4.

The scene of the crime turned out to be the Cider Hill Primary School oval. Whoever had performed this ritualistic rebirth of the Daylesford Devil had suspended the victim, a relatively new Grade 1 teacher, naked from the football goals at the far end of the ground. She had been stripped, strung up by her wrists, fed upon, then left for the poor unfortunate soul that discovered her the next morning, the school janitor, Clancy Higgins. He had arrived at the school a little before 7 and had begun his morning routine of emptying the rubbish bins for the day to come. It was a cold morning, and the fog hung as thick as a woollen jumper over the back half of the school grounds. The police had door-knocked the entire area that morning and not a single person remembered hearing anything unusual the night before. It puzzled me immediately considering the amount of noise a person would make, having someone biting a chunk of their flesh from their body. Yet no-one had heard a thing.

The police had taken Clancy back to the station and had questioned him for almost four hours. He had a rock-solid alibi and was released a little before 1, the mob of reporters anxiously waiting at the foot of the station steps, pouncing on the man known as Cloudy Clancy to the kids, as soon as he emerged from the doorway. There were a couple with cameras, the flashes popping brightly in the gloomy daylight, almost blinding the simple-minded man, yet most were the traditional pencil and notepad kind of journalists, their questions tripping over each other like a Wall Street trading floor.

"Did you kill Rita Carlisle?" asked one.

"What happened to her?" shouted another.

"What did the police ask you?" a third shouted from somewhere in the back. But Clancy ignored them all, just like Constable Rawlinson had advised him.

"Walk straight past them and speak to no one, Clancy. Straight home, do you understand?" he had told him, and that is exactly what he had done.

5.

We walked around the ground a couple of times, had stopped at several inconspicuous spots but saw nothing of interest. Behind us, the school bell clanged loudly across the open space and within seconds, children began spilling out from every visible doorway, their loud chatting and laughing drifting out to us. Several came running out onto the grass, some to kick footballs, while several girls peeled off and began to play a skipping rope game. Their song drifted across the oval to us sounding loud and cheery as one girl jumped a rope that the other two girls were twirling between them. The girl was wearing a beanie with an especially long pompom and I watched as it bobbed this way and that.

A group of boys spotted Steph and I standing back near our starting place by the goals, came to a halt and stared at us for a second. After a few moments, they cautiously made their way over to us. When they were about twenty yards away, the one in the lead, slighter bigger than the other three, held his arm out and protectively halted his troupe, judging the distance to be close enough for safety's sake. They all stood there, staring at us in silence.

"Are you here because of Miss Carlisle?" the tall one asked sheepishly. I looked at Steph, my eyes willing her to answer on our behalf. She nodded slightly.

"Yes, we are. We want to find the person responsible," she said, squatting down to their eye level. The smallest one standing to the right of the leader, took a small step back, hesitated, then stepped forward again.

"Is she coming back soon?" he asked, his voice sounding young and innocent. Someone had invaded this kid's, all these kids' childhood innocence and ripped them into the reality of this cruel and fucked up world. Rage was all I felt right then and for the briefest moment, I wanted to scream. But I bit my tongue, held it in and smiled at them.

"What's your name?" Steph asked the small one. For a moment, he just stared at her, his bewildered eyes never leaving hers.

"James, but everyone calls me Jim," he finally said.

"Wow, well guess what Jim? You see this man here with me? His name is James too and do you know what he likes to be called?" Little Jim shook his head.

"I prefer Jim, too, buddy," I said taking a step forward, then also dropping into a squat beside her. I recognized the trust they had for her; she was wearing her police uniform, me however? I was the scary stranger, the grown-up they didn't know, the grown-up that could have hurt Miss Carlisle.

The boys suddenly turned their eyes away from us and I heard footsteps approaching from behind. They sounded much heavier than a child and for an instant, I felt a sense of panic rise in the boys, even if ever so slightly.

"Can I help you?" a man's voice suddenly cried out and as I stood, I turned to see a well-dressed man approaching us. He appeared much older than myself, maybe late fifties or early sixties, his round glasses looking glued to his face thanks to an unrelenting nose that seemed to have sprouted somewhere last century. His grey, peppery hair was combed dead straight and parted on the political left. I could see he was about to repeat his question more sternly, when he spotted Steph, now also rising to her feet beside me. This time, I sensed a moment of hesitation.

"Oh, excuse me. I didn't see you there, Officer," he said politely. Steph stepped past me, held out her hand and they shook, briefly. "I'm George Bester, the principal of Cider Hill Primary."

"I'm sorry, Stephanie Connor. We did come unannounced," Steph said to him, introducing herself. She turned slightly back, willed me forward and introduced me. His eyes peaked a little when he heard my name.

"*The* James Lawson? Of the Daylesford Devil kind?" I nodded and his smile broadened so much it nearly eclipsed his nose, no simple task judging by its size, the shadow now casting across his face, looking more like a giant birth mark. His hand grasped mine so tight that for a moment I thought he would pull me completely off balance, a feat I would have thought impossible, considering I outweighed the guy by at least 50 pounds and stood a good head taller. But his eagerness tickled my sub-conscious again. I ignored it and returned his shake, smiled, then pulled my hand free when he had finished.

"You were quite the hero, if my memory serves me correct, Mr. Lawson."

"Thank you, but that was a long time ago." His face grew stern as he looked at the boys now standing scattered around his legs.

"Why don't you boys go and play and let me speak with our guests," he told them and the boys ran off almost immediately, relief visible on their little faces.

6.

George invited us back to his office so we could have a discussion. 'A trifle more private' he had said as he led the way, weeding his way through the tangles of children, then climbing the steps into the largest of the three buildings. We followed him down a dark and narrow corridor, then into a brightly lit office, where a plump lady, wearing giant horn-rimmed glasses, sat at a desk and was busy bashing her fingers onto the keys of her typewriter.

"Gladys, this is Officer Connor and Jim Lawson. Would you fetch us some tea?" The woman offered us a strained smile as she dragged her ample derriere out of her chair and headed out of the room. George opened the door to his office and invited us in, the only thing matching the gloominess of the room, being the ghastly smell of pipe smoke, which hung thick in the air. I felt my throat close a little, protesting against taking subsequent breaths.

Steph and I sat in the chairs that sat directly in front of his big walnut desk, piles of folders and books standing high on each side. It reminded me of the play-forts I had built as a kid. All it needed was a small wall, joining the towers on either side, something to rest the barrel of your pretend gun on.

"Such a terrible tragedy," he said as he dropped his butt onto the high leather-backed chair. There was very little sympathy in his voice, sounding almost dismissive. His arrogance eclipsed any compassion he may have had, and his tone suggested the loss of one of his teachers to be more of an inconvenience than a tragedy.

"Did you know her well?" Steph asked him as he wheeled his chair closer to the desk.

"I wish I could say yes, but unfortunately Rita had only been with us a short time. She came highly recommended by Miss Tuck, another one of our third-grade teachers. They had studied together back in college and were very well acquainted." He enunciated the very so particularly, as if to highlight this fact.

"Did she have any enemies you know of? Anyone that may had an issue with her?" I asked, an obvious question, but one I was sure someone had already asked.

"No, none," he replied almost immediately.

"How can you be so sure?" Steph asked him, firing the question so quick, he took a second to register it.

"I can only speak on behalf of the faculty, I guess. Everybody liked her. I don't know what she got up to when she wasn't at work, but while here, she was a happy, young woman, in the prime of her life." I felt his nerves rise slightly, a light bead of sweat break across his brow. The office had a large radiator on the far wall, and I could feel its heat from where I sat, but I didn't think his sweat came from any heating device. Steph kicked my ankle lightly, and was just about to ask another question, when the door opened and Gladys walked in carrying a tray loaded with cups, a jug and a plate of biscuits.

"Ah, thank you, Gladys," he said, almost relieved, standing immediately and taking the tray from his secretary. She muttered something at us as she turned to walk out, then closed the door.

"Please, help yourselves,' he said, Gladys does make a superb drop of tea," he said as he handed Steph a cup and lifted the jug. She held her cup up for George to fill, then dropped a couple of sugar cubes into it, using the dainty little tongs that sat beside the jar. I followed suit, minus the sugar.

It tasted fine, a little bitter for my liking, but full and rounded. Its warmth felt good when it went down, my middle feeling like it was glowing from the inside. Steph also took a sip and thanked our host, but didn't waste time.

"Did you ever see Rita Carlisle outside of school hours?" she asked, as she put her cup on the desk.

"No, I don't make it a habit to socialize with my staff." He dropped his eyes into his cup as he took another sip.

"Oh?" Steph asked, tilting her head a little. George held the tea to his face for what seemed like a long time, almost trying to hide himself behind the tiny vessel. "I was talking to June Trapnell yesterday, you know, she teaches fifth grade? Well, she told me you had visited Rita at home one evening, not long after she had commenced teaching at this school. Popped right on up to the door, all unannounced like."

"No, I don't recall ever-"

"And the reason she could tell me that for certain, was because June had been sitting in Rita's kitchen at the time. She only lived two or three doors down from her and had popped by to drop off some leftover casserole she had made. Mushroom and beef, I believe," Steph said turning to me.

"No, I defin-" he tried to protest, but Steph didn't give him an inch, enjoying watching him squirm.

"And there they were, just having a chat, when you knocked on her door. And come to think of it, June also did mention that you had dropped by her own house occasionally." I could feel Steph's anger build, her cheeks flushing with colour. George, on the other hand, also began to build his own colour, but looked more sheepish than angry, almost embarrassed. He was holding his palms up toward us, waving them from side to side, in a denying gesture. "In fact, June told me you came on to her quite strongly, wouldn't take no for an answer, even blocking her door with your foot when she tried to close it on you." His protests became more animated, his face now washed in a deep crimson, beads of sweat trickling down one side of his face. "Aren't you married, Mr-" but that was when he finally stood, ending the questioning.

"Is this a formal interview, Constable?" he squawked, anger replacing embarrassment. "Because if it is, I believe I have a right to legal counsel."

"Do you think you *need* a lawyer?" she asked, also getting to her feet. Steph took one final sip of tea from her cup, sat it down on the tray and thanked him for his hospitality. I quickly stood and followed her out of the door.

"Thank you for the tea, Gladys," I said as we walked past her desk and headed back down the corridor. As we neared the door leading outside, I took a final look over my shoulder and saw George Bester standing in the door frame, one hand wiping his forehead with a handkerchief. As we stepped outside, a cold drizzle fell, the bell clanged loudly somewhere above, and in the far distance, the Cider Hill Fire Station Whistle announced Midday to the town.

7.

"What the hell was that?" Rademeyer said as he looked out of the small office window. I could tell he was pissed just by the lack of volume in his voice. The venom highlighted the fact. Steph sat next to me, her eyes looking into her lap.

"I wanted to ask him some questions, that's all. He had a history with the victim."

"Yes, he was her boss. I've known George Bester for going on twenty years, Constable. And if you want to conduct an interview with someone like that again, I strongly suggest you run it by me first. Because, I'm *your* boss, do you understand?"

"Yes," Steph said.

"I didn't hear you."

"I said yes, Sir," she repeated, the anger in her voice sounding raw.

"And you," he said turning his attention to me. "I asked for your help to try to find whoever has decided to get some fame by mimicking the Devil. Not to harass respectable townsfolk. I appreciate you answering our call for help, Jim. But please, remember that some people have connections that go all the way to the top. Much higher than you or I." He turned to Steph. "Would you excuse us, please?" Steph didn't need to be asked twice, the door closing with a satisfying thump.

He was looking out the window again, for what seemed like a long time.

"I really do appreciate you coming back, Jim," he said without looking at me. "The first thing we did was check on Lightman. He's still locked up and tucked in at Crab Apple. I don't know whether he's recruited an accomplice or whether there's a genuine copy-cat but someone is definitely looking for fame." He looked like he had aged fifty years rather than the actual twenty. He looked ancient, the creases in his face looking like deep fissures instead of wrinkles, his head now almost completely devoid of hair, save for a couple of white strands, the thick black mane he once wore, long gone like his youth. He sighed deeply as he turned and sat at his desk. "His lawyer is fighting to have him released. Some hotshot called Lovett." It was a statement that struck me in the centre of my chest, almost knocking the air out of me. Frank saw the shock in my expression and nodded as if in agreement.

"But-" I began, but he held his hand up, stopping me.

"I know what you're going to say, and I can promise you that that is something that won't be happening anytime soon. I've also been on the phone with four separate newspapers, a radio station and a reporter from one of the New York dailies. Can you believe it? Even a Yankee newspaper is on to this. They all think we locked up the wrong man." I hadn't considered how the media would handle the news that the killings had resumed. And the media had a funny habit of following their own agenda.

"We can't let that happen, Frank," I finally said.

"That much I know, son. We have to find him. We have to find the arsehole that's doing this. And quick. I think the wheels have already begun to turn and if we don't act fast, then..." his voice trailed off, his attention drawn to the window once more. He sat like that for a long time, the silence descending on us like a blanket.

"I'll do my best, Chief," I finally said. His expression suddenly changed, and he looked surprised as if he had forgotten I was still sitting there.

"Hmmm? Oh, yes, of course."

"Are you OK?" I asked, but he didn't answer. Not at first. I stood to go, but when I reached the door, my hand about to reach for the handle, his voice, quiet and reserved, drifted to me.

"Melanie has cancer, Jim." I stopped turned and was shocked to see him crying. "The doctors have told her she doesn't have long. It's in her lungs." His voice trailed off with the last words and he looked embarrassingly at me. I walked back towards the desk, stopped next to him and offered him my hand. Melanie was Frank's wife, they married back in 24 and had lived in Cider Hill all their lives. They had met during a football match, him playing and Melanie cheering for her brother, Robert, one of Frank's team mates. He had told me their story over beers many years ago, one night after our shift ended and a bunch of us had gone over to the Railway Hotel. In the end it had just been the two of us, me a first-year constable and him, my boss. I remember feeling a little uncomfortable sitting there alone with him, listening to his half-drunk whining, but after a while had relaxed and kind of enjoyed listening to his war stories.

"I'm sorry to hear that, Frank. If there is anything I can do." He shook my hand, limply and indifferent, then dropped it into his lap.

"I'm telling you this because, well, I may not be as on the ball as I need to be right now. If you could, you know, look after Stephanie. She is a good officer, young but hot-headed and determined. She reminds me of another officer I knew long ago." I nodded and understood.

"I'll do my best, Frank." I turned and walked out of the office, glad once the door closed behind me.

8.

Stephanie was waiting for me outside, a cigarette jutting out from between her fingers. I could tell right away she was pissed. She took a long puff then jettisoned the smoke out in a short harsh stab.

"That son of a bitch is a womanising bastard who hit on every single teacher that started at that school. And He is protecting him," she cried, pointing a finger at the building behind me. I put my hands up in a surrender, smiling.

"Hey, I'm on your side, remember?" She stopped, took a deep breath and took another puff. "How did you find out about Bester?"

"I ran into one of the teachers at the supermarket, June Trapnell. I had popped in for some quick supplies and was still in uniform. She approached me and was asking me about something or other, then out of the blue she told me to watch myself. That George has a keen eye out for any single ladies that grace this township. I caught up with her a few days later, just a tea and biscuit kind of thing, and she told me the finer details. He's been harassing a lot of ladies for a long time. And that son of a bitch is married." She took another angry puff of her cigarette, so long and deep, I thought she might inhale the rest of it without stopping. Then she relaxed her lips and released it, the smoke drifting out slowly in long thin tendrils.

"Yes, I noticed the ring on his finger. Why would it concern the Chief so much though?"

"Because George Bester is the brother in law of Lachlan Murdoch." I looked puzzled, not understanding the relationship she was trying to highlight.

36

"Lachlan Murdoch?" I asked, unsure.

"Geez, Jim, don't you know anything? Lachlan Murdoch is married to Katherine Reinhart, and Katherine Reinhart just happens to be the sister of-" but she didn't need to continue.

"William Reinhart, the Chief Commissioner," I finished for her.

"Exactly. Arsehole knows he's protected. Everyone is too fucking scared to say boo to him."

"That's why he was on the phone to the chief almost as soon as we left," I said. She nodded, agreeing with me as she drew one last puff from her cigarette before dropping it into the dirt and ending its life with her boot heel. "Do you think he had something to do with that girl's death?"

"Nah, I doubt he would have the balls for anything more than raising his voice in protest. Although he was a persistent shit, his courage failed him when the girl would fight back, like telling him where to go." She was leaning against the car, her hat sitting on the bonnet, her long dark hair hanging loosely around her shoulders. I found her almost distractingly beautiful, but didn't want to acknowledge it to myself for exactly that reason. Something was telling me that this event was only just beginning, and once it gained traction, would take some clear heads to contain, if not stamp out completely. I needed my focus to be 100%, not distracted by some gorgeous girl with amazing curves.

"Let's go," I said, walking around to my side of the car.

"Where are we going?" she asked, opening her door.

"Anywhere. I think clearer when I'm moving." And with that, she started the car, drove out of the parking lot, and headed south, back towards the centre of Cider Hill.

9.

I asked Steph to drop me and my baggage off, somewhere along the main street. I wanted to reacquaint myself with some local hangouts I hadn't seen in such a long time, keen to see which were still going strong and which had fallen by the wayside. I was given a lovely surprise almost immediately after Steph left me standing at the kerb, when I saw that Mrs. Homestead's Home-style café was still bright, cheery and definitely open, the chorus of voices reaching out to me through the door. The atmosphere inside the establishment was leaking through the open windows in bouts of chatter and giggles. My stomach gave a low grumble as a familiar smell drifted into my nostrils, the unmistakable smell of Mrs. McNorton's beef pies. Mrs. McNorton was old when I first arrived in the town over twenty years ago and I doubted whether she would still be behind the counter. To my amazement, not only was she still serving behind her counter, she remembered me the minute I walked through her door.

"Jim!" she cried out when she saw me push through the strip blind, the long strings of beads getting caught around my hat. She looked old, at least 80, but moved with the grace of a lady in her 40s. She came bounding around the side of the counter, wiped her forehead with her apron, then hugged me tightly around the neck, pulling my face down to hers so she could kiss my cheek. It had been routine back in the day to pop in to this café at least once a day, for either a beef pie or a tuna and salad sandwich, both handmade and tasting divine.

"Hello Mrs. McNorton," I said as she released me from her hold, feeling my cheeks flush as other customers eyed us from their tables.

"Beef pie or tuna sandwich?" she asked, grinning a little.

"You know, it's been so long, I might just have both." She laughed at this, walked me to a table and sat me down. She returned not a minute later, carrying a cup filled with hot coffee. I thanked her, took a sip and smiled. Black and one, just as I liked it.

My lunch arrived less than ten minutes later and tasted just as good as I had remembered. A delicious tuna and salad on soft rye bread as well as a beef and potato mash pie. I practically wolfed the sandwich down in 2 bites per half, then savoured the taste of the pie, the rich gravy still tasty enough to remind me of a Sunday evening roast with all the trimmings. When I finished, I made my way back to the counter, paid and left my hostess a tip for remembering at which she laughed.

"I haven't lost the workings of my brain, yet, Jim." I thanked her again and headed back out.

Once back on the street, I saw the old Railway Hotel still sitting a bit down the road, its high tin roof visible over the feed shop that sat beside it. I needed a place to stay and as I knew of its more than adequate accommodation, decided to call it home for the next few days. If I needed longer, then I could always move to one of the many boarding houses around town, or even rent a small cottage if one was available. For the time being however, the pub would suffice.

I was just beginning to cross the street when I heard a loud squeal of tyres and a roaring engine approaching me from behind. Looking over my shoulder, it surprised me to see that it was Steph, her face flushed with concern. I could see genuine fear in her eyes as she came to a screeching halt in front of me, her voice sounding scared.

"Steph?" I asked, but she cut me off.

"There's been another one."

Chapter 3: A Horror Revisited

1.

As I sat in the passenger seat, Steph punching the throttle, my thoughts were taken back to the night of Lightman's arrest, and the terror I felt discovering my partner hanging from that rope with the knife embedded in his chest. It was a feeling I have never been able to forget, the fear and the adrenalin that coursed through my body. The total helplessness that overwhelmed me at not being able to do a God damn thing; his executioner still out there somewhere, ready to kill another. It was also a feeling that I had never felt again, save for that one moment on that one fateful night. Not until today, now, this very moment.

2.

We drove in silence for what seemed like hours, but in reality, took only five minutes. As we rounded a bend on Jackson Street, I saw a police car with its lights flashing a few hundred yards further up, parked in front of what appeared to be an abandoned storefront. The building was sitting on the front section of an empty paddock with houses scattered every couple of hundred yards at this end of town. The nearest building to this one was on the opposite side of the road and well over a hundred yards away.

Steph parked her car nose to nose with the police cruiser, as if blocking any would-be escapee. The building stood alone, deserted and almost silent as we exited the car, the windows dirty and dusty, grimy streaks running this way and that. There was a faded sign propped up in the window, but the lettering had faded to such an extent, that reading it proved near impossible. There were high weeds growing on either side of the door, the garden if you could call it that, sat maybe 10 to 12 feet deep from the footpath to the front of the house, although only a small dirt track, devoid of greenery.

There were two officers on the scene, one standing by the open door looking ghostly pale. His partner was off to one side, bent over and feeding his lunch to the weeds that grew there, a dry retching sound the only one breaking the eerie silence. There were no birds singing, no sounds of distant livestock, almost as if mother nature had flicked a switch, recognizing the horror we were about to find. As we approached the building, Officer 1 looked up, waved, made a heaving sound, then rushed to the other side of the door, also letting go of whatever he had paid good money for. My arms turned to gooseflesh as I heard the pair of them struggling with whatever had greeted them inside. Steph looked at me nervously, then led us in through the faded green paint-flecked door. The hinges groaned in agony as she pushed it open enough to allow us passage and an all too familiar smell snarled through my nostrils.

3.

If I had any preconceived ideas about what I might see this time around, they were eliminated from my mind in an instant. Steph actually shrieked as she saw the girl for the first time. She was walking a little ahead of me, the hallway not wide enough for us to walk side-by-side. She turned into a doorway a little ahead of me and the terror on her face, the anguish in her eyes, clearly visible as she raised one hand to her face. For a moment I thought that she too, would allow her stomach to get the better of her, but she was a tough girl. She closed her eyes for a moment, swallowed with a hand to her mouth, then opened them again and walked into the room.

4.

It was a lady that looked as though she may have been in her late twenties. I say 'may have looked' as half of her face had been torn away. She had an eerie expression, her teeth exposed along the left side of her jaw in an eternal grin, her left cheek, upper and lower lips and most of her nose chewed off. There were bits of skin and sinew dangling from the bones that were visible beneath the flesh. There was a fly sitting on the one finger that remained forced into the eyeball, the other just a hollow socket, a stringy nerve jutting from the darkness, the second finger lying on the floor. Again, all the clothing had been removed and it appeared as if the killer had taken great care to try and invoke as much horror as he possibly could. The flesh from one upper arm was completely gone from shoulder to elbow, the other arm missing its entire lower arm, the elbow jutting out from the meaty gristle, a single tendon left dangling. One breast was gone, the other was missing its nipple, teeth marks visibly surrounding the wound. One thigh had been chewed on, then ripped off the bone, its remains hanging down almost far enough to rest on the calf beneath it. The blood that had flooded the room had dried to a brown crust, the black and white linoleum floor that had once served this bathroom, almost entirely hidden.

It wasn't blood that was now filling its stench throughout the house. It was the onset of decay. At a guess, I would say that this girl probably died before the victim from the previous morning, and with the cold days and near freezing nights, the speed of the decay had been slowed considerably, although I was no expert in such matters. Yet the smell of rot was so pronounced that it was thick enough to taste, giving me the indication that she may have been hanging here for longer than a few days.

"Any idea who she is?" I asked Steph.

"Pretty sure her name is Rita Hayworth or Hayman or something. Works at the laundry mill by the hospital in Daylesford."

"How do you know?" I asked.

"Picked her up a couple of times. She hitched rides to work sometimes."

Steph knelt down and looked at the stumpy finger as it lay caked in blood, a tiny insect crawling across it as I felt an all too familiar feeling returning into the pit of my stomach. It was the feeling of recognition.

5.

The other two officers came back into the house, still as white as a freshly laundered bedsheet. I could see them trying to avoid looking at the girl, instead staring at the floor, pretending to search for evidence.

"It's OK, guys," I said to them, "we have this."

"You sure?" the younger of the two asked and my nodding was all the encouragement they needed, both almost running back down the hallway, as if escaping from Death's clutches itself.

"Why is this one so messy?" Steph asked me once we were alone again.

"What do you mean?" I asked in return.

"The girl from yesterday, she was, what's the word I'm looking for?"

"Cleaner?"

"Yes, that's it. She was killed a lot cleaner, if you can call it that. This looks more frenzied, as if the killer lost control."

"Maybe he was out of control and just, you know, went nuts." I wasn't sure what to think, other than the fact that this girl had died in the most nightmarish way imaginable. I wanted to find the disturbed individual responsible for this suffering and I didn't want to be side-tracked by useless distractions. I was about to share my thoughts with Steph when there was a loud crash of the front door and then multiple heavy footsteps coming up the hallway. Judging by the voices, it sounded like the cavalry had just arrived.

6.

Steph decided to head off and let the coroner do what they needed to. If they made any significant discoveries, and I was fairly positive the killer would not be that relaxed, they would let us know as soon as humanly possible. This freed Steph and I up to think-tank our next move. We went back outside, the air smelling like a spring morning after a thunderstorm, clean and fresh, my lungs sucking in the big gulps, trying to expel the nastiness from my airways. I passed on the cigarette Steph offered me, having quit a couple of years before. She, however, lit up and drew back hard, expelling the smoke with a kind of relief, judging by the low groan that accompanied the smoky streams emanating from her nostrils. I could see a tear running down the side of her face and took a few steps in the opposite direction to give her space.

"Where are you going?" she suddenly asked, and as I turned around, saw her wipe the tear angrily away as she took another drag. "We have to find him, Jim. Whatever it takes. That fucking monster…" she hesitated for a moment, looking at her feet, "we have to find him."

"We will, Steph, I promise. I will do everything I possib-" Another police car suddenly pulled up beside us. Although I heard it approaching, the urgency in Steph's voice kept me from registering it fully. It now pulled alongside our car, one window winding down, the officer behind the glass beckoning to us. He simply shouted his message to us before we had a chance to move.

"Chief wants to see you, Connor." Steph gave him a gimmicky salute then headed to her own car, turning to see if I was following. The other police car had stopped and three officers were now climbing out and hurrying towards the building, anxiety clearly plastered on their faces.

7.

We drove in silence, Steph's lighter the only sound to break it, as she lit another cigarette. The aroma filled the cabin and for a moment, a very brief moment, I wanted to rip one from her packet, spark it up and pull on it in one long delightful drag. But the temptation quickly subsided, the craving so much easier to control these days, and I wound the window down a little to let some cool air in. Steph figured the smoke was annoying me and butted it out.

"No, it's OK, seriously. I just wanted some air after smelling that shit back there." She gave me a strained smile and turned the car onto the main street, then into the police station car park a minute or so later. I could tell she wasn't in the mood for bullshit, and to tell you the truth? Neither was I.

8.

We climbed the steps to the front door and entered the watch house, one officer bent over the counter, reading a newspaper. He half jumped as we came through the door, saw Steph and gave her a half-arsed wave, his eyes dropping back down to continue reading.

"He's in his office," he mumbled at us as we strolled behind the counter, although he did give me an 'up and down' as I passed him.

"Thanks, Pete," Steph said. I followed her down a short corridor, then waited as she knocked.

"Come in," came through the door and she opened it.

Frank sat at his desk, his elbows resting on top of it, face cradled in hands.

"Tell me something interesting, Jim, please," he said, not looking up.

"I doubt whether it's him, Frank." That did make him look up. Made him sit back and ponder my words for the briefest of moments.

"You could tell just by seeing one victim?"

"No not exactly. This one just, I don't know, it felt different. It was too messy, too angry. If it was a copycat, he lost control."

"Too angry?" he asked. I wasn't even sure what I meant by it, let alone trying to explain it.

"I'm not sure how to put it any other way. Every victim that I had ever seen of his, was controlled, precise, almost surgical. This victim. Frank," I paused, thinking of the right words that would convey my gut feeling, "she looked like whoever had killed her, was in such a frenzy that he nearly tore her completely to pieces. It was a feverish attack." Frank just sat and stared at me, mouth slightly open, looking like he wanted to mouth something.

"Jim and I'll be canvassing all the houses in the neighbourhood, Chief," Steph chipped in. Frank didn't even look at her, or acknowledge her comment.

"And what do you think is the next logical course of action, besides door-knocking," he said, finally shooting a glance in Steph's direction, as if to highlight her lack of direction, then refocusing on me. "I don't want you two knocking on doors. I've got other officers for that."

"We'll get him, Frank. Just give us a moment to catch our breath."

"Just make sure you keep me informed, guys. Please." We agreed, bid our farewells and stepped out of the office, Steph closing the door behind us. We walked back down the hallway to see Pete still bent over his paper. He looked over his shoulder as we came back in, ignored us and continued reading. Once we reached the relative safety of the car park, Steph turned to me.

"What was the point in that?" she asked with annoyance.

"That's Frank showing you who's boss. Let's get this done, kiddo. I think we both know what the next step is before we even think about doing anything else." I looked at her, hoping for confirmation that she was following me.

"We have to talk to Lightman," she said, grabbing for her pack of Viceroys again.

"No." She stopped and looked at me curiously.

"No?" I could feel her temper rise, her eyes drilling little bore-holes into mine.

"No. I think for the moment it might be best if I see him alone."

"Why?" She almost turned on me.

"Steph, I have a history with him. I'm the one that ultimately put him away. I think after all these years, if he is going to open up to anybody, it might just be the guy that he is pissed off with the most."

"I understand, but I really think-"

"Hey, I'm on your side, remember? Look, come with me, but if it's OK, please, let me speak to him first." I could see she was still pissed, but my reasoning made sense to her and she was, as I would find out in due course, an excellent officer. She finally nodded, dropped her butt to the ground and walked to her car.

"Want a ride back to the hotel?"

"Sure, if that's OK. We can head to Crab Apple first thing in the morning if you like."

"Definitely," she said and hopped into her side.

9.

Crab Apple Hill had been named so because of an orchard that used to occupy the site for the last half of last century. A young Walter Hancock and his wife Thelma had made the crossing from England to Australia and looked for a place that not only reminded them of their homes back in England, but also a place that would bear rich fruit. Walter had been raised on a farm that grew apples and so the newly married couple had settled in these parts back in 1855 after purchasing a thousand acres. Walter's parents had both passed and once he was able to sell the family farm back home for a very tidy sum, it provided the financial security him and Thelma would need to re-establish a new life in Australia, then known as "the land of opportunity".

The trees had begun to yield sweet and juicy apples within 5 years and the couple enjoyed tremendous success, eventually employing permanent farm hands to help with year-round labour. They enjoyed the views from atop the solitary hill that occupied their land and around 1860, built a permanent stone cottage, now home of the prison hospital wing. It was around 1865 that Walter began to toy with the idea of planting some Crab Apple trees in a plot off to the side of the cottage, as a side project, so to speak. He chose Dolgos, a variety imported from Russia, as the tartness of the fruit proved the perfect taste he was hoping to adopt in a new line of Ciders. A local field, about 15 miles to the south of their property, had been adopted by locals as the perfect location for a farmer's market the previous year. It was still classed as crown land back then and had three of the biggest farms flanking it on all sides, the main road from Daylesford to Clunes running through its middle.

Walter's eventual concoction proved to be so popular with the locals that within a few months, word had spread far and wide about the amazing cider that was being produced in the area. Eventually, a permanent market was erected where people would come searching for goods all week long. More and more stalls were opening up as the popularity of the market gathered strength. The stalls were more of a "roof with no sides" kind of design and everyone realised very quickly that they would only serve as a temporary solution. Finally, it was decided that a hotel, named The Railway Hotel because of the train tracks that ran past the site, would be built to provide lodgings for visitors and, it proved to be the first official building ever to be constructed in the field. More businesses, including a storefront for Walter's Cider, quickly emerged and within ten short years, a brand-new town was born, named Cider Hill, after its most popular beverage.

But as with any fine story, an ending must follow, and tragedy would strike in the early 1880s. Walter, never one to pass on performing his own duties, had been transporting a wagon load of Cider to his storefront. His foreman, Will Tucker, had offered to take the wagon himself, but Walter refused, instead giving his longest serving employee the day off. His kindness and generosity had been legendary. Folklore has it that, one morning in November, this was about 1870, Walter had been making a delivery to his store when he came upon a lady sitting in the middle of the track. She had been taking her own wagonload of produce into the town when her horse was spooked, bolted, and subsequently broke a leg as well as damaging the wagon beyond repair. The lady, Mrs. Norma Purcell, was a widow, her husband having passed a few years before. Walter, of course, helped the lady into his wagon and took her straight to the

Doctor. She had suffered some bruising, a broken wrist and quite a bump to the head. Imagine her surprise, when not a day later, Walter and Thelma delivered a brand-new wagon, together with a fine animal to pull it. Mrs. Purcell had been in tears, overcome with joy and relief. This was the generosity with which his legend grew.

Anyway, it had been along the very same track, now 12 years later, that Walter had found himself, guiding his horses along about 5 miles from town. They say that it was a snake that probably spooked the horses. But unlike Mrs. Purcell, who had been thrown clear of her wagon, the horses pulled in the same direction with such a sudden fright that the wagon, including all 60 cases of cider, flipped and rolled, wedging itself against a large gum tree that flanked the track. Walter simply hung on too long and ended up beneath the wagon, his skull crushed between the wagon and the giant tree.

He was found by Will Tucker later that afternoon as he was returning from town. They say Will wept openly as he brought his employer's body into the doctor's cottage. Walter was buried in a closed coffin the very next day, on a plot he and Thelma had picked out only the year before, down by the creek that flowed through their property. He still lays there to this day, a small memorial park surrounding it, set up in his honour.

Thelma eventually sold the farm and headed back to England a widow, childless and forever heartbroken. The farm was eventually broken up into several pieces, the hill purchased by the Victorian Government, around 100 acres in total. The prison had been built in the 1920s to house the state's worst criminals, eventually including Harry Lightman. Crab Apple became notorious for harsh criminals and harsher guards, with one in particular, Arthur Dhurrin, famous for breaking fingers with a night-stick he lovingly called Mr. Knuckles. But that's another story entirely and one I may share at some future time.

Chapter 4: Meeting the Devil, Part 2.

1.

It was nearly 9 o'clock by the time Steph pulled the car into the parking lot of the Crab Apple Hill prison, its high concrete walls looming off to one side, barbed wire skirting the top of them in great bushels of twisted metal. There were no guard towers on each corner like the traditional jails as Crab Apple was substantially smaller. Rather, the prison had an inner wall and an outer wall. Each wall had a walkway built on top of it, with one armed guard patrolling between the perimeter walls and two guards patrolling atop each wall. There was no protection from the elements and each guard was expected to complete a four-hour shift without break whether rain, hail or shine. I could see one of the guards now, standing atop the outer perimeter, a rifle slung over his shoulder and staring at us. As I opened my door to climb out of the car, I felt as if the air itself had taken on a thicker, more condensed form. I suddenly found it more difficult to breathe, my heartbeat now pulsing in my temples.

"You OK there Jim?" I looked at her and offered a weak smile that felt fake. Steph's look told me she recognized my smile for what it was; raw fear. I was about to come face to face with the man responsible for at least fourteen, if not sixteen, murders of the most savage kind. A man that would have so much hatred for me that I was positive he would tear my throat out if given the smallest opportunity.

"I'm good," I said, but doubted my words as soon as they were out. Somehow, since I had received the first phone call from Steph, this moment had been playing in the back of my mind. This point in time where I would have to confront him, and do what had been the subject of so many nightmares; endless nights of waking in a cold sweat with my pillow drenched, throat sore from either crying, screaming or both. I had to face the devil, and once again, look him in the eye.

2.

I walked towards the bluestone steps that led to the little side door that flanked the big iron gate, very little enthusiasm in my step. The inner wall was visible through the railings, the huge gate standing nearly 20 feet high. There was a guard standing just inside, watching us approach. He was frowning at me, turned his attention to the woman walking beside me and smiled.

"Officer Connor, what a pleasure," he said in a surprisingly jovial tone.

"Hey, Jack. How you been?"

"Good, good. Haven't seen you at the meetings lately?" His eyes were so smitten with her that I doubted he knew I was there.

"Busy with work. You know how it is," she said casually. "This is Jim Lawson, here to see the warden. Is he in?" Steph had a tone about her that I definitely hadn't heard before. If I had to put a name to it, I would have called it flirting and doing a fine job of it. The guard was leaning against the gate for support, almost swooning over her.

"Yeah, he's in alright. And in a fine mood. People have been ringin him all day, askin if he's keepin Lucifer locked up. Really sure you want to see him?" He gave me the briefest up and down, saw nothing of interest, then refocused his attention on his prize. "You plannin on comin back to the club soon?"

"Have to see him. Police business, you understand. And yes, I will return soon. Just been busy. Wanna let us in?"

"Oh, of course, sorry. One sec." He disappeared from view as a jingling of keys and a rattle of something bumped against the smaller door. Finally, the door swung inwards revealing the guard standing with a huge grin almost eclipsing the rest of his face. He waved us through and for a moment it looked as though he was going to lean forward enough to try and kiss Steph as she walked by him. He pulled himself up at the last second, colour flushing his cheeks. Steph didn't hesitate, walking briskly toward the huge gate that served as the only entrance through the inner wall. Even sunlight struggled to reach between the walls, the space only a few feet wide. They say the walls reach more than 30 feet beneath the rocky ground, with tunnelling impossible except by modern machinery and a whole lot of time.

As I heard Jack re-bolt the door behind us, there was a loud metallic grinding, sounding like a rusty beast as the gate began to open. It slowly revealed four men standing on the path inside; 3 guards with heavy calibre rifles held in front of their chests ready to fire, and a man in a suit. The suit had an expression of grim death on his face. He stepped forward, looked at us with contempt in his eyes, then beckoned us to follow him without uttering a single word. Steph looked at me, raised her eyebrows and followed Warden Thomas toward the main building standing before us.

"What club?" I asked as we walked.

"Ball room dancing. And never mention it again," she whispered back.

3.

It was a dark and poorly lit hallway, with no windows; a single light globe trying to illuminate the passage. The air was thick with the smell of some sort of decay, like wet leaves. I tried not to breathe as we walked to whatever room we were being taken to. It wasn't a bad smell as such, but rather the smell *of* bad. I could hear muffled groaning from a room somewhere further into the building, and insane laughter from another further still.

The warden stopped next to a door, turned and paused for a moment, waving us inside. He gave a quick nod to one of the armed guards that had tailed us and then followed us inside, closing the door behind him. It appeared to be an interview room with a table and 3 chairs, a small barred window sitting high on the far wall. There were two lamps fixed to the ceiling, light emanating so bright that I was unable to look directly at them. I was thinking that a doctor would be able to perform surgery in this room as I sat in one of the chairs. Steph sat next to me, leaving the one chair on the other side of the desk for the warden. He didn't sit in it, plopping his butt on top of the desk, one foot left firmly on the concrete floor. He was tall, even taller than me, close to six eight at a guess. He had an intimidation about him that didn't need introducing.

"I don't know what the fuck is going on out there, folks, but I can tell you that I have had everyone from the groundskeeper to the God damn premier of this great state on the phone asking me whether Lucifer is locked up. The public is exactly a bee's fart from panic and some fucking psycho thinks he's the Devil. Do you people even have the slightest clue about who might be doing this?"

"We are doin-" Steph started, but he didn't stop.

"Because I sure as hell am not going to be the target of everybody's finger pointing when the proverbial hits the fan. No Siree."

"Mr. Thomas," I began, trying to sound sincere, "we are here to speak with Harry Lightman. If that's OK with you, Sir?" The room fell silent for a long time, Thomas only looking at me with eyes that appeared to blaze with anger. Steph shuffled in her seat a little and his attention was drawn to her.

"Do you think he knows? Who the killer is, I mean?" I wasn't sure whom he was asking but decided to answer, anyway.

"We don't know what to think right now. What I do know is that the killer is making no mistakes and the only person who can shed light on it at this point in time is Harry Lightman." The warden sat for a moment longer, then nodded slightly.

"Phillips!" he barked at the door, his voice projecting around the room with such a boom, that my ears flinched. There was a shuffle out in the hallway and then the door opened, the guard popping his head in.

"Sir?"

"Bring Lightman."

"Yes, Sir," the guard said and closed the door, his footsteps clapping down the hall.

"You have our full cooperation. Whatever you need. Just get whoever is doing this so we can go back to doing what we do here. All the excitement isn't good for the good order of this prison." He didn't wait for a response, standing then walking out of the room without so much as a glance back. When he was gone, I turned to Steph.

"Certainly, a warm chap." She ignored my comment.

"You sure you want me to stay?" I wasn't sure whether she really wanted to stay, but I figured now that she was here, she may as well listen in.

"Do you want to stay? I really don't mi-" but that was when the door opened and I heard the unmistakable tinkle of chains. I felt a chill race up my spine and could have sworn that the temperature in the room dropped at least ten degrees. I didn't need to turn around to know that he had entered the room, feeling evil in the air. His footsteps sounded heavy, his prison boot-heels dragging on the tiled floor in slow, laboured scuffs. His footsteps stopped next to my chair and I felt his eyes burning into the back of my head. Steph's eyes were looking at him over my shoulder, into the face of Lucifer. His footsteps resumed, Lightman walking around the back of the table. The guard padlocked his wrist chains to the metal loop that was welded into the top of the metal desk. I was still looking at Steph as I heard the padlock click loudly into place, then watched as the guard walked out of the room, closing the door behind him. The room fell silent except for the heavy and laboured breathing, coming from the man seated opposite us. I turned my head and found the eyes of the beast from my nightmares, staring back at me, a grin across his face.

4.

"Hello, Doctor Lawson." His voice sounded hollow, raspy; the tone thick with sickness. He had not aged well over the past two decades, his face a map of wrinkles and scars, mementos from altercations with either guards or inmates. His hair, short and ragged, had turned peppery, not far from almost completely white. He had also bulked up. He may have been wiry when he first came to Crab Apple, but he had grown into quite a beefy man. But it was his eyes that chilled me. His eyes still had the youth of a twenty-year-old man about them. And they were smiling.

"Hello, Harry." I had played this moment out in my mind hundreds of times over the past twenty years, maybe even thousands. The things I wanted to say to him, the conversations we would have, the things I could discover. But now that I was sitting here, the two of us sitting eye to eye, my brain betrayed my mouth by withholding every question I had ever contemplated asking. It was as if my brain didn't want to accept that the moment had finally arrived.

"I hear the killer… has started… again." His breathing sounded as if it had taken control of his body and was withholding the air from it, only allowing the barest amount through. He didn't have the breath necessary for an entire sentence, so had to speak in bits and pieces.

"What do you mean the killer?" I asked. Harry had always maintained his innocence for years, adamant there had been someone else at the farm that night.

"Come on, Doc... you know exactly... what I mean. I was... just at the... wrong place at... the wrong... time."

"You know, we aren't here to discuss your guilt or innocence, Harry. A court made that decision twenty years ago. We're here for any information you can offer us in relation to the new killings. You've heard of the new killings, haven't you, Harry?" I said with a "yes you do" tone.

"Do you really... believe that, a... killer as sophisticated... as Lucifer, would simply... let himself be caught, the... way you caught me? He outsmarted you, James." His tone had shifted to one of defiance and a touch of anger.

"It's either Doctor Lawson or Jim, Harry. Not James. Only my mother ever called me James."

"You deny the... name given to you by your... mother, James?"

"We aren't here to talk about my mother either. Do you know anything about these new killings, Harry?" I began to doubt whether we would get anything solid from him, beginning to feel like he was playing me. I was about to repeat the question when Steph suddenly spoke up.

"We just want to stop whoever is out there, hurting the women of this town, Harry. If you know anything, please." His eyes turned on her, seemed to look directly through her, then closed. He appeared to be meditating, or sleeping, I couldn't work out which, but for a moment, I thought he was just going to ignore her. Then, to my total shock, he began to speak.

"There was... a man who... visited me... a few years ago. He... told me he... was a reporter... for a newspaper... in Sydney. I don't... remember which, exactly. But... he returned a number... of times, asking me... all sorts of questions. He... told me he was... doing a piece on innocent... prisoners, people that had... been locked... up for lengthy sentences... even death sentences. He believed... my innocence and wrote a very... in-depth piece... about my story. What was his... name, again? Hank? Frank?" His forehead frowned, the deep lines growing, shadows running across his white face. He paused for a moment to catch his breath, coughed slightly, then continued. "He even let me... read the completed... article before he... submitted it to his... boss. Strange, very... strange."

"What was strange, Harry?" Steph asked him, leaning forward in her chair. He opened his eyes and looked at her, his eyes looking tired, his breathing now heavier and more laboured.

"I never ended up... seeing the... finished article... in any paper, nor... did I ever... see him again." He wheezed a couple of times, the sound drilling deep into his chest.

"What was written in the finished article? Did it read like a legitimate reporter's article?" He nodded.

"It read... exactly, like some... thing straight out... of the Daily Gossip. It was... good. It... gave me... hope. Hope that... finally, I might be... able to get... someone to... listen."

"What did this person look like, Harry?" Steph asked, now sitting forward in her seat, her interest peaked considerably.

"He was... maybe 40ish... small, clean shaven. He... had a bent... nose, kinda like... the ones boxers... have sometimes. Maybe... it had been... broken or something. He... was very well... spoken, educated." Harry stopped, coughed into his hand, the gravel sounding considerable in his chest. When he pulled his hand away, I could see blood on his palm.

"You OK there, Harry?" I asked him, now also sitting forward. He took out a handkerchief and wiped the blood away.

"I'll be fine, thank you, James." I frowned as he used my name again but didn't speak up. I didn't see the point. I suddenly had the urge to leave, just wanting to stand up and walk straight out the door. I didn't want to be in this room with this monster. I took a deep breath and fought the urge away.

5.

I had spent months, even years after Lightman's arrest, perusing the records, everybody's accounts; the entire library of court documents that were born from his trial. Even though he had been there on that farm, I always found that in the deepest recesses of my mind, there sat a tiny 1% of doubt whether he really was the Daylesford Devil. He was, after all, not exactly caught red handed. Everything was circumstantial. Even when it came to the evidence given by Tami Kennedy, it all came down to "he said, she said". There was nothing concrete that made the case a slam dunk. Harry himself, pleaded his innocence for the entire trial, and to the best of my knowledge, for all the years that had passed since. He had claimed to be walking home from the pub, a little too drunk. He had taken a shortcut across the paddock and had walked into the Kennedy property, attracted to the shouts he heard. He had seen Warren swinging from the rope, then panicked and ran outside, jumping into the car out of fear.

But it was Joe Kennedy that testified to the fact that he never saw Lightman run out of the barn. He claimed to have driven up to the shed, jumped out of his car and ran straight inside, running into me as he did, and neither of us had seen Lightman up to that point. Lightman's lawyer had pointed out that Joe Kennedy had been acting out of panic himself and probably wouldn't have noticed Lightman even if he was really there. He had been far too panicked and totally focused on reaching his little girl, so his testimony proved to be unreliable due to his presence of mind.

I had spent a total of five years on the police force. The first 18 months or so had been in Melbourne for my initial training and then on to one of the suburban stations. I think it was late in 1933 that the request came through for me to be transferred to Cider Hill police station due to an increase in duties at that watch house. During my time there, I had witnessed things no person should ever have to see in a lifetime. The Devil's victims had remained with me in nightmares for years to come, their faces permanently etched into my memories. What made the whole thing even more terrifying was the 1% of doubt that still lingered to this day, the horrifying thought that we had indeed, locked the wrong man up and the real Devil was still roaming the land, ready to begin a new nightmare.

Once the sensationalism had finished in the media and life had returned to some form of normality, I had made the decision to quit the police force. I had no real sense of direction, or any plans that I wanted to pursue so spent the first six months travelling around the country, taking in all it had to show me. But part of me remained forever in Cider Hill, the horror firmly etched in my subconscious. No matter how far I travelled each day, Cider Hill returned to my dreams each night, and each night I would wake to a scream trapped in my throat, the sheets soaking with my sweat.

Eventually I had reached Townsville in Queensland, 1936 coming to a close. I had planned to return briefly to Melbourne and spend Christmas with my Mum, but once I returned to the relative comfort of my childhood home, didn't want to leave. It was as if I had returned to the one place that I truly felt safe. The weeks turned into months and eventually, I decided to attend university to study psychiatry. My choice of campus had been the University of Melbourne as my mother had graduated from there herself. The next eight years were spent diving head first into books and learning everything I could get my hands on. I devoured each phase of my doctorate and eventually graduated with honours in 1945. I did try to enlist when called upon in early 1940, but due to a heart murmur was declined. This left me to study and when I finally graduated, was accepted to the Sisters of Charity Health Service, a hospital that was situated in Fitzroy. Although interesting, I didn't find my calling, and so within the year, opened my own practice two streets away. While I saw patients during the day, it was the writing I did during the late evenings that would eventually lead me to the financial freedom I was seeking. With my first book, Catching Lucifer, hitting the best seller list within three months, I gained worldwide attention, and an audience keen for a second helping, Nightmares Unhinged, which was released just nine months later. With the money now coming in at a steady pace, I reduced my working days to just three per week, giving me plenty of time to write, and try to reclaim a life I felt I had lost.

But throughout everything, that tiny 1% continued to linger, to float deep down in my subconscious, only to be ripped out from its hiding spot some twenty years after leaving Cider Hill. Now, sitting here before him, I wondered whether the nightmare ever truly left me, or like a predator stalking its victim, had been watching and waiting for the time to strike, when the horror would once again, stalk this land.

6.

"Jim?" Steph brought me back to the moment, her hand squeezing my arm. They were both sitting and staring at me, Lightman's lungs still rasping.

"Sorry, yes. I'm good," I said, trying to sound balanced, something I certainly wasn't feeling.

"Did you have... any more questions... for me, James?" He sounded almost cocky to me, his eyes never leaving mine. It was as if he was trying to find any sign of guilt on my face. Something that said

"Hey Harry, I'm sorry. Maybe I did fuck up." The problem was, I wasn't sure exactly how I felt.

"No, thank you. Not right now. Thank you for your time." I stood, offered him my hand which he took with both of his, his touch cold and leathery. I winced at the thought of what those hands had done and wanted to pull back instantly. The door opened as the guard entered.

"No touching. Please refrain yourself, Sir." He sounded pissed, and I pulled my hand back as he went around to Lightman's side, a bunch of keys in his hand. Another guard stood at the door; a rifle held at the ready. The cuffs were released from the table and the guard led Lightman outside. When they reached the door, Harry paused, turned and looked at me.

"I want… to help, James. I… want to… make things… right. To help catch… the real killer." He turned and walked out, the guard closing the door behind them as they left, leaving Steph and I alone once more.

"You OK, Jim?" Steph asked. Her tone sounded a little panicky. "You look pale."

"I feel fine," I replied, my legs feeling shaky. "Do you believe him?"

"About what? His innocence?"

"No, his visitor." I sat back down and was about to tell her to forget about whether she thought him guilty or innocent, when the door opened and the governor came back into the room. Another guard followed him in, carrying a large box. He dropped it onto the table with a loud thump then turned and walked back out. Thomas sat on the edge of the desk again, pulled the box closer to him and opened a flap. He reached in and pulled out a red folder, almost an inch thick and jammed full of documents.

"Here is everything we have accumulated on Harry Lightman over the past two decades. There's another one waiting at the front gate for you. They contain every disagreement, every infraction, every disciplinary issue, every sickness, cold and hiccup. Every person he has ever seen, had visited him and written him. Also, staff rosters and rotations so you know where everybody is, has been and gone to. In short, every possible piece of information we have on him." He put the folder back in the box, closed the flap and slid the box in my direction. "We have had a total of 47 guards who have been in direct contact with Lightman during his time here. 21 are still currently working here, 12 have moved to other prisons and still contactable, 11 have resigned and moved to other career paths, 1 has moved overseas to England and 2 are deceased. We are available for any questions you have. All of us. Catch this son of a bitch. As quick as you can." He didn't bother with formalities or handshakes. Thomas gave us a final glance, then stood and left the room without so much as a good luck or farewell. Steph and I exchanged a glance, read each other's thoughts perfectly and took our leave.

7.

The drive back to Cider Hill was a quiet one, neither of us speaking. As I stared out at the countryside passing us by, I couldn't help but wonder whether my doubts had been warranted, whether he was in fact, just an innocent bystander. I was just about to try to remember the moment I first spotted him on that long-ago night, when Steph broke the silence.

"We can't let him side-track our investigation with his 'I'm innocent' routine, Jim. We have to keep focusing."

"I know. But what if he is?" She butted her cigarette out in the ashtray and turned on me, more aggressive than intended.

"That's exactly what I'm talking about. He's already inside your head, making you doubt something that happened twenty years ago. Fuck!" I nodded, in total agreement. She was right. Within minutes of first seeing him, he had already planted a big, red flag inside my brain that said 'You Fucked Up' in giant black letters. I had to push it out of my mind or it would hinder any help that I could offer this investigation.

"I hear you, Constable. Loud and clear." I tried to smile and found that the grin I managed made her laugh. It sounded nice, a pleasant change to the previous ten minutes of silence.

"How about we catch up for dinner? My place. Say 7.30?" she asked.

"Why, Officer Connor? Are you asking me on a date?" I replied and noticed colour flushing her cheeks. Now it was my turn to laugh a little. "It's OK, I'm just kidding. I'd love to." As she pulled over to the kerb in front of my hotel, Steph grabbed a pen and quickly wrote her address on a scrap of paper. She handed it to me, then told me not to be late in a very serious voice. I thanked her, promising to be on time. Fortunately, punctuality had always been one of my strong points.

8.

The taxi arrived shortly after 7. Having no idea what the meal would consist of, I had purchased both a red and a white wine during a quick trip down main street, although I was far from a wine connoisseur, preferring a cold beer with any meal. Turns out, I needn't have bothered, as to my surprise, Steph was also an ale kind of girl. The taxi drove in to her driveway a few minutes ahead of schedule, I paid the driver and watched him creep slowly up Robertson's Boulevard and back to the main end of town. When I was sure it was close enough to the time, I climbed the half a dozen steps and knocked on the door.

"It's open!" Steph yelled from somewhere inside and I let myself in. "I'm just in the bathroom. Help yourself to a beer from the fridge. I won't be long."

"OK, thank you." The house bore the unmistakable aroma of a lamb roast. I had the unimaginable good luck to grow up in a house where a lamb roast was a requirement at least once a week and something I often craved when homesick. If not my curiosity, at least my stomach would be satisfied tonight.

Once I put the bottles of wine on the dining table, I headed to the kitchen to retrieve the beer. The aroma from the roast grew stronger and more intense with each step, making my mouth salivate with anticipation. The kitchen, although small, had everything necessary, including a second, smaller dining table, already adorned with place settings. To my surprise, the table had been set for three. I wondered who would be joining us as I took a long swig of beer. It felt cold, fresh and tasty, quenching the day's stresses away in an instant. The left wall of the kitchen opened up into a comfortable looking living room, complete with an open fire place that was busy snapping and crackling. The mantle above it held a number of photos which I was about to investigate when Steph stepped into the room.

"Sorry Jim. Almost there."

"Please, take your time," I said as she rushed past me with a basket load of washing. "You have a lovely home."

"Thank you," she replied from somewhere at the back of the house. There was a knock on the front door at that moment and she came back into the room, looked at me for a moment, then went to the door after gesturing to herself to calm down with her palms waving slowly up and down. I heard some muffled voices, then the door closing again. Steph came back into the room with a young girl of maybe 6 or 7 in her arms. My expression must have been one of surprise, Steph flashing me a shy smile as she put the girl down. I noticed a striking resemblance between them.

"Jim, this is my sister Judith. Jude, this is Jim." I took a step forward and held out my hand to her.

"Very pleased to meet you, Judith," I said. The girl seemed a little shy, but shook my hand none the less. She let go after a brief pause, then went back to Steph, half hiding behind her sister's leg. Steph saw the bottles on the table and went to them, picking the red up.

"Why, thank you, kind sir. I don't really do wine, but if I had to choose, then red it would be."

"I wasn't sure what we were having, so thought I'd bring both," I said, but then quickly added "but beer works for me. Truly, thanks." She smiled at that, picked up her own bottle and clinked with me, wishing us good health.

9.

The meal was amazing, and a little surprising. I wasn't expecting such a fantastic home cooked dinner from someone so young, but then felt a little embarrassed again at presuming to know her situation, or her age, or her cooking skills, for that matter. The gravy she had made from scratch, so rich and deep with a flavour that actually rivalled my own mother's in comparison. Once we had finished dessert, a warm slice of apple pie with a scoop of vanilla ice cream, Steph helped Judith prepare for bed, then tucked her in and read a story from a big red book Judith brought to her. I could hear her reading the story of Goldilocks, and the voices she was using for the bears were actually pretty good. I sat in the living room, sipping another beer, staring into the flames of the fire. It had always been one of my favourite moments of any evening, when you could just relax, and let the dancing flames and crackling pops of the wood carry your mind away.

Unfortunately for me, and probably due to the events of the past couple of days, my mind had wandered back to the first dead body I had ever seen, one of Lucifer's victims that we found only two weeks after I started at Cider Hill. Her name had been Annabelle Cruz, a 22-year-old waitress who had worked at the Railway Hotel. She disappeared after finishing work, never making it back to her parent's house where she still lived. We learnt from friends that she had a habit of cutting through the cemetery on her way home, a shortcut that saved her having to walk the three blocks down and around the lake. We don't know how the killer persuaded her to go with him, but when we found her in an old abandoned shed out on the Munro's farm, five miles out of town, she had been bound fed upon, the only injuries being those from where he had chewed on her and the marks from where she was bound by her wrists and ankles. Most of her right arm had been stripped clean of flesh, and he had begun to feed on her left arm when he stopped.

It was the Munro's dog that found her, James Munro hearing his Kelpie barking furiously at something and refusing to come when called. When he had followed the sounds of barking, he had discovered the gruesome scene, a family on the neighbouring farm some 3 miles away hearing the farmer's blood-curdling scream floating across the fields between them.

"She is asleep," Steph said as she walked into the room, breaking my thoughts.

"That dinner was amazing, Steph. Really." Colour flushed her cheeks as she sat down on the seat next to mine.

"Thanks. I'd been taught from an early age," she said as she took a sip of her wine glass. "And this wine is actually pretty good."

"Did your Mum teach you?"

"No. My Mum didn't do much cooking. She was born blind. But we had a lady that came in for most of my childhood. Old Mrs. Marsh. Four times a week she would come cook and clean for us. Then as I grew older, her visits became less frequent. But not before bestowing me with her lamb roast recipe." She giggled a little, staring into the fire, a distant memory in her eyes.

"Wow, blind. That must have been hard."

"I never knew any different, so I guess it was just the norm?"

"Of course, sorry. And your father? And please, feel free to tell me to shut up if I'm prying." I didn't want to sound like I was conducting an investigation.

"No, it's OK. I never knew my father. My mum and dad had, what you would call, a whirlwind romance. At least that's how she used to describe it. His name was Eddie, and they met by the river where my mum used to sit and enjoy the sunshine. She often told me that she could hear Eddie approach from a distance because he would always whistle this tune. What was it called? For Ellen? No, that's not it. Some foreign name. Aaahh, I can't remember," she croaked as she tapped a finger to her forehead.

"Fur Elise?" I said and her eyes instantly lit up.

"Yes, that's the one. How did you know?"

"My mum used to play piano, and that was one of her favourite tunes. I have many, many childhood memories of sitting at home, reading, building models, or just listening to her play from my bedroom." She nodded, set her wine glass on the coffee table, then took my arm and coaxed me up. She led the way, beckoning me to follow. In one of the back rooms, and to my astonishment, sat a Beale piano, the same type my mother still owned. It sat nestled against one wall, its deep chestnut covers shining with polish.

"This was my mum's. I had to move Jude and I here when she passed away a couple of years ago, but this is the one thing I will cherish forever. She always played that song too although her own repertoire of music was quite large. She loved playing this," she said as she ran a finger lovingly across the wooden fallboard. Her eyes were distant and I could tell she was having a moment. I stood quietly, leaning against the doorframe.

"How about your parents?" she suddenly asked without looking around at me.

"My father was a carpenter." I suddenly laughed at a memory of my own surfacing, "he would always say 'if it was good enough for Jesus, then it's good enough for me', every time we discussed my job prospects." She smiled at that, then slowly uncovered the keys. Her fingers began to dance lightly across the white teeth, a soft tinkle dancing around the room. I didn't place the melody, but it sounded familiar.

"And your mum?"

"She lives in Carlton. She's always been a mad knitter," I said smiling to myself, "so much so, that she could fully support herself with the money she makes from selling her wares at the Queen Vic market. Not that she needs to though. It's just one of those hobbies that's turned into much more." Her nod told me she knew exactly what I meant. The sounds coming from the old Beale sounded incredible. "You play really well."

"Thank you. It's been a while since I've played anything. I really want to teach Jude as well. Carlton, wow. That was my first station after the academy."

"Can I ask you a question?" I said, cautiously. She stopped playing for a moment, looking at me. Then she smiled, restarting the melody, and as she slowly began to tinkle the keys, I finally placed the melody. It was "In the Mood" by Glen Miller.

"Sure, of course."

"Is Judith actually your sister?" Her smile vanished, and she stopped playing so suddenly that for a moment I honestly thought she was going to throw me out, the lines on her face becoming pronounced in an instant. I put my hands up in a surrender. "I'm sorry, I shouldn't have pried."

"No, honestly, it's OK," she said, although her frown told me otherwise. "It was just unexpected, that's all. It's something that… well, I haven't really discussed with anyone in so long." She paused, looking at the piano keys with a look of puzzlement on her face. I waited, unsure of what she was thinking. Then she turned to me, seriousness replacing puzzlement. "Jim, can I trust you?"

10.

"Of course. It's not like I run the local newspaper," I replied, trying to sound humorous. She didn't smile at that. Steph looked down at her fingers for a long time, and for a moment, I thought she wasn't going to answer. And then without any warning, she began to cry, big tears streaming down and splashing onto the piano keys. She tried to muffle her sobs, but they came thick and fast, almost like an overwhelming asthma attack. I felt a little panicked, unsure of what I had opened within her.

"Steph, I'm so sorry, I didn't-"

"No, please, it's OK," she said through one hand, wiping away the tears from her cheeks. I went and sat next to her on the piano stool, putting one arm around her shoulders. She leant in and put her head on my shoulder, still sobbing lightly.

She suddenly forced herself to stop crying, stood and asked me to follow her back to the living room. As we sat back down on the sofa, the fire made her cheeks sparkle, the tears looking like glitter on her face. We sat facing the flames. Steph took a sip from her glass, took another, then held the glass in her lap protectively. It was a good five minutes before she began to talk again, her eyes never leaving the fireplace.

"His name was Toby Warner. We had gone to school in Ballarat together although he was in a higher class than me. He was a couple of years older than I was. Well, four actually. I loved him, Jim," she said, looking at me. "Anyway, his father refused to allow us to see each other. They were Jewish and Toby's father was very strict, demanding his son marry a sweet Jewish girl. It didn't stop us. I don't think anything could stop us." She paused again, staring into the flames, the occasional crackle breaking the room's silence. "We began to see each other more and more and of course his father opposed us more and more. Then, as if to bless our relationship, I fell pregnant with Jude." I could see the tears well up in her eyes again, wanted to go and comfort her, then thought better of it. "If only his father had accepted us," she croaked, her sobbing threatening to start again. She took another sip and regained control.

"Toby was so happy when I told him. He had, I don't know, this look of pride in his eyes. He told me we would marry as soon as possible and began to make all these plans." She paused again and I could see the words stuck in her throat, the raw emotion making it harder for her to talk. Taking another sip then drawing a long, drawn-out breath, she finally continued. "He was going to enlist. He told me that once he was in the army, he would send for me and we could live near the base. We could be a family. His father wasn't happy, of course. He ended up cutting Toby out of the family entirely. Kicked him out of the house before he had a chance to get any of the plans started. We ended up living with my mum for a brief time while his enlistment went through. All up, it took about 3 months for his acceptance to come through." She turned to look at me. "You should have seen his face when he read his letter of confirmation, Jim. His face, it," she hesitated, searching for the right word, one large tear, looking like a Christmas bauble in the fire light, slowly creeping down the side of her face. "it looked like he had just won a brand-new home for us. I guess, in a roundabout way, he had. He picked me up in his arms and twirled me around, that big smile never leaving his face."

Steph stood, picked up a log and tossed it into the fire. There was a sparkle of tiny embers that flew slightly out and up, the fireplace giving a couple of snaps and pops, then she settled back into her chair.

"Did you end up marrying?" I asked, but she slowly shook her head, her eyes staring back into the flames again as they took hold of the new log and slowly licked the sides, gradually enveloping it.

"Toby left on the bus for Melbourne the following week." Her voice was now almost a whisper as she fought to contain her emotion within. Judging by the tears, it was a fight she was about to lose. "The doctors told me that he died almost instantly. The bus ran off the road on a bend near Mount Macedon. The driver survived and said there had been a sudden downpour, then a car had passed them a little too close and he had tried to steer the bus away but lost control. It slid sideways, rolled and then slammed into a tree." The sobs began now, her words becoming almost inaudible. She fought them away desperately, wanting to share her sadness with me. "Toby was flung half out of one of the windows and was trapped between the bus and the tree. I never got to say-" But that was as far as she got, her sobs now putting a halt to any further words she wanted to share. I did the only thing I could think of and removed a handkerchief from my pocket, handing it to her. She accepted it and wiped at her eyes.

"I'm sorry for your loss. I, too, lost someone close to me when I was about your age." Steph looked at me, tears still flowing, but they had slowed. "Yes, it's true. But definitely a story for another day." I took a sip of my beer and waited for her to regain her composure, which she did relatively quickly, considering her grief. She took a sip of wine then lit a cigarette, blowing the tendrils of blue smoke toward the fireplace. We sat in silence for almost ten minutes before she began to speak again.

"It was just so dam cruel; you know? There I was, 16; pregnant; in school; living with my mum and the father of my unborn child dead. My mum and I spent many nights talking and crying and deciding what to do. In the end, we decided to have the baby and then move to the city. Somewhere where nobody knew us and there wouldn't be too many questions asked. For me, I wanted a job where I didn't have to be constantly explaining the situation. It was my mum that convinced me to just call Jude my sister for the time being. There was really no reason to explain anything to anyone, and once we arrived in Cider Hill years later, people didn't really know us. My mum never had a huge number of friends around these parts. She stayed home more than anything and when she did venture out, it was Ballarat that she would visit more often than not." I understood the politics with unwed mothers of newborn infants. I also know that it would have been an uphill struggle to keep the baby in the first place with most being forced to put the baby up for adoption, not that I wanted to open that can of worms.

"And now you have a job where you get to ask the questions." She laughed at that; a sound that made me smile.

"Yes. I guess that was one of the reasons I wanted to become a police constable. I wanted to ask the questions, not answer them." She turned to me again, holding her cigarette in one hand. "Thank you for listening, Jim. I'm sorry I put that on you, but I haven't really ever had the chance to tell anybody before." I held my hand up, stopping her.

"Don't mention it. And I promise you that I will never share it with anybody." She stood, walked over to me and kissed my cheek. I stood before her and held her close, hugging her tightly. She returned my hug for a moment then pulled away.

"Ok," she said, tossing her cigarette butt into the fire, "time to do some work."

11.

Steph led the way back out into the dining room and opened the top box from Crab Apple. She began to pull out its contents a piece at a time, depositing each on to the now almost empty table. There were folders, books, loose bits of papers and more folders. When the box was empty, she threw it into the far corner of the room, and started on the second one. Once that was also empty and discarded of, we began to separate all the items out individually. There were visitor logs, medical records, criminal records, disciplinary files, officer's logs and daily prison logs. There were folders with specific years from the 30s all the way to the 50s.

"There certainly is a lot of stuff there," I said when we had it all separated. Steph picked a folder up and handed it to me.

"Probably a good place to start?" she said, and I saw it was all the visitor logs that included Lightman's for the past 20 years. She needed two hands to lift it due its size, at least 5 inches thick. I opened it and discovered page after page of logs, bearing the names of prisoners and visitors.

"Do you have a pen and some scrap paper I can write on? To take notes. You know, keep track of stuff" Steph nodded, opened a drawer in a desk that sat against the far wall and took out a writing pad. She took a pen from the desktop then handed them to me. I took the folder and sat in one of the chairs, removing the paperwork and began working my way through the stack. Steph opened a folder marked "Officer's Logs" and sat opposite to me at the table. Our investigation had officially begun.

Chapter 5: The Trail Begins

1.

By the time we were too tired to continue, the sun was already breaking over the far horizon, its rays of bright sunshine creeping between the drawn curtains. I had managed to compile a significant list of people that were of interest, two in particular. One was the reporter that Lightman had already told us about. The other was a man called Clancy Higgins.

"Clancy Higgins? Isn't he the school janitor?" Steph had asked as I read the name to her.

"Unless there is another Clancy Higgins around. And get this. Clancy visited Lightman once a month, every third Saturday, never missing a single time in over 17 years. And then, three years ago he stopped. Just like that."

"That doesn't make sense. Why would he stop visiting? And why was he visiting him in the first place? Were they related?"

"It doesn't say. But if I can predict the future, and on this note I think I can with some confidence, I think we'll probably be visiting Mr. Higgins pretty soon." I showed her the list of dates when he had been to the prison and she read them with interest, handing it back to me once finished perusing both sides.

"Think I'll make a pot of strong coffee. You up for a visit to a Mr. Higgins?"

"Definitely. What about Judith?"

"Mrs. Wong is not only my lovely neighbour, she's also Jude's nanny. And my cleaner when I need one. And she wakes up every morning before the sun comes up to do her Tai Chi in her back yard." She went to the window and pulled the curtains apart. "See?" I walked over and saw that the window overlooked her own backyard as well as a clear view over the timber fence and into the adjoining plot. There was a small Asian lady doing some poses on what looked like a tiled surface. She moved gracefully from one position to another as Steph excused herself. I kept looking out the window and saw Steph pop her head over the fence and talk to the woman. She stopped, listened, then nodded vigorously. Steph came back in and went to her room to dress while I went to the kitchen and took care of the coffee situation; hot, black, strong and lots of it.

2.

We were on the road ten minutes later. Mrs. Wong had agreed to sit and keep an eye on Judith, still sound asleep while going about some light cleaning duties. She seemed undeterred with the time of day, smiling throughout the requests Steph had made of her. We were headed back to the primary school, sure that Clancy Higgins would already be busy preparing for the day ahead.

Rather than park in the school car park, Steph parked down a side street, adjacent to the school oval. She pointed Clancy out to me, a man busy scurrying from one rubbish bin to another, pushing a cart before him that resembled a small dump master. He would stop next to a rubbish bin, lift it out of a metal holder, then tip its contents into the trolley. He moved slowly and looked to be walking with a slight limp.

"Know anything about him?" I asked Steph as we walked in through a small side gate. She shook her head.

"Nothing except that he's the janitor here."

We could hear singing as we neared him, the man not hearing our approach until we were almost upon him. When he finally did realize our presence, he almost jumped at the sight of us.

"Clancy Higgins?" Steph asked him and he nodded hesitatingly. He answered with a slow, somewhat laboured voice, as if he found it difficult to speak.

"Yes. That's my name." For a moment he just stood there, eyeing us off. He offered us his hand, remembered that he was wearing gloves and removed one, then re-offered us a handshake which we both returned. He also seemed to talk with a slight impairment, but the main feature that stood out was one of his eyes appearing blind. It was milky white, the eyeball looking tired and worn out, a large cataract covering almost the entire surface. If he decided to wear an eyepatch with the rest of his natural features, I figured he would have looked exactly like a pirate.

"Clancy, I'm Constable Connor. Do you think we could talk with you for a minute?" He turned his head to her, paused and stared for a moment, then smiled.

"Sure. I could take a break."

"Thank you, Clancy," Steph replied. She looked around for a bit, then spotted a wooden table and bench near the monkey bars. Beckoning him towards it, Clancy followed her. When we were all seated, Steph on one side and Clancy and I on the other facing her, Steph began to ask him questions, although given that he appeared a bit on the slow side, she kept them short and basic.

"How long have you been the janitor here, Clancy?" He looked up at the sky and appeared to count in his head. One of his hands lifted a little and I could see the fingers twitching slightly, each one at a time, as if he was numbering them.

"I think about four years now," he said after a minute.

"Do you like it here?"

"Yes, very much. Mr. Bester says that if I work hard, then it's a job I can retire on." He broke a smile at that as if he was actually picturing his retirement.

"Can I ask you how old you are?" Steph asked. Again, his eyes went skyward, as if calculating.

"32. No wait," more calculating, fingers working and twitching, "no, 33. Yes, 33." Steph smiled at him as he corrected himself and he seemed to relax, his shoulders visibly sagging a little.

"Clancy, can I ask you about someone? A man you visited up at Crab Apple?" He considered her question for a moment, his expression vacant. Then after thinking about it for a few seconds, something seemed to switch on inside him, as if remembering something from long ago. He also appeared to cringe a little as if recalling something bad.

"Are you going to ask me about Harry?"

"Yes, that's right. Harry Lightman. Do you remember visiting him up at Crab Apple?" He looked down at his hands, interlacing his fingers.

"Is it OK to talk about Harry?" Steph asked and Clancy appeared to wince, although he began to nod a little. I reached out and touched his arm. He flinched, looked up at me, then forced a smile.

"It's OK, Clancy. Take your time," I said to him reassuringly. After a moment his shoulders relaxed again.

"Sure. I visited Harry. Up in jail."

"Yes, that's right. Clancy, how do you know Harry?" she asked him. He looked at her for a long time before answering as if trying to remember the lines to a play. His lips would begin to move, mouthing silent words, then stop. After a minute he spoke.

"Harry used to live behind our house. He was a nice man. Used to let me help him fix stuff."

"Fix stuff? Like what?" I asked.

"Harry would always have stuff that needed fixing. He had this motorbike that he loved. He would work on it often and I would hand him the spanner he needed, or clean parts. He even took me for rides on the motorbike." He grinned widely, revealing several gaps and a couple of leaners. "That was fun."

"I bet it was. And you used to visit him a lot, didn't you?" Steph continued.

"Yup. Harry showed me how to play Poker. That's a card game. Harry loves playing cards. 'Kings and Queens used to play' he would always say."

"Yes, they did. Did you happen to do anything else for Harry?"

"Anything else?" He thought for a moment. "I brought him books, too. He likes to read. And these." He pulled out an open packet of Juicy Fruit and held it out to us, showing us the name on the side of the packet. "I love them, too. I always carry a packet. Would you like one?" He took one out and held it out to Steph. She shook her head and when he offered it to me, I accepted. He popped one into his mouth, then smiled as he saw me chew, as if victorious. "Yum, aren't they?".

"What sort of books?" I asked, putting the silver foil in my pocket. He began folding his own foil, this way and that, until it resembled a tiny "W".

"Oh, Harry liked the classics. 'There's nothing wrong with reading the classics' he told me. Moby Dick, Treasure Island."

"Clancy, did Harry ever ask you to do anything you didn't want to?" I asked and his expression changed to one of fear in an instant. He slowly shook his head from side to side. "It's OK to tell, he won't hurt you anymore."

"No, Harry never asked me nothin like that. Never." He spoke slowly, almost too quietly, for fear of anyone overhearing him speak. Steph leant a little forward, lowering her own voice.

"Because if he did," she said quietly, "it would be pretty important to tell someone. So that they could stop him. Are you sure?" For a moment, I thought he was actually going to say something. His mouth opened a little to let the words come out, but after a few seconds he closed it again, his gaze never leaving the table top. His head began to shake slowly from side to side.

"No, Harry is a nice man. He never asked me nothin like that," repeating himself.

"OK, Clancy. It's OK, mate," I said to him. Steph gave me a little nod and I stood, holding out my hand. "Thank you for your time, buddy." He reached out and shook it, smiling again.

"And if you ever want to talk, Clancy, you just have to ask, OK?" Steph finished. He flashed her a big grin.

"Thank you. I will." And with that he trotted back to his bin cart, whistling as he went back to his work.

3.

Steph dropped me off at the hotel, then headed to the police station to update them of what we were doing. We agreed to meet at Mrs. Homestead's Café at 1, which would give me a couple of hours sleep. I stood on the footpath and watched her drive off, the morning still young. Once her car rounded the corner, I headed into the hotel and bounded up the stairs, 2 at a time. As I reached the second floor, almost jumping up the final steps at a run, I rounded the corner and felt my heart leap out of my chest as I crashed into someone walking the other way. They went stumbling backwards as a tray of breakfast dishes went crashing to the hardwood floor in an explosion of porcelain. The woman let out a startled scream, just before hitting the floor with a painful thud.

"Oh my God, I'm so sorry," I said as I reached down to help the poor girl. A couple of doors opened further down the hall and I saw inquisitive eyes pop out, peering at the commotion. I looked back down at the girl, now trying to prop herself up. She began to apologize quietly, the shock and surprise evident in her tone, and I was about to say how sorry I was, that I was the klutz who was at fault, when she lifted her head to look at me. Our eyes met and instant recognition enveloped us both. Inside my chest, I felt my heart stop.

4.

"Hello Jim," she said, holding a hand out. I took it and helped her back to her feet, my eyes unable to leave hers. I opened my mouth to speak but no words would come out. She giggled a little, then as she stood, winced and reached down, rubbing her knee. "You always did know how to make an entrance," she said through gritted teeth.

"Hello Tami," I finally managed, although it came out in an almost whisper. She began to pick up the spilled dishes, one shattered cup and a few bits of broken crockery scattered down the hall. The peering eyes had receded back into their doors as I retrieved the broken pieces of china. I brought them back to her, the tray now back to an almost pre-Jim state.

"Tami, I'm sorry."

"Sorry for leaving?" she replied, cutting me off. I groaned inside, remembering our last conversation, 18 long years before. I nodded my head, my gaze now shifting to the floor uncomfortably. I'm hesitant to relive the events that shaped both our lives back in the early post-Lucifer days, but I will do my best to fill you in on a bit of back-story. It's the least I can do, considering you're reading my story at all.

She began to walk past me and down the stairs, and would have continued walking if I hadn't reached out and grabbed her arm. At first, I didn't think she would stop, but she did, standing on the first step for a moment without turning around.

"I would really love to catch up, Tami. Please?" I let go of her arm as she turned to look at me. She smiled again, that joy still in her eyes. Even after all these years, it was the one thing I could always picture when I closed my own. The happiness that lived in there.

"Yes, that would be nice. I finish at 7, if you want to chat, I'll be waiting out the front. Don't be late." And with that, she turned and headed down the stairs, the tray balanced on one hand, the other gripping the hand rail. Even though her face was smiling, her tone was as stern as a brick in the face. I watched her walk down the stairs then turned and slowly walked to my room. Given the events of the past couple of days, I hadn't even considered running into her. I surprised myself with the realization that Tami Kennedy hadn't even crossed my mind. She had been as distant from my memories as the rest of this town. After I left all those years ago, the nightmares eventually subsided into the fabled place of 'best forgotten', and her along with those memories.

I unlocked my door and went into the small room that served as my temporary home for as long as I could make it work. For the time being, a room with a bed was all my wishes desired, and in the dark, gloomy room, the outline of the bed looked like paradise. I closed the door behind me, kicked off my shoes and fell forward onto the mattress. Without realising just how tired I was, I had time enough to remember her smile from a few minutes ago. Time enough to see her laughing eyes; to recall the sweet smell of her perfume; to see the lines of her face; her long brunette hair. Time enough to realize that I still loved her, before sleep stole me away.

5.

The dream that invaded my sleep that morning was a mixture of fact, fiction, horror and tragedy. None of it contributed to a restful sleep and all of it ensured I would wake in a hot and sweaty mess a short time later. At the forefront of my nightmare, every nightmare I had since my early 20s, was Harry Lightman. Although this was the younger more athletic version that I had chased along the Kennedy driveway two decades before. Harry was chasing me, carrying Tami's severed head in one hand and my Mother's in the other. And my Mother was calling out to me at the top of her voice, almost screaming.

"YOU PROMISED TO PROTECT US, JAMES. YOU PROMISED!" she cried. I turned as I ran, seeing the bloodied spittle fly from her lips, her bared teeth snarling at me. Her hair hung in ragged clumps, blood matted bits clinging to her cheeks as the rain fell in biblical proportions. Occasionally, lightning lit the sky in great spiderwebs that sketched their way across the dark, the severed heads temporarily illuminated in all their revulsion. My feet tangle as I go sprawling into the mud, my hands coming to a halt submerged in a puddle. My face is mere inches from the water's surface and as I'm about to lift myself out, Tami's face surfaces slowly beneath mine, her eyes closed, her face peaceful as if in a deep sleep. I reach out to touch her cheek and as my fingers near her smooth skin, her eyes suddenly burst open as her mouth contorts into a horrible grimace. A scream, loud enough to wake the dead, comes coursing out. I scramble to my feet and turn to run, only to find Harry standing directly behind me, his teeth, pointed and razor sharp, bared and ready to snap into my throat. He grabs me by the shoulders, pulls me nearer, then whispers into my face.

"Time to set things right, James." He lunges forward and I feel his teeth sink deep into my neck as jets of blood warm my chest. I scream, a thick gargled disappointment as I try to push him away from me to break free. I try to scream again and-

6.

-wake to the sound of a knock on my door.

"Jim?" I try desperately to climb out of bed, to wake myself from the dream still filling my mind, the world a murky mystery to me.

"JIM?"

"One sec," I yell at the door and finally manage to wrench myself out from beneath the damp sheet. I check my watch as I take the five or so steps to the door and see it's only 10.30. When I open the door, the look on Steph's face is all I need to tell me the grim news she wants to share.

"There's been another one." I groan as she confirms my hunch, walk back to the bed and begin to put on my shoes.

"Did you get any sleep, kiddo?" I ask but Steph shakes her head.

"It's OK. I'll sleep later." I watched her look in the mirror as she spoke and saw the fatigue in her eyes. I finished lacing my shoes, grabbed a jacket and followed her out. A minute later she was behind the wheel of her car driving us to the latest crime scene.

"Another teacher, Annie Wilcox," Steph began once we were moving. "I was still at the station when the call came in. Her boyfriend made the find after she failed to show for class this morning. Pete and Lewis are already on their way to the house. Should be there by now, she only lives on Clifford Lane." The car suddenly lurched to one side, tyres squealing. A dog had wandered into the middle of the road and thankfully, Steph still had quick enough reflexes to swerve around the little guy.

"Dam dog," she screamed as she fought the car back under control. I reached out and touched her arm. It felt cold.

"Rademeyer is convinced it's a copycat. Said Lightman is locked up as tight as a snare drum."

"He said that?"

"Yup. He had another 'chat' with me just before the call came in. Told me not to waste all our time chasing a ghost. He said 'follow your hot leads', or something like that."

"I know what he's saying, but what if he did find a way to get out of jail?"

"And then what? Breaks back into jail when he's done?" I hadn't pondered that part of it but now that I heard the words, wondered.

"What a brilliant alibi," I finally whispered.

"Alibi?"

"Imagine if that was his plan all along. Imagine. He doesn't mind prison, breaks out every so often to feed his hunger, then boom. Right back home each morning. I mean think about it."

"It would be a hell of a plan. *If* he found a way out of jail."

"Something tells me the key to everything is somewhere in that box we got from the jail."

"I hope you're right, Jim. Otherwise we're gonna end up chasing nothing but our tails. Anyway, Jack and Lester should already be at the latest. They were out in the car. Pete and Lewis left the station when I did."

"Wait, Lester? As in Lester Redding?" I asked with some bemusement.

"The one and only. Why? You know him?"

"Wow, I can't believe he's still around. He was like ancient when I was a cop." Steph giggled a little.

"Don't let him hear you talk about his age. He gets pretty touchy about that." She was about to say something else, but paused as she turned the car into Clifford Lane, two patrol cars visible at the far end. "There they are."

Like most country towns, houses that are more than a couple of hundred metres from the main street were spaced well apart. Privacy was a luxury many could afford and in Cider Hill, space was plenty. The road, still dirt, was about 700 yards long, maybe a couple of dozen houses in total. They were scattered, some with quite short driveways, some with quite long ones. Several had chimney smoke slowly drifting out from chimneys, fireplaces alight, keeping whoever occupied those homes warm and toasty.

The two officers that were leaning against the fence in front of 24 Clifford Lane looked as pale as ghosts. Jack Dunning was wiping his mouth, looking embarrassingly at the ground. I could tell he had recently bid his breakfast and/ or lunch farewell. Old Lester was leaning against the fence, one hand rubbing the back of the other, his face stern and pale. He watched us approach and I saw his face lighten a little as recognition crept in. He began to walk towards my door as soon as we stopped.

"Jim, oh my God. How have you been?" he said, grasping my hand tightly as he pumped it up and down vigorously.

"Lester, good to see you," I replied with a smile.

"I wish the circumstances were better," he answered back, waving a hand at the cottage behind us.

"How bad is it?" Steph asked. Lester frowned a little.

"It's not good. Prepare yourselves. She's in the bathroom. Far end of the hallway." He let go of my hand and opened the small gate that led into the front yard. It was a pretty white cottage, the two windows that sat either side of the front door, had their floral curtains drawn shut. The front veranda had a small round wooden table and two chairs sitting off to one side. There was a teapot vase on top of it, a small bunch of pink lilies sitting in it. I began to climb the three steps that led to the top of the decking, Steph following behind. Jack and Lester remained at the fence, both watching as we entered the house.

8.

As soon as we crossed the threshold, an aroma hit me that instantly raised my heart beat. It was the same metallic, coppery smell I remembered from the time I saw my very first Lucifer victim. I looked at Steph as she walked through the door, pointed at my nose and watched as she also recognized the scent in the air. The hallway was dark, the two doors either side of the entrance both stood open. On one side sat a bedroom, one small lick of light penetrating the curtain that blocked the window. It had a bed that my mother used to call 'a bed with a lady's touch'. It had a complete set of bedding including multiple pillows, cushions, a blanket and a cover, all in a pretty feast of flowers. In the middle of the bed sat a lonely teddy bear, its sad eyes looking out at us.

On the opposite side of the hallway, the door led into a darkened living room where Pete and Lewis stood, looking dazed. Pete was leaning against a fireplace that sat on the far wall, its fires not likely to burn again for a while. There was a sofa, two chairs and a coffee table. A white mug sat on one side of the coffee table, looking like someone had a hot drink before bed. Several photographs hung above the mantle and hanging on the side wall, a painting of a river scene, a fisherman standing on one bank, flanked by bright trees. The room looked cosy and inviting. The other officer was sitting in one of the chairs and never took his eyes off the floor.

There were two more doors, one on the left and one on the right further along the hallway, and right at the end, stood an open door that led into the bathroom. The light was on and I could see a shadow on the far wall, that had the unmistakable outline of someone suspended with their arms up over their heads. I swallowed hard, my throat feeling like a dry slate. I couldn't muster any spittle and my throat burned a little as I tried to swallow a second time. The house was so quiet, I thought for a moment I could hear my own heartbeat. I could certainly feel it, beating hard and fast in my temples. That nervous feeling of adrenalin burning in the pit of my stomach grew stronger with each step I took, closer to the inevitable scene I was about to endure. I slowed a little and felt something brush my arm. I jumped to one side, a small scream trying to escape my lips. I looked down and saw Steph's hand, the other over her own mouth. We looked at each other and let out a faint giggle. That small laugh relieved a lot of the apprehension that was gripping both of us.

"OK. Let's do it," I said, and walked the remaining steps into the bathroom, and the horror that awaited within.

Like so many homes in the 50s, the bathroom only had 3 things in it. A bath with a stand-in shower, a sink and a toilet. A small window sat above the toilet and I could see that it stood slightly ajar. The bath had a curtain rail that encircled it, the curtain pulled completely off and folded neatly, then placed on top of the closed toilet, as if waiting to be put away. Her hands were bound together then tied to the rail, her wrists not quite reaching high enough. She only stood about 5 foot 2 at best and the killer had to use a second rope to reach the rail. She was stripped naked, her black hair hanging down over her face. Although her face looked peaceful, as if sleeping, it was the horror below the waist that will forever fill my nightmares.

The killer had chewed on both of her thighs. The front of her legs looked almost like ground hamburger, strips of flesh hanging this way and that in messed-up strands. There were bits of sinew that jutted out from exposed muscle and both legs looked like they were fed upon for a long time. He had plugged the bath so all the blood that the victim lost was now filled with it. By the look of it, the red puddle looked to be several inches deep. I wasn't sure how long she had been hanging there, but it must have been for longer than a day. I could see maggots already consuming her, their writhing masses filling the open wounds.

But it was the eyes that once again confirmed what we were looking for. Her index fingers had been chewed off and jammed into her eye sockets, the shiny fluid still glistening on her cheeks.

We spent another twenty minutes or so carefully looking over the room, then headed out to look at the rest of the house. We were joined by more officers, as well as the coroner, and once finished made our way back to the police station. Rademeyer summoned us as soon as he became aware of our presence and we spent an hour or so going over what we had discovered. His ears pricked when we mentioned the index fingers. Rademeyer was convinced we had a copycat on our hands and said he had already assigned a number of officers to door knock the area. He wanted Steph and I to continue to build our own list of suspects and present it to him the next morning. By the time Steph and I came out from the station, it was nearing 4.30, sleep the furthest thing from my mind. Steph, however, looked ready to drop.

"You need sleep, kiddo," I said as we walked back towards her car. As if replying to me, she let out a huge yawn, her mouth almost obscuring her entire head. I chuckled a little and before she could finish, let out a snort. "I'll drive," I said and after considering for a moment, she handed me her keys.

The drive back to her house was in silence, Steph slowly inhaling one of her cigarettes. I pulled the car into the driveway just as she butted it out.

"You want to come in?" she asked, but I shook my head.

"I can't. I have to go see someone."

"Ah, yes. Tami Kennedy by any chance?" I was a little surprised.

"What? How the hell do you know already?" I said.

"Small town, Jim."

"Of course. Geez, I knew it would get around, but that fast?"

"You want me to call you a taxi?"

"No, it's OK. Think I want to walk. Clear my head a bit." She laughed as we got out.

"Drop by around 10? We can go through our stuff then." I nodded as I handed her the keys and bid her farewell, walking slowly along her tree-lined street. Thoughts were running crazy inside my head, memories of victims, the smells, the stresses. All the emotions I had forgotten about had returned in a never-ending rush since that first phone call. And now here I was, back in the same place, hunting for another killer. Or maybe even the same one.

9.

After showering, shaving and finishing all the other normal bathroom rituals, I sat on my bed reading over my notes while waiting for the time to reach 7.30. I had been steadily jotting down bits and pieces ever since we left my home a couple of days before, and the small notepad I always kept in my pocket was beginning to fill at a steady pace. There were bits about the people we've spoken to; Clancy and George Bester, Lightman himself, and of course Rademeyer. The victims, their addresses, things I noticed at the crime scenes. The times the coroner believed death had occurred, as well as how they died, although that was probably as clear to you as it was to me. I just couldn't work out how they didn't struggle. How there were no defensive wounds on any of them as if they simply had extended their hands out to him and allowed themselves to be tied up. Last time, all the victims had been spread out around Cider Hill and Daylesford, as well as a couple in the surrounding areas. This time, so far at least, they had all been in Cider Hill, and all within a couple of miles of each other. Two of the victims worked together in the same school as teachers. I ran the notes through my head and kept returning to the fingers. I just couldn't work out why. And neither could anyone twenty years ago.

I was still running this through my head when I noticed the time, 7.20. I decided to head down in case she finished early. I grabbed my jacket and headed out, locking the door behind me. There are some things that city folk will never change.

As I stepped out through the door of the pub, my heart fluttered a little as I saw her standing out on the footpath, leaning against the brick wall of the building. She smiled when she saw me, that same infectious grin I remembered. It lit her entire face up, like a kid on Christmas morning.

"Tami, hey," I said, waving to her.

"Hi Jim." I bent down and gave her cheek a light kiss and felt relief when she returned one on mine.

"Did you want to have dinner here?" I asked, pointing at the pub, but she shook her head.

"I work here, Jim, and people are already gossiping. The gossip I can't help, but their prying eyes I can. You know the saying 'A small town has big eyes and a matching mouth'" And with that, she took my hand, leading me around to a side street running next to the pub. It was a dark lane that had several small flats on either side. Tami stopped in front of one a couple of hundred yards up, opened the iron gate and waved me inside.

"Come on. I can fix us something tasty."

10.

Her flat turned out to be a one-bedroom shoebox, a single fireplace in the kitchen the only heating available. It saddened me to see her living like this. Her living room, if you could call it that, had an old worn-out 2- seater sofa made from red vinyl. There was a coffee table that needed a good sanding down and very little else. A small bookshelf adorned one wall, photos filling most of the shelves except for half a dozen books on the top one. To my surprise, I found one of them to be mine. I'm still not sure why, but seeing it, gave me a burst of embarrassment. I think I may have even blushed a little.

"Chops OK?" she asked, sticking her head around the corner as I put my book back on the shelf.

"Chops are perfect," I said, turning and walking into her kitchen. Tami excused herself for a moment and headed out into the hallway. I could hear her tinkering around in the bathroom, then returned, having replaced her work uniform with pants and jumper, as well as Ugg boots on her feet.

"How have you been?" she asked as she began juggling pots and pans, peeling vegetables and throwing food this way and that. She always had a way in the kitchen, one that I could never compete with.

"I've been alright. How about you? How is your dad?" I replied, trying to stay out of her way, a task quite difficult, given the size of the room.

"Dad passed away a few years ago now. The cancer got him."

"Oh Tami, I didn't know. I'm sorry," I said, my cheeks flushing with colour again.

"Thank you, but that's OK," she said, her smile never wavering, "he chose to smoke three packs a day. I know they say cigarettes aren't bad for you, but personally, I doubt anything that smells so bad can be good for your lungs." The sizzle that came from the thick frying pan as she dropped a number of lamb chops into it, sounded both sweet and satisfying, the aroma filling the room almost instantly. There has always been something about the smell of frying meat that I loved. It reminded me of home. I noticed something tickling the back of my mind, trying to let itself be seen, almost like a distant thought that was fighting to come out from the murkiness. I tried to pull it forward, but it wouldn't come. Was it some memory I had about frying meat? I wasn't sure and let it go, resisting its pull.

We ate in her living room, sitting on the sofa chairs with our plates in our laps. It was the way we used to eat our meals when we were still seeing each other, a long time ago. The lamb chops were seasoned with a sprinkle of salt, pepper and paprika. There was also a hint of lemon which really set them off. The potatoes were boiled and served with a generous dollop of butter and the vegie portion consisted of peas, corn and sliced carrots. It wasn't what you would call fine dining, but for what it's worth, I really enjoyed it. Tami's cooking always had a way of satisfying my taste buds.

"How's your Mum?" she asked as she picked up a chop. That's something I always found attractive about her. She was never one for elegance. She said it how it was and played it how it played. No glitter or camouflage. She took a bite from the meat then wiped lamb fat from her chin.

"She's good, thanks. Had a touch of the flu last year but she pulled through. Other than that, all good."

"Did you ever marry?"

"No, never found the right one," I said as I shoveled a load of peas in. "Did you?" Her eyes seemed to glimmer for a moment, then she looked into the fire burning in the next room.

"No, marriage was never going to be my thing. Not much of a housewife, I'm afraid." I put my fork down, then lowered the plate onto my lap.

"What ever happened to us, Tam?" I said and watched her recoil a little. Although we had a slight history, there could have been a lot more. A tear rolled down her cheek, paused, then dropped into her lap.

"The nightmares won't go away, Jim. They, just seem to change," she cried. I could see her fighting them but the tears began to fall harder, her words choking in her throat. I set my plate aside and went to her, kneeling on the floor before her. She didn't resist as I put my arms around her, hugging her tight. After a moment, she returned the hug, holding me so tight that breathing became difficult.

"I'm sorry, Tami. I really am. I wish I had stayed. I hope you can forgive me. I just couldn't." When she managed to regain some composure, Tami looked into my eyes for a long time.

"I do understand, Jim. I'm probably the only one that truly does understand why you left, and I don't blame you." And then she lowered her head on my shoulder and held me close.

11.

It was a little before 10 by the time I left Tami's. I felt happy that we managed to talk and finally settle the questions that had been left unanswered for all those years. We talked for a solid two hours, discussing everything we had carried with us for all that time. The why's, the when's and most importantly the questions that we wanted answered but were always too afraid to ask. There was no animosity, no guilt. In the end, we agreed that we would let the past remain where it was and take things one day at a time. When it came time for me to leave, she had walked me to the door and then without warning, had leaned in and kissed me. It was a long and lustful kiss, from both of us. I still found her incredibly attractive and my emotions that had awoken when I first bumped into her were now burning brightly.

"How was it?" Steph asked as she opened the door for me, her grin signalling her desire for gossip.

"It was good to catch up. Any news?" She looked at me a moment longer, then realized I wasn't about to give her any. Gossip was not one of my strong suits.

"Two crews were door knocking most of the day and didn't get a single lead. Nothing. No one heard anything nor saw anything."

"Did you manage to get any more out of the box from the prison?"

"Actually, I did. I found out about Jeremy Winters."

"Who's Jeremy Winters?" I asked, the name not registering any sort of recognition.

"Jeremy Winters was a prison officer at Crab Apple in the late 40s."

"OK?" I said, still unsure of where she was heading.

"Jeremy used to have a sister, Veronica. Veronica met a soldier called Brian Smith when she was 19. They married a year later, Veronica Winters becoming," she paused, waving a hand back and forth, waiting for me to register the name.

"Holy shit, Veronica Smith?" I finished for her, recognition washing over me, not in a good way but rather like steel wool being dragged over my naked skin. A picture of a dead girl, naked and tied to a tree stump, slammed to the forefront of my brain.

"He worked at Crab Apple?" I asked.

"He sure did. Then, in 1949, he was fired."

"Does it say why?" But she shook her head.

"No reason given."

"Do we know where Jeremy Winters is now?" Her face grew a faint smile, her teeth slightly bared, as if happy to reveal a dark secret she just learned herself.

"He's a barber in Geelong. I dropped by and visited his mother. She still lives in town, volunteering at the local Salvation Army store."

"Wow, nice job, officer, I'm impressed."

"So, when do you want to go and pay Mr. Winters a visit?"

Chapter 6: Clues and No Clues

1.

We set out early the next morning in Steph's Holden. It was agreed that I would start the drive and Steph could catch a few more z's if she was able to. If we made good time, we would reach the barber shop before it opened for business, hopefully giving us a window of opportunity to talk to the man without interruption. Steph tuned the radio to 3BA, a Ballarat station, and although fuzzy at times, the tunes still sounded alright. The Penguins were mid-way through singing 'Earth Angel', when I heard the faint confirmation of sleep as Steph's snores drifted to me.

I negotiated the twists and turns of the road, quietly steering us towards our destination. The road was almost completely deserted, not seeing another car until we were well into our journey. By the time the first car passed us, the sun had been in the sky for almost forty minutes.

The streets in Geelong proved to be almost as deserted as the roads that led us to it. The Little Barber Shop sat on the corner of Ryrie and Bellarine Streets, although this morning it looked far from the shopping metropolis it would be in an hour or so. I pulled the FX into a parking spot a couple of doors down from the barber shop. I wanted us to give the man a soft welcome instead of a full-frontal assault. I gave Steph a gentle shake and she grunted once, mumbled something then closed her eyes again. I saw a café a few doors down and decided to go in search of a couple of coffees, instead.

I returned a few minutes later, two coffees and two croissants in hand. I tapped on the passenger side window and when Steph opened her eyes, waved my goods in front of her. She smiled her toothy grin, wound her window down and thanked me for breakfast. I walked back around to the driver's door and sat inside, eating hungrily. I had almost finished the croissant when a burgundy Morris Minor stopped in front of the barber shop and a man wearing a white overcoat climbed out. I nudged Steph who was looking down the other street while sipping her coffee. She looked, winced then nodded her head.

"Looks like our man has arrived," she said. I nodded as we both got out and walked slowly towards the shop, the man now unlocking the front door. He was about to open it when Steph spoke.

"Mr. Winter?" The man turned, looking surprised.

"Yes?" he said, giving the uniformed police woman the once over.

"Sir, I'm Stephanie Connor from Cider Hill Police Station. I was wondering if you had a few minutes?" He looked a little puzzled but nodded.

"Of course, Officer. May I ask what this is regarding?"

2.

Mr. Winter took us through to the back of his shop where a small kitchenette sat. He made a jug of tea as he invited us to sit at the small table. His face had grown grey and bleak in the space of a couple of minutes, changing as soon as he heard the name of his long dead sister, the memories visibly returning to him instantly. I thought I saw his hand shaking as he filled the jug and placed it on the small gas burner.

"We appreciate your time, Mr. Winters. It's important we ask you some questions and I do apologize if it brings back painful memories. We need to get to the bottom of these new murders." Steph spoke with an emphatic voice and I was glad that I had been partnered with a woman. A feminine touch in these situations would always make it so much easier on the person questioned.

"Please, call me Jeremy," he said, not looking up as he prepared the cups. He looked older than 55, a trait I had noticed with nearly everyone involved in this case throughout the years. "You're the one who caught him, aren't you?" he said handing me a cup. It smelled majestic, rich with a hint of lemon.

"Yes, Sir, I was there that night."

"I remember seeing you during the trial. I was there every single day. And every single day he failed to meet my eyes, always looking down at his hands."

"Jeremy, is it true that you worked at Crab Apple?" Steph asked as he handed her a cup.

"Yes, that's right."

"Did no one ever question you regarding your relationship to one of Lightman's victims?"

"They didn't know I was related. Veronica had taken the surname of Brian and I waited a few of years before applying. By the time I was given access to him, Harry Lightman was well and truly old news." Steph took a sip then set her cup down as she spoke.

"May I ask why? Why would you want to work there? Close to him?" I didn't think I needed to hear his answer, knowing what his objective was.

"I wanted to look into his eyes. I wanted to tell him who I was and look into his eyes. I thought that if I could do that, I would know."

"Know what?" I asked.

"Whether he really killed her, of course." Jeremy took a packet of cigarettes out of his shirt pocket, offered us one, which Steph accepted, then lit both with a match.

"Our parents died years before, our father during the great war, our mother shortly after. I still believe Mum died from a broken heart. They were always close, my parents. When Dad was killed during the Gallipoli landings, my mother took it very hard. She withdrew into a shell no one could break her from. I took care of Veronica. She was four years younger than I was." He took a long drag from his cigarette, held the smoke within him for an impossibly long time, then expelled it slowly. I took another sip, waiting for him to continue.

"When she died, I vowed revenge, as anyone would, I'm sure. But for me, he had only added to the misery that had followed my family for such a long time. I sometimes think about what her final thoughts must have been. How terrified she must have been." Tears began to run down his cheeks. He took another drag and regained control of his emotions.

"Take your time, please," Steph said quietly.

"I wanted to wait long enough so that people would forget. They always forget. Give someone enough time and the things that don't matter to them, simply fall by the wayside. I decided to enlist and went to France to fight the Nazis. I was shot, here in the leg," he said as he pulled his pant leg up, revealing a dark scar on the side of his calf, "and managed to return early 1945. More than a decade had gone by and I knew Lightman was sitting comfortable up there in

Crab Apple. I knew that enough time would have passed, and with my service record, managed to secure a position as a guard. I began working at the prison in early 46. I didn't make a beeline for him though. Thought better of it. Instead, I worked wherever they stationed me. This unit, that unit. Eventually, in late 48, my prayers were answered. I was asked to transfer to the S-wing. It housed the worst of the worst. Ten cells for 10 prisoners you never wished to meet, and one of them was of course, Harry Lightman.

"Did he recognize you?" I asked, but Jeremy only shook his head.

"Not even close. He began to chat with me, every day, wanted to chat as if we were best mates."

"About what?" Steph asked, butting her cigarette out.

"Oh, usual crap. The weather, sports. He was a keen Carlton supporter and liked to talk about the previous week's game. Or the coming game, especially if they played Collingwood or Richmond. I'm South Melbourne myself, never could switch to the Cats, even after moving out here. Think they might go all the way this year, too, the Cats. You?" he asked, turning to me.

"Bombers."

"Good for you. Anyway, so there we were, chin wagging on a daily basis. And then, about six months after starting in that unit, I told him. I had to work a night shift, and it was me and young Angus McCredie. 'Course Angus was sound asleep this side of midnight. And, there I was, alone with nothing between me and the killer of my kid sister but a single door. A door to which I had the key." He took another cigarette out, lit it then continued. "I almost opened it, too. I often pictured just going in there and beating that cunt's brains out. Oh," he said, looking at Steph apologetically, "'scuse my language, please."

"You don't have to apologize, Jeremy," Steph said, smiling at him.

"And I cannot tell you just how close I actually came to making that daydream a reality. But…" his voice trailed off a little as he took another drag.

"You doubted it, didn't you?" I asked.

"Yes," he said, nodding, "I always had this little niggle in the back of my mind that questioned whether he actually killed her. That's why I wanted him to look at me during the trial, something he never did. So, I told him. I woke him up and had him come to the door. I had the trap down and watched him climb out from his bed and shuffle over. I shone my torch into his face, waited for him to wake up properly, then told him who I was." Another long drag, then a sip from his tea, followed by another drag. He held it again, impossibly long, the silence of the kitchenette now screaming at us.

"What did you see?" Steph asked. He looked at her for a minute then took another drag. He finally crushed his butt out in the ashtray and spoke again.

"I can tell you what I didn't see. I didn't see the man that killed my baby sister. I don't know how else to describe it. Except that the man who I saw that night, whose eyes I looked into, was not the man that ended Veronica's life." My heart jumped at the words, my stomach took a turn and I felt something give within me. I too, had the same niggle for the past 20 years and was terrified by this man now confirming his own trepidation.

"How can you be so sure?" Steph asked, pulling out her own packet of cigarettes and offering them up. Jeremy took one, lighting it and Steph's with another match.

"Because the one thing a man cannot hide, Officer, is his eyes. Whatever secrets he has, whatever words he speaks, they mean nothing if the eyes don't support them. But I didn't just leave it there. He actually told me a lot more. Like the girl he had been seeing."

"He had a girlfriend?" I asked, surprised.

"Yes, he did. Told me the whole story. But he never named her. Said he wanted to protect her from all the haters out there. He knew that if people knew about her, they would go after her. Of that, you could be sure. Harry Lightman having a girlfriend, can you imagine?"

"What did he say about her?" Steph asked.

"He said they met by sheer accident. They would never have met if his bike didn't have a flat tyre. He was taking a shortcut back to town and had crossed through a paddock when he came across her. She was just sitting in the sun. She had been singing, that's what caught his attention."

"Met where?" Steph suddenly asked. I could see her attention peak, sitting forward in her chair.

"He never said. Just that he had cut through a paddock and heard her singing. He did tell me he loved her, though. More than anything. And again, watching him tell the story, his eyes never lied. I could tell he loved this girl, whoever she was."

"Did he see her again? What happened?" I asked.

"He said they met lots of times. Although he never met her parents. Said she told him they wouldn't understand."

"He never named her?" Steph asked.

"No, never. I pressed him a couple of times, but he wouldn't say."

"Did he tell you anything else?" I asked but Jeremy shook his head.

"Mr. Lawson, you of all people should understand what I mean when I say that you can see into a man's soul by peering into his eyes. You looked into those eyes while he was still out there, free. Tell me, what did you see?" I did understand, and I knew what he was talking about, because I too, had reservations about whether he was Lucifer. It had been one of those situations where you are completely sure of one thing, but still found the minutest niggle from confirming the truth. For me, I was sitting at exactly 99/1.

There was a knock on the front door of the shop then, and Jeremy looked toward the sound.

"I'd better open, if that's OK with you?" He stood, holding out his hand to us. I took it and shook, as did Steph.

"Thank you, Jeremy, we really appreciate you talking with us," she said as she let go, turning to walk out of the room.

"If you remember anything else, please let us know. Anything at all," I said as I walked through the door and into his storefront.

"I will try. I doubt there is anything else that could be useful to you. If I was to make a suggestion though, it would be for you to talk to Dr. Levinson."

"Who?" I asked.

"He is the visiting psychiatrist that came in to see specific prisoners on occasion. One of his main patients was Harry Lightman. Although most of what he got up to was pretty hush hush if you know what I mean."

"Ok, we'll be sure to follow up with him. Thank you, Jeremy." As we neared the front door, he paused for a minute, the expression on his face lighting up, as if remembering something comical.

"Funny thing. The only thing that I do remember is probably something I'd rather forget. It used to drive me crazy about him." He chuckled a little as he spoke. Steph unlocked the door and was about to step out when Jeremy spoke his last bit of information. I now wish he hadn't.

"He always whistled that dam song. Day and night."

"What song?" I asked.

"Fur Elise," he said. In front of me, Steph froze.

3.

"Steph, you don't know," I said, trying to sound logical. She was driving now, a cigarette in one hand as it held the steering wheel, her face stern as a brick.

"I don't fucking believe this," she screamed. A woman walking along the footpath heard her, looked at us as we passed and began shaking her head. "Do you have any idea what this could mean?"

"You don't know. Just because he whistled that song doesn't mean anything. Lots of people whistle that dam song."

"My mother told me she had been sitting behind her house by the river, singing, when Eddie first found her. He had been crossing the field, using it as a shortcut. THAT FUCKER COULD BE MY FATHER!" She swerved the wheel sideways and came to a halt in the gravel, the car jolting as it stopped. She opened her door and climbed out, slamming the door with such force, that for a moment, I thought the glass would surely shatter and come flying into my lap. I climbed out after her and tried to calm her. There was an abandoned house sitting 50 yards away from the gravel pit we stopped in and Steph was throwing rocks at it, her tears falling freely around her shoulders with each rock that she launched. I walked behind her, grabbed her wrist and pulled her into me. She resisted at first then submitted, sobbing into my shoulder. I could feel her anger, her shock, her terror. Her body felt tensed up and rigid. I thought she was going to collapse to the ground, but then she managed to regain control of herself.

"Shhh," I whispered into her ear, "It will be OK, Steph. I promise, things will be OK."

She pulled away a little, then began to giggle. I looked at her, confused. She peered up at me and smiled.

"Well, this certainly wasn't the birthday present I was hoping for today."

The drive back to Cider Hill took a little longer as there was more traffic. At one point, a truck loaded with hay bales blocked our path, crawling along at an astounding 20 miles per hour. Steph asked me to drive, something I gladly agreed with, considering her emotional state. I felt much more comfortable having her sitting in the passenger seat, her emotions still coming and going in long waves that were tense one minute and confused the next. We listened to the radio for the most part, when the signal allowed for it anyway. Other times, we drove in silence, the scenery slipping past us with every turn of the wheel.

We stopped about 20 miles or so out of Cider Hill. An Esso fuel station stood there, run by Margaret Robertson. Her husband had opened the fuel stop ten years prior, figuring it would be good to have two businesses on the same land; the farm and the fuel. The farm is what proved to be his downfall, killing him back in 51. Like so many farming accidents of the time, heavy machinery played a contributing factor. In James Robertson's case, a hidden rock, a fast-moving tractor and a tired farmer taking a shortcut across an unkept paddock at the end of the day would all combine to ensure that was one work day, Margaret's husband would not be returning from.

"Hi Officer Connor," a young lad of about 15 said as we opened our doors. He was already grabbing the pump nozzle, getting ready to fill the FX's tank.

"Hey, Billy. Is your Mum inside?" He nodded and pointed at the little shop window, a middle-aged woman with a handkerchief tied over her hair standing there watching us. She waved as Steph turned to look. Steph waved back and headed inside. I stretched my arms long and hard towards the sky, groaned satisfyingly as my spine clicked, then followed. Steph was giving the woman a hug as I stepped inside and began to introduce me.

"Margaret, this is-"

"Jim Lawson, I know. I recognize you from this." I blushed as she held up my book, Nightmares Unhinged. It had a photo of me inside the back page, a photo I was never too fond of. My colour increased, making both ladies giggle a little, as Margaret held it out to me and asked if I would be kind enough to autograph it. I happily did, feeling the heat in my face.

"I've always enjoyed a decent scare. 'Specially if it's about monsters and stuff."

"Thank you," I croaked. She turned back to Steph, returning the book under the counter.

"What brings you out this way?"

"Just back from Geelong. Police business." Steph walked to the display fridge, took out a Coke and held one out to me. I thanked her, popped the top with the bottle opener that hung from one door and took a long swallow. Steph did the same, then sat at one of the tables and lit a cigarette.

"Any news on finding the killer?" Margaret asked. Steph shook her head.

"Do you remember Mum talking about Eddie?" she asked, then turned to me. "Margaret and Mum were friends since they were little."

"She used to talk about him often. She loved him very much, you know. Of course, she couldn't tell me what he looked like," she said with a giggle, and for a moment, I didn't follow. Then it hit me and I realized what an impossible feat that would have been. Her mother had been born blind. "She did say that he had a very kind face, her hands acting as her eyes, of course. His short hair was always combed straight, she said. She told me once that when they were lying on the river's edge, listening to the birds, she used to love to run her fingers through it because he would do the same to her. Is everything OK? Why do you ask?"

"It's nothing. Just missing her, I guess." Her lie came out with such ease that I wondered how often she has had to lie about her history in the past. I can't imagine it would have been easy not knowing anything about her father.

The lad walked in just then, also grabbing a Coke from the fridge.

"Not too many of those today, Franky." Her voice was stern and I could see Franky give his Mum a look that told me when she spoke, he listened.

"Yes, Mum," he said, then sat at the table with us and handed Steph her keys. "It's all filled, tyres are good and the windows are cleaned." She smiled at him, rubbed his head and thanked him. He grinned back, then blushed fiercely as she planted a kiss on his cheek. His mother began to laugh.

5.

Steph drove us to the police station after leaving the Robertson's farm. As we walked in the door, Rademeyer was standing behind the counter talking with Lester, both men appearing deep in conversation. Rademeyer looked in our direction but appeared not to notice us, his words continuing at a steady pace. I followed Steph around the side of the counter and down the hall to a small room which held a single desk. She dropped down into the chair behind it, turned it toward a box that sat on the floor and began rummaging through it, after a moment picking out a couple of thick folders. I saw a photo frame sitting on the edge of the table and picked it up. A woman with long light hair was sitting at a piano, her smile conveying her pleasure at playing the instrument.

"Is this your Mum?" I asked and Steph nodded. "She's beautiful."

"Thank you, Jim. Here, check this out," she said, handing me one of the folders. It was a folder marked "Medical Appointments" and when I opened it, found several thin books that had served as appointment schedules for Harry Lightman. They dated from the early 30s right through to this year. In the beginning, there were only the normal doctor's visits for the usual ailments. A dentist's visit in 36, the doctor for the flu in 38, stuff like that. The physician's names were written next to the patient, as well as the date and ailment. I flicked through the books, nothing really jumping out. That was until I began to flick through the book that had 1949-1950 written on the front. There was a physician's name that seemed to appear more and more often. Initially just once or twice a week, and not just for Lightman. The name was Julius Levinson.

"Here, I think I've found him," I said, pulling my chair closer to Steph's so she could see the entries as well. She set her own folder aside and pulled mine across onto the desk. I slowly began to turn the pages for the month of August 1949, seeing Dr. Levinson visit the prison twice during the first week, once the second week, twice again during the third week, then four the last week. September was similar and so was October. His appointments varied between prisoners and I saw that he saw Lightman once in August, once in September and twice in October. Then, in November 1949, Dr. Levinson saw

Lightman four times, once each week. In December he saw him five times. In January six. By April, the last month for this book, Levinson saw Harry twice per week at regular times.

As we began to flick through the following book, titled 1950-1951, the same pattern began to emerge, two visits per week, every week. Then, in November of 50, the visits increased to 4 times a week. I closed the current book and opened the next one, titled 1951-1952. The first couple of months were much the same. He would see other prisoners as well, their names written in the ledger, but none were as regular as Harry, and Harry's appointments remained much the same, four regular appointments per week. Then, in June 1950, Levinson's name disappeared. A new doctor's name was written in all the appointment slots, Dr. Lewis, this new doctor seeing all the patients at regular intervals. All except Harry. I opened the newest of the books, titled 1953- 1954. February, March, April and May continued as had the previous months before them, regular appointments with all the prisoners except Harry.

Then, in June 1953, Levinson's name reappeared in the book, his name written every single weekday in the same spot. And he was visiting a single prisoner exclusively. That prisoner was Harry Lightman. I looked at Steph as her face grew suspicious, waiting for her to speak.

"Why would he only see Lightman?" she finally said. I shook my head, unsure.

"And why take that break?" I replied, counting the months. "Twelve-month gap. Bit long for it to be a holiday."

"And a long time not to see a regular patient. Weird. I wonder…" she said as she turned back to the box, looking for another folder.

"What are you thinking?" I said, curious. She was busy flicking through papers, books and stuff when she pulled something out.

"Ah, found it," she said as she put another book on the desk. This one was titled "Visitors" and had all the visitors that came to the prison listed with their entry and exit times. Being such a specific prison with a relatively small number of residents, visitor numbers were pretty much at a minimum compared to a normal prison such as Pentridge or Beechworth. She opened the book and began at the beginning, running her finger down the list of names, stopping at each entry that read "Dr. Levinson/ Prisoner Lightman". After a moment she looked at me.

"Wow, he was spending a long time with him. Look," she said as she pointed to an entry. It showed Levinson enter the prison at 10.20 am and leave at 3.45pm. Another showed him arriving at 11.10 and not leave again until 5.30pm.

"Bit longer than the usual hour," I said, following her finger down the page.

"Can you think of any reason why he would be spending so much time with him?" Steph asked, looking up from the page. I shook my head.

"I'm not one to answer that. I didn't make it my life to treat many patients. I know I have the title, but between you and me, I was never a good psychiatrist. My heart just wasn't in it. But, if I was to have a guess, I would say he was conducting research of some description." She nodded, as if understanding.

"Think we should talk to him?"

"Talk to who?" a voice suddenly said from behind me. It was Rademeyer's.

"We've been going over some of these files, Chief. There's a doctor that's been spending a lot of time with Lightman." Steph said.

"How much time?" he asked. His tone didn't sound like one of peaked interest, sounding instead, like someone who was going to doubt, regardless of the information conveyed. Steph shuffled uncomfortably in her chair. I knew that behind me, Rademeyer enjoyed his intimidation of the girl.

"A lot," I said, turning my chair. "A lot longer than someone visiting a regular patient."

"Lightman isn't a regular patient," he said.

"No, maybe not. But in the end, he's nothing more than a killer and as such, not that different to the rest of the murderers already up there. Levinson is spending up to thirty hours a week with him. Doesn't that sound rather excessive, Frank?" I asked.

"I wouldn't know either way, I'm not a quack, Jim. That's what I got you in on this for. If you think it's worth following up then please do. But just remember, there are more bodies piling up and I don't want you two to go off on some tangent when the real killer is out here somewhere. And one more thing. I received a call from a Richard Lovett."

"Who?" I asked.

"Richard Lovett is the legal counsel for Lightman and he is going for a straight release based on the new murders. I'm told he's a pit-bull and won't lie down on this. So, you two get your fingers out of your butts and find this prick either way. We have to know what's going on before we have two of them roaming around."

"Thank you, Chief," Steph said, but he didn't respond, simply turning his back on us and walking out.

"Prick," Steph muttered under her breath and a laugh escaped my lips. She looked at me then smiled.

"Come on. Let's get a bite to eat. My treat," I said and she stood before I could say anything else, which made me laugh a second time.

6.

Mrs. McNorton greeted us with an eager wave as Steph and I walked through the door to her café. I returned her wave then followed Steph to a table in the corner, several of the other tables occupied by the lunchtime crowd. A waitress came over with a bottle of water and handed us a couple of menus, took our order for coffees, then left us again. Steph studied her menu intently, settled on something, then closed it in front of her.

"I've never been here. I normally eat at the Cider Patch further up the street," she said as she poured some water from the bottle.

"That lady who waved? She was running this place when I first started here as a cop."

"Wow, that's a long time." I laughed.

"Did you just call me old, Officer?" I cried and she slapped my arm playfully.

"No, I didn't."

"Jim, hey." I turned and saw Tami standing at the counter. I waved at her then beckoned her over. She finished paying Mrs. McNorton then made her way to our table.

"Steph," I said, "have you met Tami Kennedy?" Tami reached for her hand and they shook.

"No, not officially. Hi, I'm Steph."

"You got time to sit for a bit, Tam?" I asked, but she shook her head.

"No, sorry. Have to get back to work. You know how it is." I nodded.

"Dinner tonight, then?" I asked confidently. Her face lit up, her perfect smile returning.

"Yes, of course. That would be lovely. Same time?"

"Sure," I said. She waved us goodbye, then walked out, clutching her sandwich. I was about to ask Steph what she was ordering for lunch when I heard Mrs. McNorton's voice in the background. It wasn't so much that I heard her voice rather what she said.

"What can I get you today, Dr. Levinson?" My ears pricked instantly and I turned to see who she was talking to.

The man standing at the counter looked to be well dressed with impeccable grooming. His greyish peppery hair was neatly combed and parted on the political left. He had a full goatee beard, its near blackness almost contrasting his peppery hair. He was thin and I would guess, aged in his mid-fifties. Some people have happy faces, some have sad. Some look angry while others wear natural frowns. When I saw the face of Dr. Levinson, what I saw, was natural deceit. It was the look that I associated with the Encyclopedia Britannica salesmen that would knock on my door, the salesmen that wanted to sell me the latest magazine subscriptions. They would wear that look while telling you wild stories, always trying to convince you to buy their wares. To me, Levinson wore the face of one of those pesky door-to-door salesmen.

"That's him," Steph said over the rim of her glass of water. I nodded.

"Yup, there he is. Should we introduce ourselves?" I asked, but she shook her head. For a moment, I didn't know why she wouldn't want to meet him, considering he was our very next item on the agenda. Then I saw why.

"It looks like he already has a lunch date," she said. Levinson had ordered two sandwiches and two coffees to go. He also ordered a slice of chocolate brownie and a lamington. When he finished paying, he took the paper bag Mrs. McNorton was holding out to him and headed outside. I glanced at Steph but she was already ahead of me, on her feet and headed for the door.

"See you a bit later, Mrs. McNorton," I yelled and she waved at me as I passed her, already serving the next customer.

Levinson was getting into his car, something black and German looking, and started the engine. Steph and I headed to her car, climbed in and prepared to follow him. We watched as he reversed out, then headed down Main Street, in the direction of the prison. Steph backed out and followed him, staying back far enough not to draw suspicion.

"You don't think he actually bought him lunch, do you?" I asked.

"Six hours a day, five days a week, he certainly bought someone lunch," she replied.

We followed him all the way to the prison carpark, then waited while he picked his items out from the passenger seat and climbed the stairs to the front door. We waited a moment, then followed. He was still standing there waiting when we approached. He smiled at us as we stood there, seemingly unbothered by us. There was a rattle from inside the door, then it opened. The guard was surprised to see us standing there, but once he checked Steph's credentials, allowed us inside.

"Who you here to see today, Steph?" he asked as he closed the door.

"Need to speak to the warden, Jack," she said, her eyes following Levinson as he walked toward the main gate. "Jack, who's that?"

"That's the Doc that sees Lucifer. Spends a lot of time with him, he does." In the distance, the gate began to creak on its rollers.

"Thanks, Jack," she said, then walked toward the gate where the good doc had already squeezed through the opening and headed off toward one of the far buildings. The guards both inside and on the wall were paying very little attention to us. The two that were standing atop the wall were involved in some deep discussion, their voices carrying to us in a low murmur. I could make out several non-descript words, but when I heard one of them raise his voice a little and say 'you really think the Cats?', I knew the subject of their palaver. The two guards walking around separately beneath the wall were occupied with watching the other two guards, obviously wishing they could join in.

Steph and I watched as Levinson climbed the steps to the hospital building and walked inside, the old, thick timber door slowly creaking closed behind him. Steph hurried a little in front of me and managed to catch the door before it closed completely. Once inside, there was a front room that had a small counter, thankfully unattended. We caught the back of Levinson enter a room down one of the corridors and we headed in that direction, our footfalls echoing gently. There were voices coming from several directions, but none seemed interested in us. A male nurse came out from one of the rooms that lined the corridor, gave us the once over, muttered something that may have been 'g'day', then continued walking past us.

We reached the door Levinson had entered and waited. The door had a small window in its upper half, decorated with wire mesh for safety. Steph looked at the window, then me, and frowned. She was too short to peek through, the rolling of her eyes bringing a smile to my face. She flicked me the bird as I mimicked her going tiptoes, then let a small giggle out. She pushed past me and shoved me toward the door, pointing at the window. I edged towards the door and tried to sneak a peek.

He had bought Lightman lunch. But that's not what pissed me off the most. As dumb as it sounds, what pissed me off above all else, was that he had bought him a tuna on rye, my sandwich. At that moment, I felt as if no one was entitled to eat that amazing taste sensation except those that deserved it, and in my book, Harry Lightman didn't. They were sitting at a small table facing each other. Levinson had spread their little feast out before them and both men looked to be enjoying the meal. But then I saw something that didn't fit. Trying to describe it now, in hindsight, makes a lot more sense, but I haven't come to that part of the story yet, so I will endeavour to describe the events as I saw them in that moment.

The truth is, I didn't *know* what I saw, only that it didn't fit. There was something off. It wasn't that there was a doctor having lunch with a prisoner, nor that the prisoner, a prolific serial killer, was enjoying a two-course meal paid for by a professional. What I saw that didn't quite fit was Lightman himself. It was, if I had to put it into words, as if it wasn't Lightman at all. I know that doesn't make sense, but that's what I saw. I was about to share my thoughts with Steph when our eavesdropping came to a sudden halt.

"Can I help you with something?" The voice came from behind us and from the tone, didn't belong to someone on our side. I turned to see a guard standing there, holding a rifle in one hand. He was tall, at least six-six by my guess, and judging by the way his chiselled jaw was flexing, not happy by our presence. Steph flashed her police ID at him and never faltered.

"Officer Connor, looking for the warden. Know where he is?" She remained as calm as the proverbial, her voice both projected and confident. The guard stood there for a moment, not answering. He was about to speak when Steph took a step toward him and cut him off. "I don't have all day; now do you know where he is or not?" The guard actually took a step back and judging by the colour that rose in his cheeks, looked like he had just been slapped.

"No, ma'am. Haven't seen him since briefing this morning."

"OK then. Any ideas where he might be? I don't really have the time to go door to door, you know what I'm saying?"

"Maybe try the main building, down the right corridor. He has a room. It's-" but then the door that I had been peering through opened and Levinson came out.

"Everything OK out here?" he asked then saw us. "Ah, James Lawson," he said, offering me his hand, "Julius Levinson. And you must be Officer Connor," he said, turning to Steph. She shook with him, now faded rose colouring her own cheeks. The guard, I noticed, was almost sneering now. Levinson then turned to him, whispered something and the guard turned and walked away, slinging his rifle over his shoulder.

"Why don't you come in?" Levinson asked, opening the door to the room he had just come out of, and before I could object, saw that it now sat empty, Lightman nowhere in sight. I walked in and saw a door on the far side, now closed, but guessed that Lightman had been taken back to whatever cell he called home. Levinson waved at the chairs, offering us to sit. He pressed an intercom button on the wall and when a shrill voice answered, asked for a pot of tea to be brought.

"I'm sorry if we interrupted you, Dr," Steph said but he shrugged it off.

"That's OK. Did you manage to order your lunch before you followed me here or will you get it after?" Now it was my turn to blush, the heat rising to my ears, but again, he brushed it off. "That's OK. I knew that you two would be visiting with me sooner or later. Only makes sense considering the amount of time I am spending with your number one suspect. But tell me, do you really believe that he is breaking out of prison to kill then breaking BACK into prison again afterwards?"

"We are just following up on leads right now, Sir," Steph offered, but I could hear her anger rising in her tone already. Levinson nodded.

"Yes, of course." He suddenly rose, walked toward the door and opened it. Just as he did, a nurse approached, carrying a tray with a teapot and three cups. "Thank you, my dear," Levinson said as he took the tray from her and brought it to the table, the nurse closing the door.

"How long have you been seeing Lightman?" Steph asked as Levinson poured the tea. He paused and looked at her, smiling. The smile was as fake as he was.

"Oh, come now, my dear. You can do better than that. I'm sure you've already looked at the box of goodies that our good warden gave you, and with it, a complete history of my presence here. And if you haven't, then you disappoint me." He resumed pouring the teas then took a cup and fell back into his chair with a thump. "Oh," he groaned, "getting old is not easy, the pains just seem to creep up on you."

"Why?" I asked and he looked at me, surprised.

"Why what?" he replied.

"Why are you here? Why do you spend so much time with him? Why did you take a long break then return to seeing him with such an increase in frequency? Why?" He pondered my question for a moment, then smiled that fake smile I was beginning to dread.

"Jim, may I call you Jim?" He didn't wait for my reply. "Sometimes, and not very often, we are given the opportunity to study a human that is so evil, that nothing we seem to say or do will ever change that evil. Most of the time, they are either killed or they kill themselves, or they refuse to talk to anybody. But Harry Lightman has chosen to not only live, but share his story with me."

"Wait," Steph said, "we spoke with Harry not long ago, and he was still professing his innocence to us." Levinson was nodding.

"I didn't say he was admitting guilt, sweetheart. What I'm saying is that Harry Lightman is sharing his experiences. The one thing you have to remember is that we aren't here to extrapolate his guilt or innocence. A court of law has already determined that. You are here to see whether Harry Lightman is still safely locked up and not running around town killing innocent victims again. I'm here to learn from what he has to tell me. The experiences I talk of are from before he was locked up. Harry endured some pretty horrific experiences from an early age. Did you know that he has no penis, for instance?"

"Pardon me?" I said.

"The man has had no penis for the better part of his life. You want to talk about evil, Jim? When he was twelve years old, Harry's father took him to a whore house. Now before you get all mushy-eyed, thinking his father was giving his son a nice treat, he took him there for his own sick pleasure. You see, Harry's father had paid to see the lad suffer. Had paid the whore above the normal rate to 'inflict suffering' on him while his father sat in the corner masturbating himself. You want to talk about evil, Jim? Once she had him tied to that bed, that whore not only bit him multiple times, the scars still visible, but just before his father climaxed, the whore had bitten the lad's penis off, the blood spurting over her face as his father squirted over the floor." I felt sick, my stomach turning. I looked at Steph and saw her face grow pale, her mouth open in horror.

"I…," I began but couldn't finish.

"Not what you were expecting? The evil I speak of, was his father. Now dead of course. And by studying evil, I'm talking about the opportunity to learn about Harry's suffering. Make his life, what little he has left, actually mean something. Whether he is guilty or not is not something I ever think about. If I can learn something from his suffering, am able to use that knowledge to help others, then that is something worth learning, don't you agree?" I nodded, the nausea finally abating. It wasn't that I had an overly sensitive stomach, it was just that what he described came so suddenly and unexpected that it caught me completely off guard.

"What does he have?" Steph asked.

"A lung infection that we are struggling to control. I am simply trying to learn as much as I possibly can within the time we have left. That's why I have been devoting so much time to him. Does that about answer your questions?" I nodded, embarrassingly. I looked at Steph but she was already rising to her feet, holding out her hand to him.

"Thank you for your time, Doctor, I appreciate it." He shook with her then me, his eyes never leaving mine, as if trying to drum home his words from the previous five minutes. We walked out, closing the door behind us. As we were leaving, I heard his voice, growing fainter with each step.

"Ah, welcome back, Harry. I apolo..." but that's where his voice grew too quiet for me to hear. Harry had been waiting behind the door. I was wondering whether he had actually been allowed to listen in on us when another voice called out to us. It was the warden.

"Excuse me. Officer Connor? One second, please." We stopped and turned to find the warden actually running up the hallway.

"Yes, Sir?" Steph asked as he approached.

"You have a phone call. Its Chief Rademeyer for you."

Chapter 7: Rekindled Passions

1.

As we left the police station a couple of hours later, my stomach actually rumbled so loud that Steph looked around for a dog or something. She looked at me when I started rubbing my belly and laughed.

"I need food," was all I could manage and she nodded, pointing at her car.

The reprimand from Rademeyer wasn't as bad as we were expecting. It was actually a vast improvement over our previous meetings with him. For one, it was the warden that had called him, complaining about our unexpected arrival and subsequent pursuit of the good doctor. When Steph explained our findings in the ledgers we reviewed from the prison, the chief actually looked interested, keen for us to get any sort of sense of direction with this case. We also told him about what the doctor had told us about Lightman and he nodded.

"At least it confirms it's not Lightman. So, that means we have a killer to catch, people. Any ideas?" he said, leaning across the desk, resting on his outstretched hands.

"I think we need to speak to Clancy again," I said.

"The Janitor? Why?" Rademeyer asked.

"Just him visiting with Lightman for as long as he did. I think he knows more than he's letting on," I replied. The chief nodded his head, for once agreeing without some smart remark. Steph and I thanked him for his time then decided to head out and make a beeline for lunch. And at this stage, I didn't care where lunch came from.

2.

We ended up back at Mrs. McNorton's a little after 4. She was just beginning to clean out some of her display food when we strolled in, the smell of the place making my stomach rumble again.

"Jim, back again?" I nodded then introduced her to Steph. Steph shook her hand and complimented her on how lovely her café was. Mrs. McNorton thanked her then took our orders, a pie and sandwich for me and a tuna on rye for Steph. A few minutes later and we were both munching on food.

Neither of us spoke as we ate, the meal so good, it reminded me of home. I ended up ordering a second sandwich as well as a chocolate milk shake. It was like I hadn't eaten in a week.

"Aren't you eating at Tami's tonight?" Steph asked as I finished the last bite of the sandwich.

"Yes, but by then I will be ready for the second course, trust me. I've always been able to put away stupendous amounts of food."

"Were you serious about talking to Clancy again?" she asked as she sipped a glass of water. I nodded.

"Definitely. I think there is a little more to it than what Clancy was letting on. And if there isn't, then I'm sure he'll know something about our friend Julius."

"You don't believe him?"

"Oh, I believe what he told us was somewhat truthful, but I have no doubt that he was holding back."

"Somewhat?" she asked as she lit a cigarette.

"Aha, somewhat."

"Is there something you're not telling me, Doctor Lawson?"

"I think he's hiding something." I lowered my voice. Knowing that the good doctor was a customer from this establishment, I wasn't sure just how good a customer he was.

"What do you think he's hiding?"

"That I don't know yet, but I do know that there is more to his story than he's letting on."

"How do you know? Did I miss something?" She lent in a little closer, noticing my lowered voice.

"Because unless they were trying to cover something up, why would they call the chief on us? We weren't doing anything outside of our normal enquiries, yet the way Thomas came running up that hallway, was as if he really wanted us out of there." Realization dawned on Steph's face as she became aware of the sequence of events at the prison.

"I see where you're headed. That's so true, he really did want us out of there." I nodded. I was thinking back to when I had looked through the window in the door. Trying to place what had caught my attention. "Jim? You OK?"

"Yeah, just trying to remember something, but it's gone." She nodded, but I could tell she doubted me.

"Probably too late now, but did you want to see Clancy tomorrow morning?"

"Does he work on a Saturday morning?" I asked.

"He mows one section of the school lawn *every* Saturday morning. If nothing else, he is punctual to his own schedule according to my friend June Trapnell."

"Sure. Any plans for tonight?"

"Nah. Think once the little munchkin is asleep, will soak in a nice hot tub then get an early night if I can. I'll have plenty of reading material whilst soaking," she said with a smile. The boxes we had been given at the prison still needed well over half its contents to be perused, although now, knowing the prison hierarchy were against us, doubted whether the material would reveal anything useful. Our work would certainly be cut out for us when it came to that place.

3.

Once we had our late lunch finished, Steph dropped me back to the hotel and I watched her drive off. As I was standing there, a man walked past, looked at me, then turned back.

"You're James Lawson, aren't you?" he said. I looked at him and nodded.

"Yes, I am," I replied, holding my hand out. "And you are?"

"Richard Lovett. I've read your books."

"Pleased to meet you, Mr. Lovett. Have I heard your name before?" I didn't place it at first.

"I'm representing Harry Lightman." He spoke it almost nonchalant, as if he already had his client's innocence proven.

"And how is your client doing?"

"Should be out any day now, I think." He shuffled his fingers around in his pocket then pulled a bit of paper out of it. "Could I get an autograph? For my-" but I was already walking past him.

"Not today, sorry," I muttered at him. When I looked behind me as I entered the door, he had already crossed the street, heading towards the shops.

As I walked through the hotel's foyer, I saw Tami cleaning a table in the bistro. She flashed me a wink as I walked by, heading for the stairs. I smiled, a shot of warmth running up my spine. As I climbed the stairs, a man in a business suit was descending the steps. He threw me a glance as I passed him, grinned, then continued walking. As I rounded the corner, I saw a tall woman standing just inside a door, wearing nothing but a bra, French knickers and suspender belt. She smiled at me as I walked past, then closed the door. I had a feeling that the woman was not the man's wife.

When I got to my room, I threw my jacket on the bed and headed for the bathroom. Lunch was certainly making itself known, demanding I make some room for it. As any man does, I grabbed the newspaper I had bought with my lunch and happily obliged.

4.

Not realizing I had even fallen asleep, the knock on the door woke me with such a jolt that I nearly rolled right off the bed. I was still reading the paper by the time nature had finished its call and had lain face down on the bed, the paper resting beneath me. I must have dozed off during the interesting article I was reading about the nuclear threat that had been steadily increasing between the United States and the USSR. It was scary reading, the reporter making some damning revelations such as just how powerful nuclear weapons were compared to the atomic bombs dropped on Japan a few years ago. The dangers the fallout of these weapons posed seemed to indicate that should the two superpowers actually engage in a conflict, all life in this world would almost surely perish. It was not a happy bedtime story and had somehow, despite the horrors it was spreading, sent me off into a deep sleep.

Once I managed to pull myself out of the nap and rediscover the land of the living, I pulled myself out of bed and went to the door. I opened it and flinched a second time as the door was pushed open with such force that it nearly sent me reeling. My hand came up defensively, shielding my face from a nasty smack when arms flung around my neck and soft lips settled on my own. With shock, I initially tried to pull back, but the pattering of kisses was so adamant, that as I realised who the soft lips belonged to, was unable to resist them. Tami walked into the room, kicked the door shut with her shoe heel and willed me to the bed, her gentle lips and minty breath urging me backwards.

The back of my legs struck the bed and we fell backwards onto it, Tami hanging onto me with her thighs as we did. She was slowly opening and closing her eyes, almost as if to confirm I was still there. At that moment, I couldn't think of anywhere else I would rather be. She smelled amazingly sweet, like candied almonds, or raspberry jelly. I wanted to lap her up. Her touch was gentle yet urging, willing me to take my clothes off and take hers with it. We were naked in what seemed like a whirlwind of kisses and fondling, the tingling of excitement feeling electric. And as I entered her for the first time, listening to the moan of her desire, feeling her fingernails gently find grip in my back, her own back arching up to meet me, I took us to a place of such an intense pleasure few people are able to reach. Our climaxes came almost simultaneous, her moans erupting a short moment before the sound of her peak bringing me to mine. It felt so incredibly deep, her hotness engulfing me, clinging to me, refusing to let go.

I had wanted to be with Tami for as long as I could remember. And as I lay there, holding her closer than I ever had before, the woman I had loved for 20 years, was finally laying exactly where she belonged. And for the first time in forever, the smile on my face felt real.

It was a night of passion that I had never imagined in my wildest dreams. At some point in the middle of the night, I was woken to the feeling of inquisitive fingers gently probing around in my boxers. She had already primed me for another go and when Tami climbed on top of me, her own excitement allowed me to enter with incredible ease. She felt like satin, her pace quickening with a steady low moaning, my own excitement building to the sound of her. When it was finished in a detonation of tingling that seemed to go on and on forever, she rolled off and lay beside me, her head resting on my chest. I held her tight, one arm around her neck, gently rubbing the top of one buttock. It felt so incredibly erotic for me, I cannot explain just how intense it was. But when I saw a familiar scar on the top part of her arm, a near perfect hole of missing flesh, reality snapped me back to the present.

5.

When I awoke the next morning, I first wondered whether it had all been some intense fantasy that I finally dreamt about with such a virtual clarity. The bed lay empty beside me, no evidence Tami had ever been in my room. But at almost the same moment I was about to get up and make sure it hadn't been a dream after all, the door to my room opened and Tami came in, carrying a breakfast platter, complete with newspaper, and set it on the bed before me. Her smile was almost as long as her incredible legs. She leant in, kissed me and asked how I slept.

"Sleep was OK," I said, then pulled her on top of me and said, "but the dreams were amazing." I began to kiss her, undress her and pull her back into bed. A few moments later, our passion peaked a third time and the beginning of a new day had never been better.

6.

Tami left around 7, flashing me an incredibly cheeky smile as she closed the door. I felt something that I hadn't felt in such a long time. I don't know whether it was love, maybe something between incredibly powerful like and lust. I had been attracted to her for years, that had never been a secret, but finally having her the way I had her that morning and the previous night, was something close to fulfilling an incredible longing that had been building over time. Last night, I finally fulfilled the longing. I wanted her, not just for the act of love but more. I wanted to listen to her, learn her emotions, her feelings, her joys. Understand her passions, her hobbies, things she loved to do and the things she loathed. Right there, at that moment, it was like I ached to know my best friend, and yet I knew hardly anything about her. We had shared such a powerful nightmare together, tried to build a life afterwards but failed. I was lying on my back, one arm behind my head just staring at the ceiling, thoughts running through my head, thoughts of times long past.

7.

The recollections of that night, the one that saw the demise of a monster, came flooding back once I opened the gate, the memories dancing in my mind. I remember the flashing red lights of the approaching patrol car, the moist air that hung heavy over the paddock, the crunch of bone as boot connected with Lightman's nose, the groan of trepidation coming from the man lying before me. I remember hearing the girl sobbing as her father carried her into the house, the distant siren of the approaching ambulance. Once Lightman was sitting in the back of a patrol car, an officer flanking him on either side, I headed to the main house to check on Tami. She was the only person I knew of that had survived the Devil, and she was hurt.

She was lying on a sofa, a tea towel held over the wound on her arm, blood already seeping through it. Joe Kennedy was kneeling beside his daughter, holding the towel as tightly as he could, weeping softly, tears falling onto the sofa cushion below him. Tami had her eyes closed, but I could tell she was conscious, a low groaning conveying her pain. She also had a steady stream of tears running down her cheeks. She held her father's hand in a vice-like grip, the whites of her knuckles bulging. I could only stand by and watch as they tried to comfort each other, her nightmare almost unimaginable.

When the ambulance arrived, the two officers placed Tami on a stretcher and wheeled her to their car. They slid her into the back, her father never leaving her side, nor letting go of his little girl's hand. I asked if it would be OK to ride in the car with them and was given the nod. Chief Rademeyer arrived at that moment, grabbing my hand and pumping it up and down with much enthusiasm. He gave me a clap on the back as I climbed into the passenger seat of the ambulance and told me he would ensure I received 'a god-damn medal'.

Tami was admitted to Daylesford Hospital and spent 10 days recuperating. Her wound healed although she would carry the scar for the rest of her life. I stayed with her and her father the first night and all of the next day. The rest of the week, I would visit regularly and Joe would ask me to sit with her when he needed to run errands himself. It was during those times that Tami and I would sit and talk. She would tell me about her dreams, her ambitions, her goals. Places she wanted to visit, like Paris, London and of course Rome. She was a girl with so much ambition and a huge amount of passion. She loved drawing, and as I discovered during those days, had the talent of someone that could sketch unbelievable life-like pictures. One of the drawings that I still cherish to this day, was one she had drawn of me after I nodded off in the chair one morning. I had finished working a night shift and visited her as soon as I left the station. My eyes were so heavy and after an hour of listening to her, fell asleep while Tami had gone to the bathroom. When I awoke a couple of hours later, she had managed to create a near photographic pencil drawing of me. That drawing is framed and hanging above my fireplace as I write this.

Eventually, Tami was released from the hospital, her father picking her up, one arm still bandaged. I helped them with her suitcase, carrying it for her as her father wheeled the chair outside. Joe thanked me for my help then drove his daughter home, Tami flashing me her gorgeous smile through the car window as they headed off.

In the following weeks, I would often visit the Kennedy farm, more so during the subsequent trial. It wasn't easy for her to give evidence, but she pooled all the strength that she could muster together, and like an Anzac at Gallipoli, charged head first into helping the prosecutor find Lucifer guilty of all charges.

When the trial was over, Lightman finally sitting in a cell he would now call home, and the fanfare in the media diminished, life went pretty much back to normal for everyone. For Tami and I, we discovered our mutual interest in ancient cultures, primarily ancient Rome, and would spend hours going to the library, reading books, and discovering anything we could get our hands on. Joe Kennedy didn't seem to mind my constant visits, even offering me a back bedroom after a couple of particularly late nights of card games the three of us had played. He had taught Tami the art of Poker, Euchre and Bridge at an early age and often played together. I enjoyed playing with them, sometimes staying till late into the night or early morning.

Then, one night as we stood at the kitchen sink, washing the dinner dishes together while her father sat on the front porch smoking his pipe, Tami had lent in and kissed me. The kiss had been flirting in the air between us for weeks, but my shyness kept me from acting on it, while Tami pushed hers aside. It was such a romantic moment for me. I know, standing at a kitchen sink holding a tea towel may not sound like the ideal spot for a first kiss, but for me feeling her lips on mine at that moment, we could have been standing in the middle of a shit-storm and it wouldn't have mattered. When Tami's lips touched mine, the world of the living ceased to exist, time seemingly halted. I reached one hand out and touched her cheek as our lips danced together, gently caressing the side of her face, her tongue gently teasing mine. When it was finished, she pulled back a little and looked into my eyes, and into my soul. The passion and infatuation that came over me at that moment, has never left me in all the years since, nor has it abated a single ounce, if anything, having manifested itself further with each passing day.

Our relationship continued to grow from that moment, with Tami sometimes staying at my own home. Joe never interfered in our relationship, supporting us from the onset. At the time, it never occurred to me that our lines of communication were guarded, me holding back from completely opening up about my feelings about the horror that I saw, and Tami with the horror she actually endured. It was like we were both hiding our secrets in plain sight whilst gingerly dancing around them. We had a lot in common and it was those things that kept us strong, kept us going. But like anything, eventually the momentum grinds to a halt and for Tami and I, when conversation is limited to the fun things you share and none of the important things, conversation eventually dries up.

Our time spent together became more and more strained as we drifted further apart. Her smile began to dim and sometimes, when she did come and stay, she would fall asleep on the couch after I had gone to bed. We were intimate a few times, but the actual act? She was genuinely frightened, still healing from her event, and thus we never actually had sex.

As the days and weeks passed, Tami and I began to see less and less of each other. Neither of us, as far as I knew, saw anybody else. I remember sitting on her father's porch one night, Joe still working at the shop, wanting to talk about our future. I don't know whether it was my words or her misunderstanding, or a little of both. But it had ended up sinking into a tearful shouting match that neither of us understood. I ended up telling her of my plans to travel and she didn't want to come with me. She had simply told me to go and see what happens. I left the following week, and even though we began to write letters to each other, even they dried up after several months.

I knew I still had strong feelings for Tami, but at the time, didn't know how to act on them. In the end, I bottled them up, stored them on the back shelf of my heart, and left them there, ready and waiting for when I would once again have the strength to open them.

8.

"Jim?" It was Steph's voice that snapped me from my daydream, a gentle knocking accompanying her near whisper. "Jim? You awake?" I jumped out of bed and half walked, half staggered as I pulled on my pants and shuffled to the door. I opened it to find her standing in the hallway in her police uniform. She looked ready for official business.

"Give me a quick minute to shower? Oh, and one guess who I met yesterday?" She looked at me, puzzled. "Richard Lovett. You know, the lawyer?" Realization dawned across her face.

"What did he want?"

"An autograph," I said. Her look amused me and I giggled a little. "No, I didn't give him one. Five minutes?" I said, standing in the doorway to my bathroom.

"Sure. I'll be down in the bistro," she said and headed back down the hall.

I caught up with Steph about twenty minutes later, feeling clean and refreshed. She was sitting alone at a table, sipping a coffee and reading a newspaper. She smiled when she saw me, put her cup down and stood.

"Ready?" I asked and we walked out. Tami was at the counter and winked at me as I walked past. I felt a tingle, remembering the way I had seen her less than an hour before.

As we jumped into Steph's car, I asked, "Off to Clancy?" but she shook her head.

"I had an interesting conversation with another officer last night. You haven't met Linda yet, but she's been a cop at Daylesford for a few years. She rang me last night," she paused long enough to jump in her side of the car and once we were both inside, continued, "and what she told me made me think." She paused to light a cigarette.

"What did she tell you?"

"Her hubby has a mate who works at the old Jackson Street Mill. Has worked there for the better part of 30 years. Can you guess who used to work under him?"

"Lightman?" I asked, already knowing the answer.

"Yup, and I'm hoping that he might have an idea of anybody Lightman hung around with that may have some input on the recent killings."

The mill was about 20 minutes out of town, almost halfway between Cider Hill and Daylesford. We chatted as we drove, coming up with some questions that we wanted to ask, hopefully finding some sort of lead. God knows we could use a good one.

9.

The parking lot out the front of the wood mill was almost completely deserted. It wasn't common for the mill to be operating on a Saturday, but Richard Sadler had always insisted that a skeleton crew spent the morning cleaning the machines ready for a new week, paying the men double their usual rate for the four hours. He had taken over the running of the mill after his father, John, retired ten years earlier. Richard had been quite young at the time, only 28, but took to running the 40-man operation in his stride. Darren Fermaner, the mate Steph was talking about, had been working at the mill for the better part of 35 years, the last 10 as the mill's foreman. He was also famous around town for another reason; his unbelievable ability to sink beer. It was how he earnt the nickname "Keg".

Richard Sadler came out of the small side office as we pulled into the parking lot, almost on cue, as if he had been expecting us. He wore a warm smile and greeted Steph with a hug as soon as she climbed out of her side.

"Steph, so good to see you," he said with a welcoming tone.

"Rich, this is Jim Lawson," she said, turning towards me. Richard held out a hand and shook with me.

"Pleased to me you, Mr Lawson."

"Jim, please," I said.

"Rich, could we speak with Daz, please?" Steph said. The man looked at her for a moment, his smile fading slightly. Then it returned almost as quick.

"Keg? Sure thing. He's down at the dumping shed," he said, pointing towards a small track at the far end of the parking lot. Steph waved a thank you at him and we headed for the track, Richard walking back to his office.

The track was a tiny walkway, no more than a foot wide at best and was covered in weeds and low shrubs. A small shed stood at the end of it, flanked by a small dam, the water brown and very silty.

There was a pump near the shed, a pipe snaking towards the water and a bald man with a great big belly was hunched over, performing some sort of maintenance on it. He looked up as we approached, then smiled when he recognized Steph.

"Officer Connor, what brings you out this way?"

"Hi Daz, this is Jim Lawson. Can we ask you a couple of questions?" The man also shook with me. He struck me as a gentle giant, someone you would trust with your own mother. I think it was his eyes that conveyed his calming nature.

"Hello, please call me Keg" he said to me, then, "anything I can help you with, Steph. But please, would it be too hard for you to call me Keg, Steph?" He listened as Steph told him about the new string of murders, something he had already read about, no doubt. His face grew grave when we told him about our non-existent leads.

"There's not much to tell about Lightman. He was a loner, stuck to himself pretty much, never mingled and never came out for a drink. Not coming out for a drink is what I think kept most of the lads here at a distance. Working men don't like loners, but a man that don't drink with others? Something untrustworthy about them."

"Did he have any friends? Anyone at all?" But the man just shook his head.

"None that I remember. Lightman was one of those guys who always turned up on time, did his work, and did it well, then went home at the end of the day. It's not a crime not to drink and certainly not a crime if you choose to keep to yourself. The boys never beat him up about it, it just kinda went from one day to the next. Became his routine, I guess." I was about to suggest talking to Richard again when he looked up at the sky and put a finger to his mouth.

"There was that one afternoon, though," he said and my interest peaked.

"What's that?" Steph asked. Keg was still looking at the sky, thinking. He took a packet of cigarettes from his pocket, offered them around, Steph never one to pass one up, then lit his with a match, sparking Steph's as well.

"There was this one time, where he wanted to leave a little earlier than normal. I remember it so well because Lightman never took off early. If anything, that man was punctual and honest. He was always here ten minutes before shift and never left until at least ten minutes after. Anyway, it had been a Friday, and he asked if he could leave at 2 o'clock."

"Did he say where he was going?" I asked.

"Said he wanted to surprise a girl he'd been seeing. Some girl over in Daylesford."

"Did he say what her name was?" Steph asked, her tone becoming low with dread, but the man shook his bald head.

"Nah, sorry. Can't help you there. He never struck me as the dating kind, you know. Some of the lads even thought him queer. Just struck me as odd when he told me, that's all. I'm sorry there's not more to tell." Steph shook his hand and thanked him for his time. I shook then followed her back to the car, walking behind her single file along the narrow path.

"Steph, you OK?" I said. She only nodded. "Don't forget, kiddo, Lightman doesn't have a pecker, remember?" She stopped and turned to look at me.

"Does he need one? I mean, is it all gone, half gone, all the bits gone?"

"I don't know. Just try not to think about that now. I know it's difficult but-"

"Excuse me, Steph?" It was Richard waving his hand from his doorway, trying to get our attention. We turned toward him, then heard him ask, "Does this have anything to do with Clancy Higgins?"

10.

He waved us into his office, then sat behind a modest-looking desk, which to me, was surprisingly clean for a timber yard manager's. Steph and I sat in chairs facing him, anxious to hear what he had to say.

"How do you know Clancy?" I asked.

"Clancy is famous in this neck of the woods. And not for any good reasons." I shuffled in my seat slightly, in anticipation of something useful.

"How do you mean?" Steph asked.

"Clancy worked here a few years back. Was just a work hand at the time, nothing too technical. As you know, he has a few sheep short in the top paddock, if you catch my drift. Not all there. Was my Pa that put him on, said everyone deserved to earn an honest living."

"How long did he work here?" Steph sat forward; her interest also peaked.

"He started in, oh, around 42, and I let him go in around 45. I remember 'cause it wasn't long after Pa retired."

"You fired him?" I asked.

"Ah yup. Had to. On account of all the animals."

"Animals?" I asked, glancing at Steph, but her eyes were locked on Richard's, as if waiting for the punch line.

"It was old Graham Roberts that found him first, but he never said anything to him. Instead, came and got me. Took me down past the shed you was just at. The path continues into the bush another 4 or 5 hundred yards or so. Graham had been working on the pump down at the dam. Had been there a couple of hours, and the whole time he was there he swore he could hear a kind of yapping, like a dog in pain. So, he followed the noise and came across the gully that sits at the end of that path. He saw Clancy down in one of the holes down there, watched him for a bit, then came 'n fetched me." He stood, walked out into the next room and came back a second later, carrying three open bottles of coke. He handed one to each of us then clinked our bottles together, wishing us good health. After a long swallow, he continued.

"I could hear the poor dog from almost 500 fucking yards away, 'scuse my French. When we broke through the trees and stood at the edge of the clearing, the gully opened up maybe fifty or so yards in front of us. It's quite deep, maybe twenty feet in some places. And there he was, doing his freaky shit." He took another swallow, his hand visibly shaking.

"Take your time," Steph said, sipping her own coke.

"He had that poor dog pinned to the ground, tied to stakes that he had hammered in. The poor mutt had no chance. That fucken creep's face was covered in blood. He was biting chunks out of the dog's leg and shoulder. Biting chunks and chewing them." He was almost yelling now, his anger raw. He had to put the bottle on the table, the shaking almost uncontrollable. Steph's face was grim, as I was sure mine was. My heart felt like it was beating in my temples again, adrenalin making my stomach feel like it was doing cartwheels.

"What happened?" I asked.

"I picked up the nearest stick I could find and almost ran down to him. He never heard me coming, never knew I was there until the first swing connected with his head. It almost sent him sprawling, his goofy expression never leaving his face. I could have sworn the fucker was smiling at me. Then I swung again and this time his good eye closed as he went ni-night. Graham already had a pistol which he got from his car when he got me, and now he used it to put the poor animal out of its misery. Then we noticed the smell. At first, I wasn't sure where it came from, but then we looked around a bit and that's when we found it." He paused again, finishing his coke in two large gulps, then holding the bottle in his hand, looking at it, as if trying to read the fine print. He suppressed a belch into the back of his hand as we waited patiently for him to regain his composure, both too dumbstruck to speak. Steph took out her cigarettes and I saw that her fingers were also shaking.

"It's OK, Richard. Take your time," I said, trying to sound in control, but I noticed my voice was a little shaky.

"Could I bum one of those?" he asked Steph. "I quit, but, under the circumstances. Just don't tell my wife, she'll kick my butt." He took one, Steph lit it for him and he inhaled deeply.

"We saw a large sheet of tin lying on the ground some way off. At first, we figured it was just some junk, there's a shit load of it down there, old car bodies and stuff. But then we heard movement from beneath the sheet. We walked over to it and Graham lifted one side. There was a hole dug underneath it, maybe 7 or 8 yards wide and almost as deep. In the bottom of it, were animals, some alive, but most dead. We counted 6 dogs, 12 cats and a goat. Of them, only 1 dog and 4 cats were alive, and those *should* have been dead. He had been eating them alive, their skins matted with blood. Their faces were all skinnier than you could imagine, probably all starved, eyes sunken into their skulls. The dog was trying to chew on one of the cats. They all had wounds that were weeping blood, pus and God knows what else. And then there were the maggots. It was like their wounds were alive, crawling with those filthy things in some tangled, writhing mass. I can still hear the noise when I close my eyes, like a fucken nightmare. I wanted to kill him, Steph. Right then and there, I wanted to grab Graham's gun and shoot the son of a bitch. But, of course, I didn't. Instead, Graham jumped in the hole and put the animals out of their pain. Then he went back to fetch a shovel and when that bastard came to, we made him bury the animals. We stayed there for almost three hours and made him fill in the hole, watching as he panted and groaned, covering his evil one shovel load at a time." I was stunned into silence, my mouth dry as a dust bowl. I looked at Steph and could see her mind in overdrive, looking down at her fingers, each hand firmly grasping one of her legs.

"Did you report this?" she finally asked.

"Yup, but guess what? Rademeyer didn't want to hear it. Said he wasn't going to waste valuable police resources on a retard culling the town's vermin problem."

"He said that?" I asked, again shocked. Richard nodded, his fingers closing around a pencil so tight, I heard it begin to splinter.

"And now that retard is working at the school, hanging around kids," he said. "I fired that freak and warned him that if I ever saw him again, I would end his miserable life. I saw him down the main street a couple of times but was glad when I saw him cross the street to avoid me." Steph rose to her feet and held out her hand. Richard shook it, then held it out to me.

"Thank you, Rich. I appreciate your help," she said as she headed out the door.

"No problem, Steph. Anytime."

11.

"That crazy fuck," she said as we headed back into town.

"Still keen to talk to him?" I asked, but again she shook her head.

"No way. We need to follow him. Watch him. I want to know what he gets up to after the sun goes down. Fancy a stakeout?" she asked, turning to me.

"Whatever it takes to end this nightmare," I said, "whatever it takes.

Chapter 8: Trailing Madness

1.

As we reached the outskirts of Cider Hill, I asked Steph if she was going to report this new information to Rademeyer, to which she shook her head.

"But it's not new information, Jim. Rademeyer already knows. Now why would I bore him with details he's already aware of?" The cheekiness of her grin told me exactly what she was thinking. "I say, we head to the school and keep an eye on him. We know he'll be there and it's a good a place to start as any." I agreed as she turned the car towards the school, approaching it from one of the roads that ran adjacent to it on its western side. The road sat on the edge of a small hill, thus providing us with an elevated vantage point. We could see Clancy mowing the grass on the far side of the oval, cutting a strange myriad of shapes into the grass as he went.

"There he is," I said as Steph turned the car off. After a few moments, she said, "I wish I had my binoculars."

"You have binoculars?" I asked.

"Sure. They were my mum's," she said with a straight face. It took me a second, then I burst out laughing. Steph looked at me, surprised. "What are you laughing at?" she asked, and I realised she didn't understand.

"What was your mum doing with binoculars?" She nodded, then giggled a little, as she understood.

"They belonged to her father, silly." She looked around, first over the school yard, then the road behind us.

"What's up?"

"Do you mind waiting here? My house is only a couple of blocks behind us. I can go grab them, and maybe some supplies as well."

"OK, but don't be long. Looks like he's almost finished that patch and I don't know if he'll start another." She agreed and hopped out, hurrying down the footpath behind us. I slid across to the driver's side to look less conspicuous.

I watched him, fascinated, as Clancy weaved in and out of strange patterns in the grass. It was like he was creating some amazing piece of artwork that only he could see. He had his shirt off and had suspended it from his belt. Every so often, he would pull it from his belt and wipe his brow with it, looking up at the cloudless sky as he did. Round and round he went, the remaining grass patch growing smaller and smaller. I figured he would finish in the next ten or so minutes and hoped Steph would be back by then.

She returned less than ten minutes later, carrying two bags, one in each hand. She hopped in the passenger seat and slung the bags in my direction. I took them and handed them back to her once she closed the door. She reached into the first and pulled out a brown leather case with a long brown leather strap. She popped the top and took out an old pair of binoculars. They looked like something from the first world war, but when I looked through them, saw they were in amazingly clear condition. With the binoculars, I could see Clancy close enough to pick out the beads of sweat on his forehead. She also took out two thermoses, two bottles of coke and a bottle of milk.

In the other bag, Steph had packed a loaf of bread, an entire length of salami, a jar of mustard, a whole sponge cake and a container of mixed nuts.

"Wow, were you expecting anyone else?" I laughed as she handed me the container of nuts.

"I wasn't sure what you liked and I don't know how long this will take." I took the bag and put it on the back seat, returning the spyglass to my eyes. Clancy was walking the mower back to a small shed next to the main building, the patch finally complete.

"How are we going to follow him when he walks to wherever he goes after this?" I asked. It was a small town with very little traffic, and he would surely notice a car trailing him, regardless of his IQ.

"We drive from corner to corner for some of the time, other times, one of us gets out and walks. Although I would probably suggest you hop out. I have no doubt he would notice my uniform." She had a point and wondered why she hadn't changed when she was home. I figured it didn't matter at this point and agreed with her.

3.

We followed Clancy for the best part of an hour as he made his way up Main Street. I had to get out a couple of times to follow, but Steph kept coming at just the right moments to scoop me up and continue behind him. He stopped at a couple of shops, one to buy cigarettes and another to buy an ice cream. Each time, he would come out of the shops whistling, throwing a set of keys in the air, then catching them triumphantly. He dropped them once, cursed, then picked them up. It was almost comical to watch him, and under different circumstances, maybe even funny. But our reasons for trailing this person were far from anything enjoyable and so we had our game faces on.

The further he walked toward the outskirts of town, the harder it became for us to follow. On one occasion he stopped to tie his bootlace just as I had jumped out of the car. I considered jumping back in but there was a woman walking her dog past and I didn't want to draw unnecessary attention to us. He took an insane amount of time to complete the task of tying the lace and in the end, I had to walk straight past him. I turned my head as he glanced up, trying to shield my identity from him. I think I achieved this with some success as he didn't utter a word to me. The problem was though, he had seen me, knew I was there. If he continued walking much farther, and I was forced to hop out again, he would surely know I was following him.

4.

His final destination couldn't have been described as anything more than a run-down shack that sat beside a larger run-down shack. A rickety picket fence surrounded the dwellings on three sides, the left side remaining open, sharing its space with a field devoid of livestock. There were, however, several piles of rubbish dotted around the yard and paddock, one old rusted-out car, a small tractor with rotting tyres and what may have been a chicken pen sometime in the previous century. The buildings weren't in any better shape, the larger having two of its four windows boarded shut, cracked glass visible in one uncovered corner. Neither building had seen a taste of paint in like four hundred years and the roof of the smaller building had scraps of tin nailed to it in little spits and spats. It would seem that Clancy Higgins lived in squalor. Steph parked the FX a couple of hundred yards from the house, saw a dirt track that led up past the paddock and decided to investigate where it ended. To our relief, the track ended in a bunch of trees that flanked the northside of the paddock, sitting atop a slight hill. From here, we had our second perfect vantage point of the day, both buildings visible, including clear uninterrupted views of the front and rear of the buildings.

Steph tapped my shoulder and pointed to something sitting on the far side of the paddock, almost hidden from view by a tree and large clumps of grass. It was a sheet of roofing tin, roughly 7 to 8 feet by about 4 to 6 feet. I looked at her, thinking the same thing she was. I made it my intention to investigate it once darkness fell. I checked my watch, saw it was a little before 11 and groaned. It was going to be a long day.

Steph grabbed a coke and popped the top, handed it to me then grabbed the other. I took a long gulp, burped into my hand, then set the bottle on the floor. Steph took an even longer swallow, belched like a frontline soldier and giggled when I looked at her wide-eyed.

"OK, puts mine to shame. Just warn me if you plan to cock your leg, yeah?" I said, making her giggle harder. I grabbed the box of nuts and threw some into my mouth. Steph followed suit then grabbed the binoculars, scanning the buildings for signs of life. She didn't see any and put them back in their case.

"Can I ask you something?" I asked her after a while. The only sounds out here were a couple of magpies sitting in the trees above us, and an occasional cow, bellowing in a paddock down the road.

"Sure."

"The car. It's a pretty sweet ride for someone so young."

"It belonged to my uncle before he died. He never married and had no children so it came to me."

"I'm sorry to hear that."

"Don't be. The guy was an arse." That was what I really liked about this girl, she said it how it was, no glitter, no bullshit, just plain and simple.

5.

The afternoon slipped by with nothing noteworthy. After a lunch of salami and mustard sandwiches and a generous helping of sponge cake, Steph drifted into a nap while I stayed on duty. Around 3, we swapped, sleep taking me much easier than I anticipated. I don't recall dreaming, but do recall almost jumping out of my skin when Steph began shaking me. It was pitch black outside and it took me a moment to realise where we were.

"Jim," she said, close to my ear. I sat up, rubbing my eyes, trying to focus on what she was pointing at. I could make out a blurry mix of lights, but due to sleep stuck in my eyes, I couldn't focus on the individual lights that were shining out there. I rubbed my eyes a second time and when I took another look, made out three separate sets of lights. One set was the large house, one was the smaller house. For a moment I couldn't work out what the third set was. I looked at her, questioningly.

"It's a car," she whispered back.

"Do we know who?" I asked.

"I think we do. It's a German make," she said.

"Levinson?" I asked, sitting bolt upright. My head hit the roof, making a loud thump inside the car. Steph opened her door and quietly climbed out. Even though the house was several hundred yards away, noise had a funny way of travelling, especially at night. A sound could easily travel for miles, as was evident by the barking dog we could hear, somewhere out of sight. I climbed out of the car and walked toward a tree, leaning behind it and peering around its trunk. There was no moon, so the darkness worked in our favour, the cloud cover even shielding us from the starlight. From this distance, all we could make out were the distant lights, shadows occasionally walking in front of them. We had no idea how many people, or who the people were for that matter. We suddenly heard some muffled yelling coming from the house, a crash sounding like a door slam, then two distinct car doors being slammed shut. I looked back at Steph who was standing just behind me. The car started up and began to reverse.

"What do we do?" I asked, panicking.

"Have to split up. You stay here, I'll follow Levinson," she said, turning to run back to the car.

"Steph," I whispered after her, "be careful." I watched as she started the car, then slowly began driving back down the path we had come down, not turning the headlights on until she was hidden behind the hill. I listened to her as she slowly idled the car back to the main road, but didn't see her, figuring she probably killed the lights as she neared the road. I could still see Levinson's lights in the distance and was hoping Steph would get close enough to his car that she could feed off his lights.

I looked back to the houses and the lights that were still on. There was no noticeable movement and for a moment a bolt of fear ran through me that everybody had gone with the Doc, leaving Steph to deal with them on her own, while I sat here twiddling my thumbs watching an empty paddock.

There was something I did want to check out though, and that was the sheet of tin that was lying at the far side of the field. Dreading what I would find under it was an understatement, but to my relief, once I had slinked across the paddock and lifted the sheet up, found it to be nothing more than a discarded sheet of roofing iron, nothing of interest beneath it. That at least meant no animals were harmed in this location at least. Although that didn't mean Clancy had given up chewing on dogs and cats. That was something we still had to confirm.

I decided to sneak to the houses and see if I could learn anything of interest. There was a very low sound coming from one of the buildings, and as I neared the larger of the two, made out the distinct sound of music. It was some sort of classical orchestra, like Beethoven or Mozart. Classical music was definitely not one of my strong suits, but as I crept closer, I recognized the piece that was playing immediately because it was a piece my mother was quite fond of. I knew it was called Symphony No. 40, but couldn't remember who had written it.

There was an open window nearest to me and the music was emanating from there. I crept closer and closer, edging my way towards the sound. There were no other sounds coming from the house and at first, I thought that the house was empty. But then as I neared the window close enough to peer into it, saw an old woman sitting back in a sofa chair, her nightgown pulled tightly around her ample bosoms. She was sporting a dozen or so hair curlers on her head, reminding me of pictures I had seen in a book of Greek mythology. It reminded me of the picture I had seen of Medusa, the mythical titan. There was a glass of what looked like whiskey or bourbon on the table in front of her and in her fingers dangled a lit cigarette, its tendrils of smoke slowly snaking towards the open window. Her eyes were closed and I thought she must have fallen asleep while listening to her music, but then she lifted her cigarette to her lips and drew in a puff.

Without any warning, her eyes suddenly shot open and her head turned towards me. I found myself staring at her less than 3 feet from her face. Her eyes grew wide behind her oversized glasses as she sat bolt upright and that's when she began to scream, a long shrill screech that drilled into my head. I put my hands up trying to quieten her, to show her that I meant no harm, but then I heard footsteps running from another room.

"What's wrong, Ma?" I heard, and when I saw the rifle in the man's hand as he came through the doorway, it was all the motivation I needed to get my arse out of there. Instead of running towards the road, which meant running past the front door to this wonderful dwelling, I decided to turn and run the other way, back up the hill and further from town. I figured it would be easier to double back once I gained enough distance between me and whoever the man with the rifle was.

The back door suddenly crashed open and I instantly fell flat on my face, then wiggled forward a few yards to hide in some thick weeds that were growing in a clump. The patch was almost large enough to hide me and was also close enough to the house that I could make out the man now looking for me.

"I'LL FIND YOU, YOU PERVERT!" he yelled, getting closer to my hiding spot. I could just make out the rifle he was now raising in front of him, the butt end nestled into his shoulder. "COME OUT YOU QUEER!" I lay completely still, unable to move a single muscle. Something began to crawl over my fingers and I nearly yelped in surprise. I swallowed the shock and held my breath. The man suddenly fired the rifle, the crack so loud, I heard it echo back from the hill behind me. The bullet whizzed above my head and I was sure that he had spotted me. He fired again but had aimed off to my right this time. "DON'T COME BACK, YOU HEAR ME?" He finally turned and began to walk back to the house. He climbed the step, turned for one final look then went in, slamming the door behind him. I heard the muffled sound of garbled conversation and breathed a sigh of relief. It was a good five minutes before I finally had the nerve to move, and when I did, I ran like the actual Devil was chasing me.

By the time I had reached the main road again, it was close to 8 o'clock and Steph had been gone almost an hour. Clancy's house was at least a mile behind me, and as there were no other cars that I could see, figured I was pretty safe walking along the road. If I spotted a car coming towards me, then I would duck into the bushes until I was sure it wasn't Levinson. I needn't have worried. About another mile down the road, I saw Steph's car parked down a side lane about 30 yards off the main road. As I approached, I saw that the car was turned off and abandoned, the driver's door open. I peered inside and was about to close the door when a hand grabbed my arm, the scream unable to be held in this time. My arm came up to hit out, but I saw Steph's face in the nick of time.

"What the hell," I cried, "you scared the shit out of me." She giggled a little then pointed to something further down the lane. I could see some sort of shadow also sitting beside the small lane, but it was too dark to identify.

"It's Levinson's Mercedes," she said.

"Are they parked there?" I asked, beginning to walk toward it.

"No, it's empty. I don't know where they've gone. They just disappeared."

"Disappeared?". Just then something illuminated not just Steph and I, but her car, the Mercedes and the rest of the lane. As if to confirm any doubt about who it was, revolving red lights began to fan across the trees, cars and landscape as the patrol car came to a halt beside us.

"Steph?" A voice asked.

"Yah," she replied.

"Chief wants to see you."

"Pete, what are you doing here? How did you find me?"

"We got a call from Irene Higgins. Apparently, someone's been sneaking a peak at her through a window. Some pervert looking to get his rocks off. We saw your car from the road."

"Is that the only call you got?" I asked, but he didn't answer, ignoring me.

"Anyway, Chief's lookin for ya."

"Thanks," Steph replied and didn't wait for any formalities. She jumped in the car and waited for me to climb in. Judging by the slam of her door, her frustration had grown considerably.

132

"Think someone tipped them off?" I asked as she swung the FX back onto the main road.

"I'd put a fiver on it," she said, lighting a smoke.

"He's up to something, I know it," I said, looking through the window at the approaching street lamps.

"Of that, I'm pretty positive," Steph said as she inhaled. Ten minutes later we were sitting in Rademeyer's office.

6.

"Before I tell you about a phone call I just received, I just want to make it clear to you two that I am on your side. Despite whatever differences we may have had in the past, however you feel about my ability to run this police station or even what names people are calling me these days, I need you two to get it through your heads that I am on your side. I can't help you if you don't help me." He looked at us from across his desk, all the years of stress clearly visible on his face tonight. I wanted to believe him, and I think on some level I did, but the doubt that lingered wouldn't go quietly. It hung in the air between us, both sides of the desk aware of its presence.

When neither of us answered, he continued. "I received a call from William Reinhart. I trust you two know the name?" I nodded. "It seems that Commissioner Reinhart has a history with a certain Doctor that is currently doing some work up at Crab Apple." I groaned inside, but when Rademeyer's eyes flashed in my direction, I realised I had groaned externally. "Yes, Jim, that's right. Levinson and Reinhart go all the way back to high school. And he's been using his connections to conduct his research anywhere he damn well pleases." Rademeyer stood, went to a shelf that hung on the far wall and rifled through a folder. He pulled out an envelope and sat back down.

"Chief, I wanted to-" Steph started but Rademeyer held a hand up, stopping her words. I felt a flash of anger and was about to say so, but then he looked at me.

"Do you really think I would ask for your help if I didn't respect you as an officer, Jim? I know we have a history, but this thing is bigger than us and we need to put our differences aside." He turned to Steph. "Steph, I don't mean to be as harsh as I am to you. I respect you as an officer too, I really do. I don't always have the right words, and to be honest, I get worried about you out there." Steph's jaw dropped and I thought she was about to fall out of her chair. "I have a daughter who's about your age and it would scare the shit out of me if she was out there doing what you do. I don't mean to stand in your way, it's just," he paused for a moment, looking down at the envelope, then continued," it's the father figure in me, I guess." He handed me the envelope which I took, unsure of its contents.

"Chief?" I asked, hesitating.

"I know the rumours, I've heard them all, Jim. I know what was said when we finally nailed that bastard. That I held out on you, that I took your glory. Open it. Maybe it's time for unanswered questions to be laid to rest," he said, pointing at the envelope. I tore it open and read the single note that was inside. It struck me how old it looked; the paper yellowed around the edges.

To the Office of the Chief Commissioner of Police
Dear Sir,

It is with much pleasure and pride, that I am formally advising you of the apprehension of the wanted criminal known as the Daylesford Devil, responsible for the torture and murder of 14 Victorian citizens. The investigation and subsequent arrest had been made possible by a vast number of men and women, both in uniform and out and it is my honour to pass on their names to you in the attached list.

There are, however, two names that I would personally like to put forth to you, for the raw courage and bravery they displayed in ensuring the arrest of the offender.

I would like to put forth the name of Leading Senior Constable Warren Smythe (killed in the line of duty) to be considered for the Victoria Police Star.

I would like to put forth the name of Constable James Lawson to be considered for the Valour Award.

Sir, these men have shown incredible bravery and sacrifice in the course of their duties and I believe deserve the appropriate recognition.

With Respect
Frank Jodey Rademeyer
January 28, 1934

Reading the letter a second time didn't help diminish my embarrassment. I always figured he just ignored my input, forgotten the hours and hours that Warren and I had put in. When I finally met his eyes again, he was smiling, a warm almost apologetic smile.

"Frank, Chief, I'm sorry," was all that would come out.

"They overruled me, Jim. Three times I tried and three times they pissed me off, telling me it was a group effort, no single officer deserved recognition over anybody else. And then when they implied that Warren had acted with bravado rather than calling for back up, they didn't want to acknowledge his sacrifice either." I didn't know what to say. The best I could think of was to hold out my hand and shake his. He shook my hand, tightly, as if releasing some long held-on pain.

"Now," he said as he let my hand go, "tell me what's going on."

7.

We told him everything that had been happening the past couple of days, including the interviews we held, the meeting with Levinson and spotting him out at Clancy Higgins' house. He listened intently, nodding here and there to confirm his understanding, even asking questions of Steph. It was like being in a room with a completely different person. When were finished, he sat back in his chair, pondering the information he had now been made aware of. After a few minutes, he lent forward, clasped his hands together and put his arms on his desk.

"The one thing I have learnt in this job is that the more reason you have to hide what you are doing, the higher up the chain you climb to shield yourself. This arsehole, Levinson, has climbed almost as high as he could possibly go. That means he's up to some serious shit. Agree?" We both nodded. "There's really only one person higher than the commissioner and we all know who that is. We also know that given the commissioner's relationship to our premier, that one higher phone call is a real possibility."

"But Chief, we have to-" but Rademeyer stopped her with his hand again.

"I know, Steph. We have victims piling up faster than they did back in the 30s and everyone seems to be fighting against us. Just be subtle. Do what you have to do; you know I have your back. But try not to stick your necks out far enough for the entire town to see. Subtle." He waved his hand up and down to highlight slowly, as if beckoning us to slow down. "Listen, why don't the two of you drop by the house tomorrow night. Melanie would love to see you, Jim. And you too, of course," he said, turning to Steph. "Nothing fancy, just dinner and a couple of brews. Say around 7?" There was a sudden scurrying above us, sounding like a small animal moving around in the ceiling space.

"Dam possums again," the chief said and reached across to a broom that was leaning next to his desk. Without standing, he lifted it and began banging the handle on the ceiling which I thought, given by the banging, was going to punch right through the plasterboard. "We only had old Bill catch a couple yesterday and take them away. Dam tree next to the cop shop gives 'em easy access. Anyway," he said, returning the broom to its original post, "dinner tomorrow night, OK?"

"Yes, of course, Chief." Steph stood and then was visibly surprised when Rademeyer also stood and offered her his hand.

"You're a good cop, Steph." She blushed fiercely, and then, to try and take some of the focus away from her, I made the chief blush, the three of us enjoying our one and only laugh together.

"One question, Sir." He looked at me.

"Shoot."

"Your middle name is really Jodey?"

8.

I expected Steph to drive me back to the hotel, she instead headed for her home.

"Steph? It's kinda late."

"I want to show you something. I didn't notice it on the first go around, but something struck me as odd."

"Odd?"

"Wait till we get to my place. Better to show you and have you decide for yourself." I was intrigued and patiently held my tongue until I was once again, sitting in her living room. Steph quickly ducked next door to grab Judith and when she came back with a sleeping munchkin in her arms, went to lay the girl into her bed. When Steph returned, she was holding one of the ledgers from the prison. She sat next to me and I saw it was the visitor's log.

"When I was going through this the other night, I was trying to see if there were any sorts of patterns to the times when Lightman was being either visited or seen by medical staff. Nothing really jumped out, everything looking as random as the rest of them. I got frustrated and threw the book across the room in frustration and when I went to pick it up, it had opened to a specific page. As I bent down to pick it up, half the page was covered and all I could see were the visitor's signatures. Here, like this." She folded one of the sheets across itself, leaving only the column with the signatures visible, but I wasn't picking up what she was trying to show me.

"I don't see it," I said after a minute.

"That's because you haven't seen this." She unfolded the page and flicked a couple of pages back. Once again, she folded the page over itself, but once again, I wasn't picking it up.

"Steph, what am I-" but that was when I saw it. She began to smile as she saw my expression change. I took the book, held one finger on the page we were on, then flicked a couple of pages forward. The signature that was next to Dr. Levinson's name was different. And not just by a little bit. It had been written by a different hand entirely.

"It's fake?" I asked and Steph nodded.

"It's fake," she said, confirming it for me.

"Why would he fake the signature?" I asked, but had a feeling I already knew the answer. "Because he was coming and going whenever he chose. Someone *else* was filling the book in for him to keep it all official. I don't get it, though. Why would he *need* to fake it?"

"Because I'm guessing, he wasn't only visiting during normal hours. My guess? He practically has a key to the front gate."

"But that would jeopardize the security of the prison," I said.

"Yup, but who's going to tell him off?"

"I don't get it. The man visits Lightman for years, almost on a daily basis and everything is legit. Then he takes off for a year, leaving his patient in the hands of someone else. Then, when he returns, he sees Lightman daily like clockwork but now needs to make up the times that he actually comes and goes. Why?"

"Wait, do you have the prison rosters in that box?" I asked, an idea flashing into my mind like something tapping me on the shoulder.

"One sec, I'll check." She left the room again, returning a minute later carrying the box. She set it down on the table and began taking out piles of old books. She found what we were looking for with the second pile she pulled out.

"Here, is this it?" she asked, holding a book out to me. I took it, opened it and nodded. On the front cover were the words "Staff Schedules" and when I opened it, found a section titled "Rostering". After flicking through a couple of pages, I found what we needed.

Each officer was assigned a post, which they held for the duration of their employment. Transfers between duties occurred, judging by the names changing places, but not often. Each guard worked a 12-hour shift, meaning each position had 4 officers that rotated between days and nights. Crab Apple had the inner wall with its gatehouse and it was in this gatehouse that the visitor's log was kept and signed by all the visitors to the prison. Guards with the number 1 behind their name, worked the day shift. Guards with the number 2 allocation, worked nights. The first three names that were written next to "Gatehouse" meant nothing to me, the fourth however did. The name was Lee Higgins.

"Do you know who Lee Higgins is?" I asked Steph, but she shook her head. Even though she had lived most of her life half way between Cider Hill and Daylesford, most of her life took her to Ballarat, about the same distance from Cider Hill that Daylesford was. She had only been in Cider Hill since being posted here and in that time, hadn't totally grasped all the 3500 or so names that resided in this town. "Could he be any relation to Clancy?" I was thinking of the man that chased me with a rifle not too many hours ago.

"I don't know," she said, then held up one finger, as if about to announce something," but I think I know someone that might." She walked into the kitchen and picked up the telephone that hung on the wall. She spoke in a low voice, Judith's bedroom across the hall from where the phone hung. A couple of minutes later, Steph returned, smiling triumphantly.

"Margaret says hello. And, she also said that Clancy has one brother. Lee Higgins, who's been working up at Crab Apple for the past 5 years." I told Steph what happened when she left me at the house, me peering in on the woman and about the man who fired the gun at me.

"You were shot at?" she said when I finished. I nodded. To my surprise, she began to giggle.

"What's so funny?" I asked.

"You're the peeping tom that Pete was talking about, aren't you?" She laughed harder, then stifled it when she remembered the little girl sleeping down the hall.

9.

It was decided that we would take a drive to Melbourne the following morning. I was beginning to feel inadequate without my own transportation and asked Steph to take me home so I could get it. She phoned her trusty neighbour, asking if she could pop over early in the morning to watch Judith, then brought me a blanket. We figured it would save a lot of time and hassle if I just camped on her couch for the night. Neither of us were too fussed with rumours and I knew Tami wasn't the jealous type.

I snuggled into the cushions on the couch, wished Steph a goodnight as she switched the lights out, then closed my eyes, the noises of the house and the night outside slowly receding as sleep took hold of me quicker than I was expecting. I don't think I even heard Steph climb into bed before I was out.

10.

The drive to Melbourne was a quiet one, given the day of the week. We didn't talk much, not because we didn't want to speak to each other, the landscape just looked incredible in the morning light and we just kind of went with it. I did engage Steph with an incredibly important plan I needed help with and as usual, she obliged. There was very little traffic, a couple of farm tractors slowing us, but when clear, Steph negotiated the FX around them with ease. It really was a fine automobile and I loved riding in it. The weather had been kind to me, the days almost spring-like once the morning fog had cleared. When the sun broke over the distant horizon, almost an hour into our trip, I could see a few clouds scattered over the sky, but for the most part, it was looking like it would turn into a fine day. As I've mentioned before, hindsight can be a wonderful thing. It can also be a savage bitch with bared teeth and if I could have had the slightest inclination of how that Sunday would end, I would have turned around and headed back to bed.

Chapter 9: When Words Are Not Enough

1.

Steph beat me back to Cider Hill, partly due to us being separated in the traffic whilst driving through Melbourne, but also because her car was a lot quicker. Her FX handled the pace a lot easier than my Beetle, plus it was also a lot more comfortable when tackling the roads around town. My small car felt every single bump and pothole, each thud sending jolts up my spine. I also had one minor errand to run and promised to see her later that day, although visiting one's Mum probably shouldn't ever be referred to as 'running an errand'.

It was a little before 1 when I finally rolled down back through town, the streets empty except for a few cars parked around the half a dozen hotels that dotted the road. It didn't matter which town or city you visited on a weekend; the busiest establishments would always be the nearest watering hole.

I turned the beetle down a street just before the hotel I currently called home, stopping out the front of Tami's small unit. When I knocked on her door, she opened it so fast and had her arms around my neck before I had a chance to speak, her lips on mine in an instant. I reached into my pocket and brought out a small gift, wrapped in yellow and gold paper. When the kiss subsided, I held it out to the side, waving it a little from side to side until she saw it. Her eyes gleamed with excitement when she realised what it was.

"You remembered?" she said, taking the gift as I held it out to her.

"Happy birthday, beautiful lady," I said and gave her another kiss, breathing in the sweet scent of her perfume. She thanked me then held my hand and led me inside, kicking the door closed with a heel. Her living room was bright today, the curtains tied back with pieces of red ribbon, sunlight streaming in with fierce rays. She sat on the couch and pulled me down beside her, then looked at the gift excitedly.

"Well? Go on, open it," I said, waving a hand at the present. She tore the package open, revealing a small, square jewellery gift box. She opened the lid and exhaled loudly when she saw the drop-pearl earrings that were dangling from the inner board.

"Oh my God, Jim. They're beautiful," she said, almost whispering, one hand held over her mouth.

"They were my mum's. When I told her that I was seeing you, she insisted I give them to you on your birthday."

"Wow. They're stunning." She put the earrings in then stood and ran to the bathroom to admire them.

"When did you see your Mum?" she called down the hall.

"Oh, about 3 hours ago," I said and grinned when I heard her laugh. When she came back, she flashed a wide Cheshire grin at me, twirling a little, as she paraded the jewellery to me. She was about to sit in my lap but a knock on the door stopped her. I looked at my watch and saw it was 1pm; right on cue. I stood and grabbed Tami by the wrist. She resisted at first, then understood and allowed me to guide her to the dining table. I sat her down, motioned for her to stay, then went to answer the door.

2.

Steph had not only arranged for a 3-course meal to be served at Tami's home, but she had organised two of the waitresses to dress in complete formal attire and serve each course as if we were sitting in the middle of a lavish restaurant. The curtains were drawn and a large white candle placed between us, its flame creating dancing shadows on the walls in her tiny room.

The entre we were served consisted of pan-fried scallops, served on small dollops of cauliflower mash. I remembered Tami's love for seafood and had spoken to the head chef in the hotel kitchen the day before. He showed me a list of things he had on hand and was relieved to see a generous choice of seafood.

Tami clapped her hands together as the mains were brought in. Whole fried snapper on rice, the smell of garlic and lemon filling her tiny abode. She ate with gusto, conversation ceasing as she wolfed her fish down. It was such an enjoyable sight to see.

But, as it had always in the past, it was dessert that finally made her gush with glee. The waitresses brought in an entire pavlova, made especially for her, the fruits adorning the marshmallow and cream looking juicy and sweet. Strawberries, raspberries and blueberries were piled on top, their juices creating intricate patterns of red and black trails like roads on a map. Tami and I ate almost half the entire creation by ourselves, then rubbed our bellies which felt close to bursting.

Once the dishes were removed and we were once again alone, Tami took my hand and led me back into the living room, sitting beside me on the couch. She held my hand as she looked into my eyes, her face as radiant as ever. I was awestruck at her beauty, had been since I first saw her after that fateful night. I didn't know whether our feelings were purely because we had shared such a traumatic episode, and to be totally honest, I didn't care.

"Jim?" she whispered to me. She looked at the window, the curtains open again, sunlight now creating its own shadows around the room. She turned her face toward me again and lent in a little closer, her face now just a few inches from mine. "I love you, Jim." The words hung in the air, momentarily caught between the seconds, as if temporarily halted in time. The moment where you *think* you know what was said and the moment where you *realise* what was said seemed to mingle. Once I let the words sink in, I smiled and said the only thing I could, the words that had been jumping around my own mind for too long already.

"And I love you, Tami, with all my heart and soul." She smiled at that and gently pressed her lips on mine, our tongues gently probing and exploring. I could still taste the sweet residue of the pavlova and it made me want her more. I pulled her in closer, my arms wrapping her tightly into me. Then the kiss ended as she tilted her head onto my shoulder, resting it there as she stared out the window.

"I've wanted to say that for such a long time, Jim. But," she paused, contemplating her words, "but my father wouldn't allow it." I pulled away, looking at her, the words hitting me in the chest.

"He what?"

"He didn't want me to see you. He kept saying that you would be too scarred, like me, and that life would be too difficult for two scarred people to make a go of it."

"That's horseshit," I cried, my anger building.

"He wanted me to find someone normal, unhurt. Someone who wouldn't suffer from anxiety and depression."

"Anxiety and depression? You mean like him?"

"I'm sorry." I could see tears begin to form, building behind her eye lashes, threatening to spill over at any moment. I pulled her in tight again, hugging her in a fierce embrace.

"I will never let you go again," I whispered in her ear. She returned my embrace, pushing her face into the crook of my neck, her fingers grasping my shirt. And as I held her, I heard the tiniest whisper from her as she fought back the tears.

"Forever."

3.

I stayed for as long as I could with Tami, but around six that evening had to bid her a good night. She was OK with me having to attend Chief Rademeyer's house for dinner, and perfectly fine that I was going with Steph. As I said, Tami was not the jealous type. But she made me promise that I would return the second the dinner was over.

"I promise, Baby," I said as she kissed me good night. I looked over my shoulder as I jumped in my car and saw her leaning against her doorframe, flashing that Cheshire grin.

4.

It didn't take me long to get myself ready for the Chief's house. Men never seem to take much time to prepare. What's there to take care of? You shave, shower, comb and splash some sort of cologne on. Brushing your teeth adds a couple of minutes. And unless you needed to shine your shoes with some good old spit n' polish, that was pretty much it. Women on the other hand. WowWee, that's another ballgame entirely. I cannot even begin to work out just what the hell takes over an hour. Hair and make-up almost require the previous day to plan and execute. There were a couple of ladies whom I dated in my younger years and every one of them required a couple of days' notice and an entire vacant house in order to prepare.

But Steph was different. That lady could get herself ready and looking a treat almost as fast as me. When I pulled up in front of her house at twenty to seven that evening, she didn't come out. I hopped out of my beetle and went to the front door. She answered, still wearing a bathrobe, her hair dry and looking the way it had before lunch.

"Steph, it's nearly a quarter to," I said, pointing at my watch. She smiled.

"And?" I didn't know what she implied, so went into the living room as she detoured to the bathroom. A second later, I heard the shower start and groaned. I knew the Chief did not like to be kept waiting.

Mrs. Wong was sitting in one of the sofa chairs in the living room, an open book in her lap. She smiled when I walked in and gave me a little wave which I returned. Judith was sitting at the dining table, a menagerie of pencils and crayons sprawled out before her, as well as several blank sheets of paper.

"Hello Mrs. Wong, hi Judith." She looked up from her drawing and gave me a little wave, her face unsure of me. But she shot me a smile none-the-less, then resumed her drawing, a kindergarten scene with swings and see-saws with a slide in one corner.

"Say hello, Jude," Steph suddenly said from behind me. I was startled, not only by her presence but also at how fast she had showered and dressed. I felt she had done both in the time it took me to take half a dozen steps or so. She whizzed past me, then whizzed back again, going to her room, as Judith whispered a 'hello' at me. I swear it was less than two minutes and she was back, dressed, hair up and face as pretty as a picture. I thought she had hypnotized me to finish everything so fast.

After the usual "have her in bed by 8, call the station if you need anything, I won't be late, behave yourself" to Judith and Mrs. Wong, we left the house.

"Take mine," I said as Steph headed towards her own car, parked in the driveway beside the house. She paused for a moment as if considering. "I think it's my turn to taxi you around for a bit." She didn't argue, instead, walking towards my car, flashing me a grin as we climbed into the Beetle.

5.

Frank and Melanie Rademeyer lived out on Crescent Lane, a humble neighbourhood where an unfamiliar person could tell immediately what type of people occupied the dwellings that were dotted along the road. Every home along Crescent Lane seemed to sit on its own hill, the blocks ranging from 2 to 5 acres, and every single home was two storeys high. Most enjoyed a swimming pool in their back yards and fruit trees in the front, a couple of them even sporting rows of grape vines for amateur wine makers. A large hill, maybe 300 yards high, dominated the land on the western side of the road with Crescent Lane running north to south. The Chief's home was the last one on the western side, the only one to have a beautiful mature palm tree growing by his driveway.

Back when I was still a young constable, the Rademeyers still lived in one of the working-class areas of Cider Hill. The Chief would commute to the station via his bicycle on a daily basis, telling me on one occasion, that the ride to and from the station was quality thinking time and gave him the brain space he needed to unwind by the time he arrived home. It also helped with his waistline, he once chuckled.

They had raised two children, a son called William who was born in 1926 and a daughter named Elizabeth who was born in 1930. The family seemed to be such a happy one when I first made the transfer to Cider Hill, meeting the family at a police Christmas barbeque, held behind the station. All the officers and families attended, Melanie holding little Lizzie by the hand while William had been hanging around his Dad. He was a doting father, proudly showing off his son's ability to kick a football.

"Play for Carlton one day, he will," he would say. But William Rademeyer would never play for Carlton. Or any other team. Two days after Christmas Day, in 1933, while his parents slept soundly in their room, little William decided to go into his father's study and play cops and robbers. He took the service revolver Frank always kept in the drawer of his desk, and began to pretend-shoot make believe robbers that were hiding behind the furniture. The doctors said that little William never knew what hit him, the pistol discharging as he tried to open the cylinder. The bullet pierced his forehead just above his right eye, the crash of the gun waking his parents instantly. The neighbours told a lone reporter that they heard Mrs Rademeyer's screams from their own kitchen, her blood-curdling cries of anguish continuing until the ambulance arrived ten minutes later.

The funeral was held at St. Johns Anglican three days later, attended by everybody in town, me included. He was buried in Hope Cemetery out on One Stump Lane, his grave next to his grandfather and grandmother. I still remember the sobbing from the heart-broken parents, the umbrellas that were held above them not enough to shield them from the prying reporters that were dotted around the small grave yard.

From what I could gather, little Lizzie Rademeyer became one of the most shielded children in Cider Hill, Melanie almost refusing to allow the little girl out of her sight. In the years that followed, there were many confrontations when Liz wanted to live a little, like spending a night at a friend's house or attending school camp. She eventually left home to attend the University of Melbourne. I met her once at one of my book signings. I didn't recognize her but she told me who she was just the same, looking relaxed and happy. She told me she was studying nursing and keen to travel the world. I imagined she was happy just to travel to the local shops without being watched. We chatted for a few minutes and then I signed the book she was holding, Nightmares Unhinged. I never saw her again but hoped that she enjoyed her newfound freedom.

6.

By the time Steph and I turned the Beetle into 29 Crescent Lane, dusk had turned into night, as all traces of the fiery red sunset were erased with the dark sapphire glow of night. The house stood large on its wooden stilts, towering above the surrounding landscape. The driveway was flanked by petite lights that were suspended from little poles, leading the driver towards a large circular driveway that had another palm in the middle of a round garden bed. The Chief's own FX was parked in a car space that sat underneath the home and a patrol car was parked off to one side of the driveway. There was a large balcony above it and I could see table and chairs sitting on one side of it as well as a telescope in one of the large windows that looked out over the land. There were lights switched on in what looked like the living room, its timber ceiling beams visible from where we now sat.

I parked the Beetle behind the FX, climbed out and made my way around to Steph's side. She climbed out and I closed the door for her. We stood looking at each other, both taking deep breaths.

"Ready for this?" I asked. She took another deep breath, exhaled, then nodded.

"Let's do this."

7.

When no-one opened the door after the third knock, I looked at Steph with a surprised expression.

"Do you think he forgot?" I said, getting ready to knock again. She put her ear to the door, listening for approaching footsteps. The house was made from timber and sat on stilts and I knew that any movement inside the building would be heard from here. The house sat deathly quiet, the only sound a distant dog barking at some night-time critter. When we heard no sounds, she pulled away and looked at me.

"Are they home?" she asked.

"The cars are here," I answered, pointing below us, "and I'm pretty certain that Melanie doesn't drive."

"A walk maybe?"

"Now? With guests coming? No way." I thumped on the door again, harder this time, the echoes reverberating through the house. "CHIEF? MEL? ANYBODY HOME?" But after a few seconds of no reply started feeling that sinking feeling. Either he *had* forgotten, or something was wrong. I tried the door knob and wasn't surprised when it turned, the door opening a little. It was, after all, 1954 and people hardly ever locked their doors, especially country folk. I peered in, sticking my head through the crack, still holding it closed somewhat. "Chief? Mel?" No sounds, just that same, eerie silence.

I could smell cooking though, some sort of meat, its aroma strong and pleasant. Steph held the back of my shirt as I opened the door fully and stepped inside. The only sound I could hear was my own breathing as we tiptoed towards the light that was coming from the living room. As we peered around the corner, it looked too big to be just a living room, a massive open space comprising the lounge-room with a huge dining table in one corner, a billiard table in the other corner and one entire wall of glass. The floor to ceiling windows looked out over the driveway and the land beyond, now unseen except for the night-lights that dotted the area.

"Chief Rademeyer?" Steph said. I listened again, hoping for a reply but deep down knew none would come. We walked slowly back out into the hallway and headed toward the only other light that was on. It was a room further down the hallway, its door almost shut except for a small wedge, where the light emanating through was settling on the opposite wall. I held the doorhandle for a moment and looked at Steph hesitatingly, seeing something in her eyes. I knew that look because it was telling me that she knew what I knew. It was the smell. She could smell it, too. That overwhelming coppery smell that most police officers were only too familiar with. It was the unmistakable smell of blood. Lots of blood.

8.

As I slowly swung the door open, the horror that the room contained exploded before us in all its evil. Melanie was hanging to the right of us, suspended from the rafter in front of her dressing table facing the bed, her arms tied above her head. She was completely naked and her throat had been torn out, the spray of blood hitting the facing wall. Her eyes weren't gone completely, the gelatinous weeping from both sockets turning her cheeks into shiny mirrors. It looked like someone had pierced them, popping them with something sharp. Her mid-section had also been torn open and her insides hung askew in a twisted tangle of intestines and organs, the blood, vomit and faecal matter pooled together in a pile beneath her. The bedroom had floorboards so most of the body fluids had nowhere to go, instead congealing where it fell. There were bite wounds on her breasts, arms and shoulders, blood leaving long trails as it coursed down her body. My stomach heaved and for a brief moment, I thought my lunch was about to reappear before me. I swallowed hard and tried to limit my nasal breathing, trying to shut that part of me off and instead breathe through my open mouth. A thick aroma of blood and shit hung heavy in the air and as I sucked in deep breaths, I was horrified to think that I had the faintest taste of the stench in my mouth.

Sitting opposite to his beloved Melanie and tied to the headboard of their bed, was Frank Rademeyer. He was also naked, his throat slashed wide open, the windpipe jutting out at a precarious angle. The blood had been extensive, pooling beneath him, then seeping into the mattress. His penis and scrotum had been sliced off and the coroner would find them during the autopsy, lodged in his wife's windpipe, forced to swallow them as she was fighting blindly for breath. His eyelids had been cut off, preventing him from shutting out the horrific scene playing out before him; forced to watch the horrific torture of his wife as his own demise now faced him.

I heard Steph hyperventilating beside me and pulled her from the room. She was a strong girl but not even her strength saved her from the horror she saw, a low scream escaping her before she doubled over and vomited into the hallway. I left her and ran back into the living room, finding the phone on a coffee table beside the couch. I called the police station, Pete answering after half a dozen rings. He didn't understand me at first, repeating my words several times, then when I enunciated the chief's name, he finally understood.

I went back to Steph and found her sitting in the hallway crying, shaking like a leaf. I knelt down and put my arm around her, trying to get her to her feet. When she didn't, I bent down and picked her up then carried her back outside, sitting her carefully on the steps. She felt cold and I wish I had my jacket to give her. I remembered that I always kept one in the back seat of my car and went to retrieve it. By the time I returned, the lights and sirens were turning into the driveway.

9.

We had missed the killer or killers by sheer minutes, the coroner putting time of death for both parties at between 6 and 6.30. Several patrol cars turned into the driveway, as well as the local ambulance and one from Daylesford a short while later. Chief Edward Richards from Daylesford Police arrived just before 8 and took over command, directing half a dozen officers to immediately door knock the surrounding homes and the rest to walk the surrounding countryside by torchlight, looking for anything. The ambulance officers gave Steph the once over and advised her to go home and rest, noting that the shock she was suffering would subside in a few hours.

One of the officers offered to drive her home, but she refused, as I knew she would. She wanted to catch this arsehole as badly as I did and there was no way she would sit this one out. Once she had herself under control again, we both went to see Richards. He was trying to coordinate some road blocks around town to try and catch anyone attempting to flee the area by car. A number of officers from Ballarat arrived and were given the assignment.

"You two have any ideas who could've done this?" he asked, but we shook our heads. I couldn't think of anyone that would want to hurt this family. "No one?"

"There's no one that stands out, Chief," Steph said.

"It's going to be a long night so try and get yourselves sorted. Put your heads together and come up with names. Any names. The Commissioner is already on his way and he's going to want some answers." He didn't wait for our reply, turning toward another group of officers that had arrived. Steph grabbed my arm and pulled me away, leading me back to my car. It was boxed in and I could see it was going nowhere fast.

"Wait here a sec," she said and went off somewhere, back toward the group of officers. She returned a few minutes later, shaking a car key in front of her. I followed her to one of the patrol cars and she climbed in. As we drove back out onto the road, she lit a cigarette, then wound down the window.

"Who the hell did that, Jim?" she asked. I didn't know. But there was something that struck me as odd about the whole thing.

"Don't you think it's a strange time to go and commit such a planned execution?" I said. She looked at me.

"What do you mean?"

"If you were going to kill a man and his wife in such a horrendous manner, would you do it in the early evening or wait until later in the night? You know, when there were less people around, less chance of getting caught."

"Not if it was a spur of the moment killing."

"Steph, you think that was a spur of the moment?"

"No." She puffed on her cigarette.

"That was planned. Whoever did that, knew that they would be home, knew that they would be alone. And whoever did that to them had a major fucken issue with them." I looked at the passing houses, their lights burning behind closed curtains; lives shielded from the outside world by thin sheets of cotton.

"Do you think they knew?" I suddenly said.

"Knew?"

"Knew we were coming."

"Why do you think that?" she said, crushing her cigarette in the ashtray.

"Don't you think it's a little too brazen for it to be some random killing? I mean, whoever did that wanted to do what they did, yet managed to finish just in the nick of time, right before another police officer knocked on the door." I was running it through my own head more than telling Steph. It was like I was following my own trail in my mind.

"How would they know? Think the Chief told someone we were dropping by for dinner? Wouldn't have thought it was that important." But I had another thought entirely.

"Can you swing past the cop shop?"

"Sure. You got an idea?" She sounded hopeful but I didn't want to raise her hopes too much.

"More of a hunch. Curiosity. I just want to check something out."

10.

Steph pulled the patrol car into the station car park and I climbed out. She jumped out and began to run toward the front door. I didn't follow her, instead walking around the side of the building, looking for something.

"Jim?" She called out, but I rounded the corner. "Where are you going?" I heard her call out. As I rounded the next corner, she came up behind me.

"This is what I'm looking for," I said, pointing at the gum tree that grew behind the station. It was quite tall, one branch growing out over the roof of the building. I shone a torch up into its branches, then at the building. I turned to look behind us and saw a vacant block, itself flanked by one abandoned building and another vacant block. Behind those was a paddock which I knew had several cows living in it.

I shone the torch up at the branches again then handed the torch to Steph.

"Here," I said, holding it out to her," hold it for me?" She grabbed it and watched as I grabbed the lowest branch and swung myself up.

"You looking for possums?" she asked.

"I don't think it was a possum at all. I think someone was listening." Realization dawned on her face as I continued to climb. When I pulled myself onto the roof, I motioned for her to throw the torch up to me. She did and I caught it easily, shining it from one side of the roof to the other. There was nothing out of the ordinary, just a standard tin roof. I was about to climb to the other side when I saw what I was hoping for.

It would be almost impossible to be aware of it during the day, given the similar colour of the two. But light from the torch focusing on specific points of the roof made the roofing nail stick out like the proverbial. About a quarter of the way up one roofing incline, the four roofing nails that held that particular sheet down, were missing. I could see slight indents in the waves of the tin about half way up the sheets as if they had been slightly bent. Lying on the roof, beneath that sheet, lay a single nail. I walked gingerly toward the holes, carefully following the nail line with my feet to save myself a nasty fall.

"What did you find?" Steph called out from below.

"One sec," I called back and bent down to feel the tin. I grabbed the edge and wasn't surprised when it lifted easily. I peered beneath it and saw the roof space, dark with cobwebs. I shone the light around, looking at the floor and shuddered, dread hitting me like a brick.

"Steph?" I called, "can you climb up-" but she was already stepping on to the roof behind me. I waved her over then shone the light at something on the floor. She knelt down beside me, then reached forward, picking up a tiny piece of foil. She looked at me, held it up, its unmistakable w-shape highlighted by the torches' beam. She slowly began to uncurl it, carefully trying not to tear it. When she finished and the shiny piece of wrapping was flat and open, she held it up. It was a juicy fruit wrapper. When I smelt it, the distinct aroma filled my nostrils.

"This possum catcher," I began but Steph was shaking her head.

"Bushy Bill is the pest man around here, Jim, and Bushy Bill has no teeth." I shone the torch around some more, looking deeper into the cavity. We could see drag marks in the dust, like someone dragging themselves through the space. I climbed into the roof, asked Steph to wait and she sat, holding the tin up far enough to watch me. There wasn't a lot of space in there so lying on your belly was the only possible way to move around. I also noted it was the quietest. I shone the torch before me and followed the drag marks. They stopped directly ahead of me and I noted some vents in the ceiling, scattered around the space, light seeping through some of them. When I reached the spot where the drag marks ceased, I saw a vent directly beneath me. I didn't need to look through to know which room sat below me. As I peered through the grating, the Chief's desk now clearly visible, I slammed my fist into one of the timber beams, the pain shooting up my arm.

"Jim, you OK?" Steph yelled to me but I was already crawling back. She held my arm as I maneuvered myself back out onto the roof and told her what I had seen. "I'll call it in. Get the guys to keep an eye out for Clancy. We'll find him."

"Wait, Steph, this isn't Clancy." I said to her.

"But the wrapper," she began.

"Even if the wrapper was Clancy's, and if we find out that the person that crawled up into that roof to eavesdrop on the Chief was him, someone put him up to it, Steph. Someone is leading him, getting him to do these things. And I'm not sure that Clancy would be capable of inflicting that damage to those people. They aren't small animals." She began to nod again, understanding my point. If we were going to get to the bottom of all this, we needed to find out who was guiding him. "OK, let's put the call out for him, see if anybody can pick him up. Worst case is we get to question him. I'd prefer to catch him ourselves. Be a lot easier to question him in private without someone looking over our shoulder."

"I'll make the call," she said and began to climb back down the tree. A few minutes later, I followed.

11.

After she had contacted Chief Richards, we climbed back into the patrol car. We wanted to go by Clancy's house and see if he had returned. It was a long shot but Clancy was feeble minded and he may just be stupid enough to return home. I asked her to swing by the hotel first. I wanted to pick up a jacket and also to see Tami quickly, to fill her in and also ease her mind in case she had already heard. I wasn't sure if she had returned to work and gossip in a small town, regardless of how delicate it was, had a way of making the rounds quickly. Sometimes, too quickly.

She dropped me out the front and told me we would meet back in 15 minutes. She wanted to duck home and check on Mrs. Wong and Judith. I jumped out of the car and watched her drive down the street, then raced up the stairs, three at a time. I retrieved my jacket from the room, used the bathroom, then headed back down. The bistro was empty and the main bar only had half a dozen or so patrons, quietly sitting around with beers before them. It was just another quiet Sunday night in Cider Hill.

I went back outside and waited for Steph by the lamp post. I was leaning against it, running the previous hours' events through my mind when I heard a noise off to my right. I looked and barely made out a shadow standing across the street from the far side of the pub. Because I was standing under the light and the shadow was standing in darkness, it was impossible to see who it was. I took a few steps out of the light but the shadow began to walk down the alley, its head never turning, as if watching me. As I stopped, it stopped. I took another couple of steps and the shadow took a couple as well. I started getting a bad feeling in the pit of my stomach, panic setting in. The lane that he was standing on was where Tami lived. If he was watching me, then maybe he was planning something.

Without thinking, I sprinted to the corner, rounding it just in time to see the shadow jump one of the fences that fronted the line of flats. There was at least a dozen or so and, in the dark, found it difficult to know exactly which one he had jumped over by the time I had reached the spot. I was only a couple of doors away from Tami's and could see her kitchen light on. I couldn't see into the window as the curtain was drawn but I knew she would be home. Keeping an eye behind me and walking slowly, I opened her gate then walked to the door, knocking on it gently while listening for any noise.

The door opened and she flung herself out at me. I almost raised a fist as she leapt from the doorway, throwing her arms around my neck as she always did. When she finally pulled away a little, I saw her trademark Cheshire grin, her eyes beaming with happiness.

"I'm so glad you're back," she said, taking my hand and pulling me inside. Those words were the last words I ever heard my beautiful Tami say. It was also the last time that I saw her alive, her beautiful smile extinguished from this world forever.

"Tami," was all I had time to say as I heard the click of the gate behind me. "Too late," was the only thought I had as I saw Tami turn her head back towards me, our eyes meeting for the final time, then looking past me, her face contorting in terror. The scream that followed sounded a thousand miles away as something hard exploded to the side of my head and I fell, not only to the ground, but also into darkness.

Chapter 10: Remembering

1.

The events that immediately preceded and then followed that terrible night are still mostly flashbacks as well as information given to me by the people that were there. I need you to understand that I am writing this book many years in the future and have the passage of time to help me. But at the time, things were much more difficult. For one, Tami's final moments didn't come to me again until a good week afterwards. The head-wound I suffered put me into a coma for three days and I woke up at Daylesford Hospital on the Wednesday night. Whoever decided to thump me, also very nearly broke my left leg as well as actually breaking 2 ribs on my left side. It was believed to have been a metal pipe that took me out and the doctors told me that I was extremely lucky. Any harder and I would have been eating my food through a straw, or worse, not at all.

When I finally regained consciousness, Steph had been sleeping in a chair beside my bed. The table next to me was covered in flowers and get-well cards. A jug of water was also there and that was what I needed first. The dryness in my throat was painful, the scratching unbearable. I reached for it with my right hand, almost managed to grab it, then pushed it off the table, the explosion of glass sending shards in all directions. Steph leapt from the chair, a pistol in her hand ready to fire. I flinched a little and a bolt of pain went shooting down my left side from my shoulder all the way to my toes.

When she realised it was me, she holstered her pistol and bent over me.

"Jim, oh my God, you're awake." She hugged me as the door suddenly opened and another officer as well as a nurse came rushing into the room. When they saw that I had awakened, the officer left while the nurse went to fetch a broom. She returned a minute later, carrying a fresh jug of water. Steph stepped back a little as a doctor came in and began doing some tests on me, torch in the eyes, listening to my chest, stuff like that. He asked me my name, James Lawson, whether I knew what day it was, Monday, and who the lady standing in front of me was, Stephanie Connor. When he was satisfied that I was OK, he waved Steph forward and after informing me that it was actually Wednesday, left the room.

"Jim," she repeated. I looked at her, my heart in my mouth.

"Where's Tami?" was all I could ask, the only question that was burning into me. She looked away, hesitated. "Steph, where is Tami?" I repeated.

"Jim, we can talk about that later. For now-"

"NO," I cried out, "NOW. WHERE IS SHE?" She still didn't answer me and I began to sit up, trying to get myself out of bed. Steph lunged forward and pushed me back down, trying to keep me down. I did as she wanted, then took hold of her hand until she looked into my eyes. "Steph, please. I need to know." My voice sounded so quiet; I wasn't sure whether she heard me. But when she began to nod and sit on the edge of my bed, never letting my hand go, I knew to expect the worse.

"She's," she began, then paused and looked away as a tear spilled down her cheek. "She's dead, Jim. I'm so sorry." The words punched a hole through my heart, my own tears then coming in streams. I don't remember screaming, but she later told me that I did.

2.

They didn't find Tami for two whole days. After the killer had taken care of me, he had hidden her. By the time Steph found me, she was gone. She had known to look for me at Tami's because she knew I was going to pop in to make sure she was OK. When I didn't show up out the front of the pub, she had driven down the lane and found me crumpled up at Tami's front door, bleeding profusely from a wound to the back of my head. An ambulance had taken me straight here, to Daylesford Hospital, while Steph remained in town, partnering up with Alec Rawlins, another young constable from Daylesford.

They had gone to Clancy's house but only found his brother and mother at the house. He still hadn't been found by the time I woke up. They spent almost 36 hours straight following up any lead that the police were able to get hold of. One person thought that a car, a Mini, had been seen driving erratically from town, out towards the old mill, but the mini was never found, the mill standing abandoned. Up to 40 officers and hundreds of volunteers had begun searching the surrounding farmland; searching every dam, lake and puddle. Every shed, building, home, stable and outhouse was examined. There were even volunteers making the trip from Melbourne to help with the searching, all the radio stations covering the events of that Sunday. Steph showed me the newspapers, local, national and even one international, all including Cider Hill in their dailies. The Herald Sun had a four-page spread, including the front. It had a picture of Tami taking up almost the entire page, except for a small picture of the Chief and Melanie. Their story was on Page 3.

Tami had been found in the unlikeliest place imaginable. They say that the chances she was still alive by the time Steph found me, were almost 100%. They believe she was still alive an hour later as officers walked through her home, looking for any sort of clue to her whereabouts, the killer keeping her silent either by rendering her unconscious or subduing her into submission.

It was only because of the passage of time that they found her. Time had allowed for certain events to take their course and combine to reveal her location. A heavy thunderstorm had hit Cider Hill on Tuesday, hard enough to cause flash flooding in some parts, damaging roofs and uprooting trees. Her roof had sprung a leak, one of the tiles damaged. When the rain water had leaked into the roof cavity, the congealed blood that had pooled beneath her body became watery again, slowly weeping through the ceiling plasterboard. A large red patch of moist sludge had formed in the middle of her living room ceiling. When Lester and another officer had returned to the home on the Tuesday afternoon to search for any missed clues, they made the grim discovery, finding my Tami tied to her own rafters in the ceiling space. She had been there the entire time.

3.

It took a lot of pleading for Steph to finally show me the photos of Tami. At first, she refused to even listen to me, saying that they were police evidence and she was unable to get them. The she said that she didn't want to show them to me, that they weren't for me to see. One look into my eyes and she knew that that line was not going to work. I practically was police as much as she was. Then she told me that it wasn't a good idea with my injuries, needing rest and relaxation to heal quickly. But with each plea, I could see her walls slowly crumbling. I eventually told her that if I didn't get them from her, then I would get them from someone else, like Lester. She knew that I was right and so, with dread in her eyes, she handed them to me the following morning.

"You can have these, Jim, but I won't stay while you look through them. I don't think it will make things any easier for you, but if you insist, then I won't stop you." She let the envelope go, then without another word, turned and left the room, closing the door behind her. I held the envelope for close to ten minutes, tears building, then slowly tracing their path down my cheeks. My heart was truly aching, my belly on fire with rage. My leg was throbbing and my chest felt like a spear was lodged in it, a piercing bolt of pain cascading through my body with every hitching breath. I tried to prepare myself as best I could, trying to picture the horror I was about to see.

Nothing can ever prepare you for the moment you see the love of your life dead and lying on some slab, the inflictions of a madman visible in the slashes and cuts and bites that would adorn her body. Her Cheshire grin now gone forever, her beautiful eyes closed, the happiness in them extinguished for all eternity. I took another painful breath then slowly opened the envelope.

There were six photos in all. I don't know how many I was expecting but as I held them in my hand, they felt meagre compared to the life-changing event they were about to show me. The first photo was of her face and I felt a wave of relief as I saw that it was untouched, her beautiful eyes closed as if in an eternal sleep. The second was of her legs, again, untouched and unmarked. The third photo showed her back and buttocks while the fourth was of her wrists, deep ligature marks showing how the rope that held her had bitten into her soft skin, leaving identical wounds on each wrist. The fifth photo was of her upper torso and showed her naked breasts and stomach as well as her upper arms. The scar she had suffered twenty years earlier was visible on her upper left arm, just below her shoulder, a deep hole that had healed itself over time but never able to replace the missing muscle tissue. There were no visible marks of any kind.

I was beginning to think that maybe he had simply strangled her, her body seemingly untouched and devoid of major trauma. But then I looked at the last photo, and my tears began to flow, the levee broken. It was a photo of her neck. It had one single bite mark on its left side, deep enough to open the carotid artery that pulsated with each beat of her heart. He had taken a single bite, then watched her bleed out, if he had indeed waited to confirm her death. My guess was that he probably did wait, long enough to ensure that she was gone. But something struck me as odd.

I suddenly wanted to speak to Steph, the urge almost overwhelming. I called out but no one came. I yelled louder, then waited. After a minute of nothing, I screamed at the top of my lungs. The door crashed open a few seconds later and a nurse and a policeman burst through the door. I sat up, looking at the cop and asked him to get Steph. He looked at the nurse and when she nodded to him, he left the room.

4.

We waited for the nurse to finish her checks and leave the room before speaking. Once the door was closed, I pulled out the photos and held them in front of Steph.

"This makes no sense," I said, shaking them up and down.

"Jim, I know how you feel."

"DAM IT, STEPH!" I yelled, my emotion temporarily overwhelming me. She flinched away and I pulled back a little, embarrassed. "I'm sorry. I don't mean to yell. Steph, this doesn't fit."

"I'm listening," she replied as she lit a cigarette.

"You've seen Clancy, spoken to him. Do you think that he has the strength required to lift Tami and drag her up into the roof of her home?" Steph looked at me with an expression of intrigue. "And the wound. Tami, you saw the chief, you saw Melanie. That was a different person, I'm sure of it. It's almost like we're chasing two different people. The controlled one like Tami and Rita Carlisle and the out-of-control one. Whoever killed Tami had the presence of mind to control their emotion. The chief and Melanie, and that girl," I clicked my fingers in the air, trying to remember her name," Rita Hayman, they were all pure rage." At that moment, there wasn't the slightest doubt in my mind that whoever was killing these people, had an accomplice. An accomplice also capable of taking a bite out of someone.

"We have to find Clancy, he's the key to everything now. Without him, we have nothing."

"A lot of officers are out looking for him," she said, stubbing her cigarette out, "and there's also the Levinson thing."

"The Levinson thing?" I asked. She frowned a little.

"I went to see him again. He's got a house in Daylesford and Alec and I went to talk to him. You know, to ask him about Lightman again, to see if he knew anyone else that could be involved."

"What did he say?" I asked, trying to prop myself up, but the bolt of pain that shot through my chest convinced me not to.

"Never got to talk to him. Guess who was standing on his porch talking to him when we arrived?" I didn't have a clue.

"Richards."

"The new chief?" I asked, surprised.

"Just the temporary one, but yeah, the chief. And they weren't having a friendly conversation either. He was right up in Levinson's face, finger pointing and stuff."

"Did you hear what they were talking about?" I asked but Steph shook her head.

"They stopped the second we pulled up. Didn't see them at first, a big bush near the front gate shielding them. But when we came up the path, there they were. Richards stepped toward us and asked us what we wanted. When I said we wanted to speak with the good doc, he shook his head. Told us that he was questioning him personally and we were to return to Cider Hill and help locate Clancy Higgins."

"Why would he-" but Steph stopped me with a hand held out, motioning for me to wait.

"Wait, there's more."

"More?"

"Aha. Alec is stationed in Daylesford and remembers pulling over a car a couple of months ago, out on the Daylesford- Ballarat Road. He was sitting on the side of the road watching for traffic when this car sped past, driving erratically. It was a black Mercedes."

"The doctor's?"

"Yeah, but that's not the interesting part."

"Steph?"

"The doc had a passenger." I looked at her, unsure of why she wasn't just telling me.

"Who was it?"

162

"Jim, it was Tami. And Jim, she wasn't just a passenger. He said she was sitting pretty close to him. VERY close to him."

"What? Are you positive? How can he be sure?"

"It was her smiling eyes. And the fact he had seen her a few times before. In the company of other men around town." My anger suddenly boiled to the surface, my face feeling flushed and hot.

"No, that's not true. It's a lie," I cried out.

"Jim, you have to know. He was driving erratically because," but she stopped herself.

"WHY? WHY WAS HE DRIVING ERRATICALLY?" I yelled, my heart beat feeling like it was hammering at my temples again.

"He was trying to do his pants up as Alec approached the vehicle. Tami was blushing while the doctor sat grinning at him." Suddenly, without knowing I was going to, I picked up the glass of water sitting beside me and threw it at the opposite wall. It exploded on impact, the water hitting the wall and ceiling in a spray of liquid as glass shards clinked around the room. I felt confused, unsure of my memories, trying to remember back to when I had seen her, the tears sitting hot in my eyes, almost stinging them as I wiped them away. How could she not tell me? How could she betray me? But she hadn't. I tried to slow my breathing, taking great gulps, holding them deep. Our chance meeting was still weeks in the future and then, what reason would she have to discuss her past with me. I wasn't anyone to her then, and he was no one to me when I first saw Levinson, the connections between the three of us still not complete. There was no reason for her to tell me.

The door burst open for a second time, the nurse and officer coming in again. The nurse came at me and immediately began scolding me for my outburst, performing a number of checks on me. I didn't respond, sinking lower into my bed and closing my eyes. All I wanted to do was be alone and cry. As if reading my thoughts, Steph bent and kissed me on the forehead, wished me a good night and walked out.

5.

It took another two excruciating days for the doctors to allow me to leave the hospital, the Friday dragging slower than any day I had ever endured. Steph didn't return the next day and I began to wonder whether I didn't push her completely away with my outburst. But she was simply tied up with work and her own responsibilities. She came back in on the Saturday morning, dressed in casual attire, Judith's hand held in her own. Jude was holding a bunch of flowers and handed them to me when they walked in. I thanked her and watched her run from the room, excitedly looking for a nurse to find a vase for them.

"How are you feeling?" Steph asked when we were alone.

"Much better, thanks. I'm sorry for my outburst, Steph. I shouldn't have." But she shook her head.

"There's nothing to apologize for. I can't imagine what you went through. Any news when you can get out of here?" she asked.

"Saw the nurse this morning and she thinks the Doc may let me out today. Just have to wait for him to finish his rounds." Jude came back in, carrying a large glass vase.

"The nurse asked if you can please refrain from breaking this one," she said as she handed it to her mum. I laughed out loud, Steph giggling as she filled it with water from the sink.

6.

The Doctor came shortly after Steph and Judith had left, telling me that he needed to consult with another doctor early in the afternoon. He returned a little after 3, telling me I was free to go. I called for a nurse and asked her to contact Steph. She was about to leave the room, when Steph stepped into the room, pushing a wheel chair before her.

"Who's that for?" I said, pointing at it.

"Hospital policy, Mr. Lawson," the nurse said, and judging by her tone and steely eyes, I wasn't going to win the argument.

Ten minutes later, I climbed out of the wheelchair and into the FX which was parked at the hospital entrance. She pushed the wheelchair back in through the doors then returned and climbed into the driver's seat. We began driving, heading back towards Cider Hill.

Steph?" I asked as she drove. She looked across at me. "Could you take me to Tami's?" I asked. She frowned a little, but nodded. I watched the scenery flow past the window as we drove along the road. I felt alone. Although we hadn't been together for so many years, just knowing that she was in Cider Hill, knowing that she was there doing whatever she was doing, gave me some sort of comfort. I know we didn't have the closest of relationships, but Tami and I had shared something unique and even though it was a nightmare, it had given us a bond that time nor distance could ever take away. Now that she was gone, I felt truly alone for the first time in twenty years.

7.

After dropping Jude to Mrs. Wong, Steph drove us back to the lane beside the Railway Hotel. I admit, I had butterflies as we pulled up in front of the flat. Tami's home looked exactly the same. There was no sign of the horror that took place inside just a few days before. The only thing that was different was a small padlock that secured her front gate. I climbed out of the car as Steph parked by the kerb, gingerly trying to keep the pain in my chest to a minimum. Steph had the key to the padlock as she was the lead officer in the investigation and unlocked it for me so I wouldn't need to jump the fence, a feat I knew to be near impossible with my injuries.

We walked to the door and she unlocked it, swinging it open. I was standing on the spot where I saw her for the final time. I looked at my feet and saw tiny spots of blood which the rain had failed to wash away, like eternal stains. I could feel the apprehension in my gut. Steph led the way inside and I could smell the dampness in the air. I looked around and took in her home. Steph headed for the hallway, probably checking out a back bedroom. I decided to have a look in the living room, the last place we sat and talked. I lowered myself on to the couch, sitting quietly and closing my eyes, trying desperately to feel her. I didn't. I opened my eyes and scanned the room for anything that might give me a clue as to who had hurt her. The ceiling plaster had been removed, the exposed beams now staring at me in an almost menacing grin. My eyes fell on her bookshelf and I saw my book again, sitting amongst others up on the top shelf. I stood carefully and shuffled over, standing before the shelf for a moment, looking at the familiar black cover with my name on it. I reached for it, meaning to pull it out and flick through the pages, pages that she had no doubt read.

But just as my fingers brushed the spine of my book, the book sitting to its left suddenly highlighted itself to me, its words hitting me like the metal pipe did a few nights before. It was a book similar in thickness to mine, with a rich red spine. The name of the book was "Splitting Hairs" and the name of the author was Dr. Julius Levinson.

"Steph," I called as I reached for it, pulling it out from between the others.

"Yeah?" she called back.

"Check this out." I sensed her shuffling about then heard her footsteps coming down the hallway.

"What did you find?" she asked as she came into the room. I held the book out to her, her eyes growing wider as she read the name of the author. She opened the front cover and saw what I hadn't yet seen. There was a hand-written note inside the front sleeve. I watched as she read it, her eyes moving slightly from side to side. She held the book out to me when she finished, her eyes lit up.

To my darling Tami,

For being there when I needed you most.

Julius

I was stunned, feeling the urge to sit as my legs felt like they were about to fail me. I turned, book in hand, taking one step toward the couch, then dropping into it. I looked up at Steph, about to ask her for a glass of water, when I noted that she was staring open-mouthed at the blank wall behind me.

"Steph?"

"Something Alec told me when he was telling me about pulling him over with her in the car. He said that Levinson had gotten out of the car and asked her to remain. He had ushered Alec to the back of the vehicle to tell him something."

"What did he tell him?"

"That these kinds of indiscretions were best kept quiet, if he understood. Then he had held his ring finger up and flicked the wedding band there, indicating to Alec that he was married. He's married, Jim."

"So, was he her sugar daddy or something?"

"I doubt that. He doesn't strike me as someone that has the time for a marriage and a girlfriend. Sorry."

"Do you know if she had any friends, Steph?" but she shook her head.

"Could always ask around at the hotel. Maybe there's someone there she was close to." But I was already getting to my feet, knowing who to talk to. I indicated to Steph to exit the home. I took a final look around the room then followed her out the door.

8.

"You want Jackie," the head chef told us, pointing out to the bistro. He was the only friendly face I knew since staying here and had arranged for the beautiful meal I surprised Tami with. "I'm sorry for your loss, Mr Lawson." I thanked him, shook his hand then headed for the bistro, Steph in tow. There were 4 ladies sitting in the far corner, congregating around a fifth who was sitting in a chair. As we approached, one saw us and threw me a smile. The others saw her and followed suit.

"I was after Jackie," I said as we neared the group. The others looked at the girl sitting in the chair then turned and left, leaving us alone. "Jackie?" I asked and she nodded. Judging by the swollen red eyes, she looked to have been crying intensely not too long ago.

"Hey," she said. I offered her my hand and she shook it.

"I'm Jim."

"I know. Tami told me about you."

"Jackie, were you and Tami close?" I asked. She nodded. She looked past me for a moment, then back at me. When she didn't answer, I continued. "Did she ever tell you about a man she was seeing?" Her face grew dark and her eyes darted back behind me for a second time as if looking for someone. I turned to look but only saw the front door. "Jackie?"

"You mean other than you?"

"Yes, other than me." Her eyes kept looking past me and I was about to ask her another question when Steph spoke from beside me.

"Jackie, would you like to go somewhere more private?" She was on her feet in an instant and waved at us to follow. She turned down a hallway then into a room at the far end. It was a vacant guest's room, a curtain hiding its lone window. Once we were all inside, she closed the door, then locked it with the chain. I looked at Steph and she shot me a wink. We were about to find out something we weren't expecting and she knew it. Or, she already knew and wanted me to find out for myself. In any case, Jackie was about to let loose. Jackie went to the bed and sat down. Her lip was quivering in a familiar fashion and I wasn't surprised when she began to cry. Steph went and sat beside her then put an arm around her. Jackie sobbed into her hands then began to regain control, wiping her eyes with a hanky she pulled from her pocket.

"She loved you, Jim. I just want you to know that. She hadn't seen anyone since she saw you. No-one. She even stopped doing it."

"Doing what?" I asked. She frowned, looked at Steph then back at me.

"This town has everything one could want. Everything one could ever need. Everything except," she paused.

"Everything except what?" I asked, unsure of where she was headed. She looked at Steph again and I knew that Steph already knew what she was about to say.

"Everything except somewhere for the lonely man to go and, you know."

"And?"

"Well, Tami was, well, she had been seeing a couple of men over the past couple of years. There's a few of us that do it. She asked me about it one day and I, I took her to meet with," she paused again and for a moment I wasn't sure she was going to continue. Then she did. "With Mrs. McNorton." I choked on my own spit, began to cough, the pain in my chest exploding with each rasp. Steph looked at me alarmingly then came and began clapping me on the back. Jackie went to the sink and got me a glass of water. When I had managed to breathe again, I looked at her in stunned silence.

"Sweet Mrs. McNorton runs a brothel?" I asked in total disbelief. Jackie nodded.

"There's some pretty high up people that use her services, Jim. Tami had seen a couple of them, but then she began to see that doctor that goes up to the prison a lot. And at first things were going really well. He was treating her like a princess. Bought her some pretty expensive jewellery and stuff. But then she fell pregnant." I looked at her, completely stunned a second time.

"Pregnant?"

"She didn't tell you?"

"You mean to tell me she was pregnant when she died?" I asked, my heart feeling heavy as it sank into the pit of my stomach. Steph squeezed my shoulder then turned to Jackie.

"How many girls does Mrs. McNorton have doing this?" she asked her.

"Seven. Well, six now. She's a lovely lady, always making sure we're OK. She doesn't advertise her girls to just anybody, you know? She deals with some pretty well-off clientele, if you know what I mean."

"Like who?" Steph asked.

"Married men mostly, the ones that can afford it, anyway. Mr. Jacobs the Commonwealth Bank manager, Mr. Sutton the Supermarket owner, Chief Rademeyer-"

"Wait. The Chief?" Steph interrupted, her face showing what I was feeling. Jackie just nodded.

"Yeah, he was really nice. I spent some time with him. He was so gentle. Also Dr. Levinson, Dr. Gibbs, Chief Richards-"

"Richards?" I asked, interrupting her this time.

"Yup, he's been seeing girls for longer than anyone else."

"Where do you go?" I suddenly asked, curious.

"Go? Oh, you mean where do we take them? They come to us. At the Railway." For a moment I didn't comprehend her words, then as they suddenly sank in, began to understand.

"You mean the Railway Hotel is a brothel?"

"No, well, maybe, kind of, I guess. Mrs. McNorton says that as long as she rents more beds out for sleeping than she rents out for, you know, the other stuff then it's fine."

"Wait, what do you mean if 'she rents out more rooms'? Does she own the hotel?" Jackie was nodding again, as the surprises continued to explode before me. I had been boarding at a brothel, had been eating food prepared by a madame and been infatuated with a pregnant whore. My skin broke out into gooseflesh as I thought about Tami with Levinson, then hated myself for thinking of her as a whore.

"Jackie, how long have you been working for Mrs. McNorton?" Steph asked.

"About 4 years now."

"And Tami?" I asked.

"About 2." I was gutted, gob-smacked, in total disbelief. The ramifications of what had been happening in this town, the leads that would need to be followed up following this conversation were going to take a lot of effort. And Steph and I were going to have to walk on very fine egg shells. There was no way that we could even discuss this conversation with the new Chief, especially if he was involved with the town whorehouse.

"Jackie, did Tami say anything to you about Levinson? I mean, did she say that he was threatening her, or anyone else threatening her for that matter?" She shook her head.

"She did give me an envelope. Asked me to give it to the cops if anything should ever happen to her."

"Did you?" Steph asked.

"No. If I ever had to, I was planning to give it to Frank, but then he got himself killed and, I was scared. The new Chief isn't as nice as Franky was."

"Do you still have the envelope?" I asked.

"Yeah, it's upstairs." She stood and began walking to the door, unlocked it, then checked to make sure we were following. We did, and once we reached the room where her things were stored, followed her inside. The room had a row of lockers down one wall and a door that led to a bathroom. A bench ran the length of the opposite wall, resembling one I remembered from the gym's locker room back in high school. Jackie went to one of the lockers and opened it. After rummaging through some clothes, she pulled out a brown jacket and reached into one of its pockets, pulling from it, a small rectangular envelope. She handed it to me and I took it, putting it in my own pocket.

"Thank you, Jackie," Steph said as I shook her hand.

"We really appreciate your help. Thank you," I said and she shot me a smile.

"She loved you, you know? She wouldn't stop talking about you. Drove me crazy."

"Thanks again," I said and left the room, Steph following me. We didn't say a word until we were sitting back in her car.

9.

"Holy shit," Steph yelled when we were safely back in her car and driving away from the hotel. She switched the windscreen wipers on, the weather turning murky as the first spots of rain began to fall. I

170

wasn't sure where she was taking us but made sure the windows were rolled up tightly. We couldn't risk anyone overhearing our conversation. "Holy shit," she repeated.

"That is some serious information. Like fucken hell. What the hell! Old sweet Mrs. McNorton is a madam? What the fuck is that about?" I still couldn't believe it, my mind now a frazzle of names and places, all inter-mingling in a labyrinth of material.

"We need to go somewhere, Jim. Somewhere away from here, for a couple of hours, at least. Go through this shit. And the envelope," she said, pointing a finger at my pocket. I pulled it out and looked at it for a moment. I lifted it, holding it in front of my face. It was sealed, the front and back blank. I slid a finger along the seal and ripped it open, reached in and pulled out three sheets of paper, all folded twice over. The first was a hand-written letter. I recognized Tami's handwriting immediately and noted that it was addressed to no-one specifically.

Should anything happen to me, I want it known that I have been in the company of Doctor Julius Levinson for almost 8 months now. I'm currently pregnant with his child. I have been threatened by this man on a number of occasions, namely trying to force me to abort my baby. He has also offered me money to relocate me to Queensland, which I have refused. I have discovered that Dr. Levinson has been conducting experiments on prisoners at Crab Apple prison and have enclosed some papers that I discovered while looking through his desk for anything that I can use to guarantee the safety of my baby and me. The rest of the diary has been hidden by me in case this letter should also fall into the wrong hands. I pray this nightmare will end soon.

Tami Kennedy
12th May, 1954

I read the letter a second time, out loud so Steph could hear it. When I finished, I unfolded the other two bits of paper, at first, unsure of their purpose. One appeared to be a page torn from a magazine. It was an article about a dangerous serum that was being developed and tested on psychiatric patients in Hungary. It had been initially developed back in the mid-30s, had been adopted by the Nazi's in hundreds of experiments during the war, then gone underground after the war ended as evidence of its extreme side-effects became apparent. The page had been torn out of a German magazine called "Die Dunkle Offenbarungen" or "The Dark Revelations". According to the magazine, the serum and any experimentation linked to it, had been banned in 94 countries, including Australia, The U.S. and England. Serum MB17471 had been deemed too dangerous to continue trying to research and develop.

I read some of the magazine's writings to Steph while she drove, randomly choosing streets to drive down. I looked at the other sheet and saw it was a page that had been torn from a diary. There were notes about MT17471, named in a couple of places by name, stating that the test subject had shown some signs of mental "re-alignment" and that the test subject "may be able to control the dispersion of their consciousness thus preventing the mental blockages they currently exhibit".

"Think Lightman is his test subject?" Steph asked. I didn't know. What I did know was that this web was beginning to weave itself faster than I could comprehend. The twists and turns beginning to look like a maze of deception and murder with the roots of the whole mess growing deeper than I ever imagined. I still believed that Clancy was going to be the ultimate key to unravelling the whole farce.

"We need to find Clancy," I said to Steph and she agreed.

"I may have an idea," she said. I looked at her with anticipation in my eyes, hoping that she was serious. "You remember the talk we had with Richard Sadler? Out at the mill?" I nodded. "Remember how he told us that they found Clancy out the back with those poor animals?" My interest peaked a little, understanding where she was headed. "What if that's his, you know, his "space"? You know, the place he feels comfortable."

"Comfortable enough to torture and kill animals. Probably comfortable to hide out while this shit storm is blowing," I said. She swung the car around and we began heading towards the Jackson Street Timber mill. Steph lit a cigarette, offered me one out of politeness, and to her surprise, pulled one from the packet.

Chapter 11: Win One, Lose One

1.

We arrived at the mill just as the rain began to bucket down in an actual wall of water. We could see it sweep across the car park in the rapidly fading light, running left to right, the wall instantly turning the dirt lot into a minefield of puddles and quick-flowing ripples. Steph growled a little.

"Of course. And I didn't grab the umbrella," she said, reaching for the door handle, then hesitating.

"I got news for you, kiddo. You're gonna get wet," I said and opened the door, the rain instantly soaking me to the skin. Steph jumped out of the car and squealed a little. We had taken a few steps in the direction of the dam, when Steph suddenly growled again and ran back to the car. She opened the door and lent in, staying bent over for what seemed like an eternity in the miserable dusk. When she came running back, she was carrying a torch in each hand. She handed me one and stuck the other into her pocket.

By the time we reached the edge of the parking lot, we both resembled drowned rats. There was a sudden rumble of thunder overhead and I hoped that the lightning would pass us by. I didn't want to be walking through a nest of trees with lightning strikes in the vicinity. We walked single file, me in the lead and Steph three or four steps behind. There was still enough daylight to see where we were headed but judging at the speed of darkness falling, I was guessing that we would be walking by torchlight within the next ten minutes. The rain was still falling at a steady pace, just heavy enough for it to be uncomfortable. I had to wipe the water from my face every couple of minutes as it began dripping into my eyes.

We passed the dam with the small shed a few minutes later, the pump still sitting where it had the previous week. It was turned off now, the only noise coming from the non-stop rain falling on the roof of the shed and our feet trudging through the mud, occasionally snapping a twig that crossed our path. We continued walking past the dam, up over a small hill and a long stretch of cleared land that resembled an old walking track. The light was almost completely gone, but thanks to our eyes adjusting with it, we were still able to navigate our way along without using the torches. I preferred not to use them, in case Clancy saw them from a distance and either hid or decided to run from us, either option to our detriment.

As we came to the top of a small hill, the land before us suddenly cleared of trees and brush, the landscape barren and muddy. There was a lot of rubbish strewn about, from bits of machinery, sheets of tin and abandoned cars. I groaned at the sight of it, knowing that if Clancy was hiding out there, it was going to be near impossible to locate him. But just as I was about to tell Steph, she grabbed my shoulder and pulled me down as she lowered herself to her knees. She pointed at something in the distance and at first, I couldn't make out what she was trying to show me. Then as I allowed my eyes to relax and take in the poor lighting, I saw a very faint glow coming through the window of an old abandoned pickup truck. It was down in one of the gullies, about 200 yards directly in front of us. Its tailgate was hanging down at an angle, one side torn from its hinges. The roof looked dented and by the look of it, I was guessing that whoever was trying to stay out of the rain, was lying across the seat. I nodded at Steph to show that I saw.

"How do you want to do this?" she asked. I wasn't sure. I didn't want to risk losing him again and also wanted to avoid a confrontation. Then I had an idea. I pulled Steph toward me and lent in close, whispering to her. She listened intently, then gave me a big grin and a thumbs up, agreeing to my suggestion.

2.

It didn't take long to find what we were looking for. We found the first almost immediately, lying only a few yards from the edge of the clearing. The second took a little longer and I asked Steph to remain on watch while I searched for it. When we had both, we carefully lifted them and made our way towards the truck.

When we were about forty yards away, I motioned to Steph to wait. I dropped my cargo very carefully onto the ground, trying to remain as quiet as possible. Then, almost slithering the rest of the way on my stomach, I made my way closer to where he was hiding. Before we could proceed with our plan, we had to confirm that the person in the truck was actually Clancy and not some random drifter, taking shelter in an out-of-the-way metal hut.

When I was almost twenty yards away, I heard my confirmation from the voice that was singing.

"Ring-around the Rosie, a pocket full of posies," the unmistakable voice sang. He sang quietly, the small vent-window slightly askew. I made a mental note to remember that when it came time to execute my plan. We needed time to set the plan up and if he heard us, would jump out of the truck and escape into the bush. If that happened, particularly with the weather, he would disappear as soon as he ran behind the first bit of undergrowth. I made my way back to Steph, one step at a time, slowly edging my way through the mud. The slightest twig was going to warn him. When I got back to her, I confirmed that I had heard him and directed her to the other side of the truck.

We each carried our cargo, tree branches around 8 feet long and about 4 to 5 inches thick. They needed to be substantial enough so that they wouldn't bend or break. My plan was simple. Wedge each branch against one of the truck doors and trap the bastard inside, preventing him from opening the doors. If he wound either window down, we would have enough time to run around to the window and stop him.

The crawl back to the truck was much more difficult carrying the branch. I was almost at the door when it slipped from my fingers, threatening to fall to the ground. But I had just taken a step forward and caught the branch on my foot, holding one end about an inch off the ground. Clancy was still singing, the same song over and over again. I carefully pushed the thicker side into the mud, praying it would be deep enough not to slide if the door opened, while the thinner side of the branch I carefully wedged above the door handle. I waited for Steph to finish her side, peaking under the truck for her signal. I could see her feet moving this way and that, then saw the branch lean against the door. A few seconds later, she peered under the truck and gave me a thumbs up.

"The time had come," I thought to myself. I was about to get to my feet right next to the window and make my presence known when a massive explosion rocked the ground beneath us, night instantly turned into day. A bolt of lightning had struck a tree about 50 yards in front of the truck, the tree now sending sparks into the night sky. Clancy let out a shriek and for a moment I was sure he would bolt from the truck. But when I peered in through the window, he had covered his head with a jacket, hiding beneath it. He was still singing that damn song, louder than before. He seemed to know only the first line, sounding like a scratched record, stuck in the same loop, over and over.

"Ring-around-a-rosie, a pocket full of posies, ring-around-a-rosie, a pocket full of posies, ring-around-a-rosie, a pocket full of posies," over and over and over. It was driving me a little insane as I kneeled beside the door, cold rain running down the back of my neck.

3.

"Clancy!" I shouted, knocking on the window as he cowered beneath the jacket. He jumped in fear, lifted the jacket off his head and just stared at me with one terrified eye. I shone my torch into the cabin and Clancy did exactly as I predicted, rolling himself to the other side and trying to push the door open. But Steph had the presence of mind to shine her torch in through the window, the man in the cabin screaming with fear. Because Steph had stood back and shown the torch in from a couple of feet away, it lit the entire window up in a burst of light, her face hidden in the shadows. I didn't know whether he would be scared of a woman standing there but as he couldn't see her, he didn't know who it was that was guarding the other door.

"CLANCY! SIT THE FUCK DOWN!" I screamed through the window. I heard a loud metallic tapping coming from the other side of the truck and when I looked through to the other side, saw Steph tapping her revolver against the glass of the window, holding it in front of her torch so that only the gun was visible. It was a smart move and Clancy immediately sat still, the jacket held in his lap, his hands visibly shaking. He stared at me with one good eye so wide that I thought it may just pop out if he didn't relax a bit.

"Clancy? Do you remember me?" I asked, trying to sound calm. He didn't respond, just continuing to stare at me with his good eye. I remembered something I had picked up from the shop earlier in the day and now took out a packet of Juicy Fruit from my pocket. I held one out to him through the small vent window. He didn't move at first, just stared at it, then back at me. I shook it slightly and after a few seconds, he finally reached for it, snatching it from my fingers and pulling it back to safety. He never took his eye off me as he tore the silver foil off and popped the strip of gum into his mouth. As the taste filled his mouth, his eyes closed and a small grin dawned across his face, as if the familiar taste somehow soothed him. He chewed a few times, then remembering his audience, resumed staring at me.

"I need to ask you some questions, Clancy. Is that OK?" At first, he didn't seem to hear, just chewing and staring, staring and chewing. But then his head began to nod ever so slightly. "Do you remember the Chief, Clancy? Chief Rademeyer?" He nodded. Chew, chew, chew. "Do you know where he is now, Clancy?" He paused a little, then nodded again, his eye locked on me. Steph kept the torch on him from the other side, never letting it dip. The torches lit the interior of the truck like a search light in full blaze. "Clancy, can you tell me where the Chief is?" He nodded again, his mouth contracting and relaxing as his teeth continued working the gum. I didn't think he was going to answer but then his jaw relaxed as I saw him move the gum into the hollow of his cheek. I waited patiently, anxious for him to respond, to begin the dialogue that I so needed him to help me with; to answer all the unanswered questions that he held the answers to. After a couple of minutes, his mouth opened slightly and a low, trembling voice began to talk.

"The Chief is dead. And his wife, Mrs. Chief. She's also dead." He began chewing again, chomp, chomp, chomp.

"That's right, Clancy, Mrs. Chief is dead too. Do you know who killed the Chief and his wife? Do you know who hurt them?" His expression suddenly changed, his face turning pale and grim, his eyes turning into his lap as his lips pursed tight. "Clancy, it's OK, buddy. No one will hurt you now. We will protect you."

"YOU CAN'T PROTECT ME!" he suddenly screamed at me, bits of spittle hitting the window and slowly dripping down, leaving a sparkly trail as it sank. He looked into his lap again, tears spilling down his cheeks. "You can't protect me from the Devil," he whispered.

"The Devil? You mean Harry Lightman?" I asked, trying to sound calm again. But he shook his head.

"Not Harry, the other one." Chew, chew, chew. I looked across at Steph, her eyes wide with hope.

"Which other one? There's another Devil?" I was hoping for a name from him, something we could use, someone we could track and arrest.

"No, there's only one Devil," he said, his voice still quiet and frightened, "only one Devil and I don't want to say his name. He comes out when you say his name."

"When who comes out, Clancy? Who is the Devil?" Chew, chew, chew, his eye fixed on mine. "I need to know, Clancy. So that I can stop him hurting more people. Clancy? Can I ask you something else?" He nodded, as if happy that we were no longer talking about the Devil. "Do you remember Tami? Tami Kennedy?" His face suddenly contorted, twisting itself into a mass of agony. He put his hands to either side of his head, covered his ears and began to scream. I took a step back, the scream catching me off guard. I began banging on the window, trying to get his attention again. The scream went on and on and on as his fingers grabbed his hair in large clumps, pulling it from side to side. "CLANCY!" I screamed, banging the window again. The scream began to fade, low sobs now coming from the broken man sitting before me.

"The Devil will kill us all," he said, then as if trying to soothe himself, began to chew vigorously as he stared at his lap. I was about to ask him another question when another loud clap of thunder rolled across the sky, the flash of the lightning striking something a split second before. When the thunder had rolled away, I tried again.

"Clancy, I need to know who the Devil is. I need to know so I can stop him hurting people. Is he the one that hurt Tami?" I was hoping he wouldn't begin screaming again at the mention of her name and to my relief, he just turned his eye at me. "Clancy?" He lent forward toward the vent window and beckoned me to come closer. I went in, ready to listen. His words came out a little louder than silent, the whisper barely registering to me. But seeing his lips at the same time, gave me an advantage.

"Loui," he mouthed at me.

"Loui?" I whispered back to him and he nodded his head. "Clancy, who is Loui?" I asked.

"It's his brother," he said, sitting back in his seat.

"Who's brother?" I asked, unsure of the name. I hadn't heard the name Loui before and I didn't know anyone's brother.

"Harry's brother," he whispered.

4.

What I have known about Harry Lightman, probably the only piece of information I was 100% sure of, was that Harry Lightman was an only child. His mother had died when Harry was 6, the only child to the proud parents.

"Clancy, Harry doesn't have a brother," I said. He looked at me.

"Harry has two brothers," he said in a matter-of-factly tone. I could see Steph peering at me over the windscreen, waving a hand at me. I took a brief glance at her and she was pointing at something in the cabin of the truck. I took a look but didn't see anything of note.

"Clancy, have you met Harry's brothers?" I asked. He nodded almost immediately. "Who's his other brother?"

"The one I don't want to say, Harry and Eddie, Eddie is the nice one," he said, then resumed his chewing. I heard Steph gasp a little as she heard the name and for a moment, I didn't understand the connection. Then I remembered what she had told me about her father, the one she never knew, the way Margaret had spoken about him at the Esso. I still didn't understand what he was talking about. Harry Lightman had no brothers.

"Clancy, I don't understand. Who is Eddie?" My frustration began to boil over. I smashed my elbow against the window, screaming at him.

"FOR FUCK SAKE, START MAKING SENSE!! WHO IS EDDIE? WHO IS LOUI? TELL ME!!" I screamed at him. He shrank away, trying to sink deeper into his chair, his face terrified again. "TELL ME, CLANCY!"

"They are all Harry," he finally whispered through tears. "Harry becomes Eddie and when he gets really angry, he becomes Loui. He talks different when he is a different one. But when he becomes Loui, he just gets angry and hurts people. The doctor knows."

"Doctor? What Doctor?" I asked.

"Dr. Levinson," he said, and I suddenly had a recollection, a vague memory from long ago, as well as a memory from earlier in the day, like two things finally coming together to reveal the complete picture. The first memory that came drifting back was from the night I

179

had chased Lightman from Tami's shed, had chased him down the driveway as he ran from me. When I had managed to force him to the ground, he had said "It wasn't me, it was Loui." It made no sense at the time and none of us had paid the slightest attention to it. He had only said it that one time and I had completely forgotten about it until now. The second memory was from earlier today, when I saw Levinson's book on Tami's bookshelf. The book had been called "Splitting Hairs" and when I flicked through it, didn't really take too much notice of its content. But a couple of words did jump out to me, words that now came flooding back to me in a bright flash. "Multiple personality disorder" and "Split Personality" were written on the back of the book. The doctor was studying the disorder and was experimenting with different treatments. As those memories began dancing around my mind, another one surfaced. The page that Tami had included in her envelope, the one about the banned serum.

It all began to come together like the pieces of an intricate jigsaw, each one having its very own place on the table. Harry was the Devil, but suffered from some type of multiple personality disorder. I was trying to build the pieces in my head when Steph began screaming at me. I looked and saw her pointing into the cabin again. This time I saw what she had wanted me to see. Lying in his lap, partly hidden by the jacket, was a revolver. Clancy held it in one hand, his finger on the trigger. He had the cylinder open and was flicking it with one finger, sending the cylinder spinning on its pin. Whilst he was doing this, he had resumed singing his song, looking at the bullets as they spun, round and round and round.

"Ring-around-a-rosie, a pocket full of posies," he sang, over and over again. He was staring at the cylinder as if he was in a trance. The thunder boomed above us again, the boom rolling across the sky. The rain had eased a little but was still falling in great sheets.

"Clancy? Clancy, give me the gun. You don't need it, mate," I said but he just shook his head, singing, over and over again. Steph also began to bang on the window, but he ignored her. Either he didn't register her presence, or he didn't care.

"Clancy? Clancy, give him the gun," she yelled, but his singing never stopped. He suddenly flicked the cylinder back into place and cocked the hammer back.

"CLANCY! CLANCY, YOU DON'T HAVE TO DO THIS!" I screamed but he never looked at me, just singing that damn song.

Then he grabbed the rusty steering wheel with his free hand and raised the pistol to his head, aiming the barrel at his bad eye. In his final seconds, he turned his head to me and spoke one last time.

"You can't beat the Devil, Jim," he said. I saw his finger begin to flex, but as it did, an explosion suddenly rocked the truck, a brilliant flash blinding me as I was thrown backwards by a force so strong that I flew through the air like a ragdoll. I hit the ground hard, slid a few feet, then came to rest in a large puddle some fifty feet from the truck. My arm throbbed like a son-of-a-bitch and my chest felt like it was going to explode. I couldn't catch my breath. I looked at the truck and saw that the interior of it was ablaze, a figure sitting in the driver's seat screaming in agony as it writhed around, flames leaping from the shattered windows. It looked as if Clancy was trying to open the door, his screams so high and loud that it drowned out every other sound, including the rain. And then darkness took hold of me, dragging me beneath its surface.

5.

Harry was chasing me again; chasing me through a field of dead weeds, a full moon illuminating the landscape all around me. I was running from him but knew he was gaining. I could hear the voices getting louder and louder with each step. The voices belonged to Steph and Tami, sounding angry as they screamed profanities at me.

"You killed us, you cunt," they yelled in thick gurgling voices. I took a quick glance over my shoulder and saw Harry now just 30 yards behind me, a severed head in each hand. In one hand he had a handful of Tami's beautiful dark hair, her neck looking like it had been torn from her body. In his other hand was the severed head of Steph. Her eyes were missing, dark holes squirming with maggots staring at me.

"Why did you let me die," Tami called out, accusation in her tone. "You let him kill me, you piece of shit. You were supposed to protect me."

"I didn't. I tried to protect you," I call back, but all three begin to howl with laughter. My feet suddenly tangle up, something caught in between them and I go sprawling into the dirt. I look down to see what had tripped me up and see a long bone, bare of flesh. Then I see dozens of bones lying all around me, if not hundreds. Skulls devoid of flesh, their dark sockets staring at me. I jump to my feet and begin to run again, the laughter gaining ground.

"Isn't this your bitch?" Harry suddenly yelled at me and I steal another glance, trying not to fall again. He is holding Tami's head up, her eyes staring at me with their beautiful shine, her trademark Cheshire grin over her face. "I tasted her cunt as she died," he cried and they all laughed again, howling in glee as I tried to run faster.

"He tasted me, Jim, tasted my cunt," Tami yelled after me. I tried to run faster, my feet feeling like they were floating across the ground. I turned to look again and saw that Harry had stopped, holding both heads up high in front of him. Steph had eyes again, wide, horrified eyes.

"Jim? You can't beat the devil, Jim, Jim, Jim-"

6.

"Jim," the voice cried out as I was shaking from side to side. My eyes slowly opened and I could see a shadow bent over me. It was Steph, her voice distant and afraid. There was a sickening smell in the air and for a moment I had no idea what it was. But as I began to remember where I was, remembered the lightning strike and Clancy caught inside the truck, I recognized the unmistakable smell of cooking flesh.

I tried to sit up, a stabbing pain almost stealing my breath as it tore through my chest. Steph helped me sit up and I saw that the truck was dark again, the fire fully extinguished. The rain had stopped and I could see stars shining in the sky above us.

"How long was I out for?" I asked, but she shook her head.

"I don't know. My watch was fried," she said. I looked at my watch, the phosphorescent dial staring back at me, but I couldn't see the second hand moving and held it up to my ear instead. It was also quiet, the time displayed as 8.04. If there had been a moon, it wouldn't have helped with the time as it didn't appear as consistently as the sun, and as there wasn't one, it didn't make a difference. It was dark and that meant it was still night time. We would just have to walk to Steph's car and drive back into town.

Steph helped me to my feet, an act requiring a lot more effort with broken ribs and whatever other injuries my recent flight left me with. As I gained my balance, I glanced at the distant horizon and saw the unmistakable colour of impending dawn. The sky was beginning to turn a dark purple. I pointed at it and Steph groaned.

"How long were we out for?" she muttered. I walked towards the truck and felt no heat coming from it. I touched the bonnet and felt its cold rusty metal, any hint of the fire long gone. The charred remains of Clancy were still sitting in the seat, now reduced to just a bunch of springs. One hand was still grasping the wheel. I could smell the remains of his flesh, now just ashes, his eternal grin glaring at me. Steph came and stood beside me, saw the skull then turned away, never looking back at the remains of Clancy Higgins.

7.

The walk back to her car took us a lot longer, both of us now hobbling and me still nursing my broken ribs. We rested often, sitting on some fallen down tree or high mound of earth, talking about the information we had heard from Clancy.

"A split personality," I said in wonder as I sat on a damp log. I realised that it may well be the reason that Jeremy Winters never saw what he wanted to. Probably because he had spoken to either Eddie or Harry. It suddenly dawned on me that if Levinson had been experimenting on Lightman, and Lightman was actually killing the people of Cider Hill, he was somehow smuggling the serial killer out of the prison, as well. I was about to mention this to Steph when she beat me to the punch.

"Levinson has been getting him out of that prison to do his dirty work," she said as she puffed on a cigarette.

"You think he put Clancy up to spying on the Chief?" She nodded, inhaling a drag.

"I'd put money on it." I agreed with her, but still wondering how he was getting him out.

"Can you believe it? Harry Lightman, 3 different personalities. I wonder if that's the reason there has been two distinct differences between the killings. You know, the angry one and the controlled one."

"All I know is that Lightman is the killer and Levinson has been feeding him. We have to get back to town and tell the Chief," Steph said, stubbing her cigarette out on the log then getting back to her feet. I did the same and we resumed our walk, the sky now growing brighter as the first hints of orange began seeping around the edges of the dark purple night sky. Dawn would be less than an hour away and that meant it was close to 7 in the morning.

8.

By the time we reached the edge of the car park, the sun was beginning to break, the first rays striking the trees above our heads. I was walking towards the lonely vehicle sitting at the far end, but saw Steph making a beeline for the small office we had sat in when talking with the mill owner.

"Steph?" I called out to her.

"Gonna try the phone," she called back over her shoulder. When we reached the door and tried the knob, it surprised us both to find it swing open. We walked in and found the phone on the desk beside the door. Steph picked up the receiver, listened, then pushed the cradle buttons a couple of times. She listened a second longer then returned the receiver back to its cradle.

"It's dead," she said. She walked into the far office, tried the phone in there and found it to be as useless as the one in here. As we walked out of the office, I saw a tree that had fallen behind the building, a tangle of cables caught within its branches.

"There's our problem," I said, pointing at the tree.

We walked back to her car and got in. Steph inserted the key, turned it and groaned when the car remained silent. She tried again, then again. She was about to try it a fourth time when I noticed our problem. In our haste to go and find Clancy, neither one of us had noticed that the headlights were still burning and during the night, had completely drained the battery. Steph punched her fist against the steering wheel, screaming.

"Of all the stupid things to do," she said when she got herself back under control. We climbed back out, pondering our options. As we were standing there, I heard an approaching car driving along the main road. The car park was mostly hidden from the road by a thick line of trees but the entrance was clear. Without needing me to point it out, Steph began to run towards the entrance, already waving her arms about. The man never turned towards us, his eyes remaining firmly fixed on the road in front. I could see his hat pulled down tight over his ears, both hands on the wheel. As the noise of his engine began to dwindle, Steph launched into a new tirade. I walked towards her, then gave her a squeeze as I walked past, heading for the road. With luck, another car would pass by shortly. But that morning, luck was definitely not on our side.

9.

It was almost an hour and a half before another vehicle came slowly ambling up the road behind us. Behind the wheel of the truck sat the oldest man I had ever seen. We had to shout into his face for him to recognize our words. He looked foreign and his words were as alien to us as ours were to him, some foreign tongue neither I nor Steph understood. But he was happy for us to climb into his cabin, his final destination unknown to us. He was however, wearing a wristwatch and when we motioned the universal hand signal for the time to him, he turned his wrist toward Steph.

"8.52," she muttered. "How can there be no traffic at 9 o'clock on a Saturday morning?" Her question was answered around the following bend, as first the rear end of one car, then another and then another began to show. All up, there was a line of maybe a dozen cars. There was a large gum tree that had been brought down through the night and we could see as many cars on the other side of it, some of which were workers from the mill. Most of the cars were small European ones. They wouldn't have the power to budge the tree, but if we could somehow find a strong enough rope or cable, we had the vehicle that could do the job.

Turns out our driver knew exactly what we were thinking. He never slowed down, driving past the line of cars, then turning the truck in an arc and finally reversing it so that it was parked in front of the tree's lower branches. Another driver approached the truck and as we climbed out, began to shake hands with our driver. We found out his name was Jacob and he was an Italian immigrant. The man followed Jacob to the back of the truck and removed a large chain.

10.

What we didn't know, and what I can tell you thanks to writing this in the future, is that Richard Lovett was living up to his reputation and was about to make the "fuck-up" of his career. A monumental mistake that would cost more lives. The Chief had called him a "pit-bull" and true to his name, wasn't letting go. For the previous 5 days, Lovett had been busy on the phone, waving his flag about and spreading the word that a free man had been locked away for twenty years. And people were beginning to listen.

3 days ago, a High Court judge had received a letter from Lovett, detailing the latest developments, the lack of solid evidence in the initial case and the fact that it now appeared that the original perpetrator had returned to his killings. The judge, the Honourable William Pasco, conveyed the letter to four other judges, all of whom agreed to review the case. The five judges had spent the past two days going over every piece of information that had been presented back in 1935. They looked through all the latest evidence provided to them about the latest spate of murders, including the similarities that reappeared at most of the crime scenes. Then, last night they had come together for a late afternoon meeting that continued through until 8pm, right around the time poor Clancy was riding the lightning bolt. A motion was passed that would see the release of one "Harry Lightman" at the prison's earliest convenience.

He was going to be freed. The time had been set at 10am, Saturday 12th June. Lovett had ensured that there would be as much publicity as possible, calling every newspaper and radio station he could. He worked for a prestigious law firm in Melbourne and one thing prestigious law firms enjoyed was free publicity, especially when it's favourable to them.

11.

The guards later told me that Harry sat in his cell patiently waiting for one of them to come and escort him to the front of the prison. His belongings, half a dozen books as well as his toothbrush, sat in a box on the floor next to the door. He kept looking at the box, almost meditative and when the guard watching him asked how he felt, he mumbled something about thinking just how little a person truly needed to live in this world. Not survive as such, but rather just to live. He said he didn't need the clothes he had accumulated as they were mostly prison uniforms. His artwork he had given to one of the other prisoners, together with his paints and brushes. He certainly wasn't going to need them anymore. Once out in the real world, he'd be able to attain some proper supplies for his art. Proper brushes, paints that had actual brand names and canvases that were purer than white. Ralph said he also asked him how his monetary situation was and Harry gave him a big grin, saying his finances were especially plump, thanks to "a rich uncle". And as the minutes ticked by, Harry just sat on his bed, hands in his lap and eyes staring at the floor, that grin never leaving his face.

12.

Jacob was attaching the chain to his truck while Charlie was trying to push the other end under the branches of the tree. The men on the other side of it pulled the chain through then swung it back across the top. Charlie pulled the chain tight and tightened it around the trunk, pulling smaller branches this way and that to make sure it sat snug. When it looked like it was ready to go, Jacob hobbled back to the driver's side and climbed in.

I hadn't noticed her leave but Steph had spotted a car on the other side of the tree. The driver was June Trapnell, the fifth-grade teacher from Cider Hill Primary and Steph grabbed the opportunity. She climbed a fence on the side of the road, rounded the big gum tree then climbed the fence on the other side of it. As Jacob was starting to crank the truck over, I heard my name being called somewhere from the other side of the tree. I peered over the branches and saw Steph yelling my name, madly waving her arms.

I followed the path Steph took, ripping my jacket on the barbed wire as I tried to climb through, then hurried toward the two women looking at me.

"Jim, this is June. She's offered to drive us to the prison," she said as I neared them. She seemed more than impatient as she held the door open for me.

"Wait, the prison? Why the pr-" I began, but she slammed the door closed before I could finish. I was getting ready to ask her again as she climbed in but she spoke first.

"Jim, they're letting him go," she said, as June climbed in and fired the engine up.

"WHAT?" was all I could ask, my mind bursting with shock.

"It's been all over the radio, and the morning paper had it on the front page," June said as she sprayed gravel behind us, the tyres squealing a little as she turned the car around.

"Why would they let him go?" I asked.

"The lawyer, some guy named Lovett had sent a letter to a judge in Melbourne and that judge showed it to a bunch of other judges," June said, trying to convey what little information she had.

"DAM IT!" I screamed, punching my arm on the door. "I'm sorry," I said to June, my face burning, unsure of whether I was embarrassed at hitting her car, or angry at what was about to happen. "Did they happen to mention a time?" I asked.

"The radio said 10 o'clock this morning." She gripped the wheel tightly as she sped us along, her Mini rattling and bouncing with each pot hole it hit. Steph lent in to look at June's wristwatch.

"It's 9.24. Should only take 10 minutes to get there. Let's hope," Steph said. I was considering stopping at one of the farm houses we were passing but then more thoughts jumped out. Not everyone had a phone and what if we chose one that didn't. We'd be wasting more time. And what if it did work, who would we call? The new Chief? Even if we could convince him over the phone, which I doubted considering our lack of history, then he would still need to make the call to the prison. And if we called the prison direct, we'd have to wait to be put in touch with the warden, and after our last interaction, I knew that his cooperation would be minimal, if at all. No, we would have to do this one on our own. Ten minutes. June was doing good time, her foot a lot heavier than mine or Steph's. It was our only blessing that morning.

13.

"Ready, Harry?" Ralph had said to him through the bars and then watched as he picked his box up and waited for the door to be unlocked. He noted that the grin was still there and nearly asked him whether there was something else that was making him smile, then decided not to. Ralph escorted Harry to the reception building and had him fill out the final documents then walked him to the big iron gate.

It swung open slowly on rusty and tired hinges, creaking and sounding like a movie soundtrack from one of those horror flicks they play down at the Mayfair on a Saturday afternoon.

Harry turned to the guard, thanked him for his respect, then shook his hand. Ralph later told me he hesitated for a moment, as it was an unwritten rule not to shake an inmate's hand, but Harry had stuck his hand out to him so fast that it caught the young guard off balance, grasping it tightly. He looked him in the eyes and felt his blood turn cold, a dark shadow hiding behind the man's gaze. Then he let his hand go, turned and strolled out, whistling, as if heading out for a morning stroll. Ralph said he felt a chill as he watched him, gooseflesh popping across his arms. His lawyer was waiting out the front, saw his client emerge from the gate and went to embrace him. Then the gate closed and he was gone.

14.

I could see the first glimpses of the prison through the trees as we neared it, Crab Apple sitting high on its hill. As June turned the car into the driveway that led into the carpark, we could already see the line of cars that had come to see the release of Harry Lightman. As June drove into the carpark, we heard the crowd. And they didn't sound happy. When she found a space near the back, Steph and I climbed out, thanking June for her help. I tried to listen to what they were shouting. At first, I thought they were angry that he was being released. It made sense, considering this was the community that he had terrorized. But then my stomach sank and terrified realization set in as I saw who the crowd was. They weren't the people from the community, townsfolk who came to watch. They were reporters, photographers, people that Lovett had contacted to come and witness "the righting of a monumental injustice", as he put it.

"What's happened?" I asked the first man I came to, a young guy, carrying a notepad in one hand and a pen in the other. His cheeks were flushed, his expression far from happy.

"They let him go early," he said and my worst fears surfaced.

15.

189

Of course, they had. To avoid an already embarrassing situation from becoming an outright spectacle, the prison had sent a messenger to Lovett's hotel room before dawn that morning, which also happened to be at the Railway Hotel. The guard advised him he had five minutes to get ready and accompany him back to the prison.

Lovett had jumped in his car and followed the officer back to Crab Apple, the guards on top of the wall watching him to ensure he didn't attempt to contact anybody. That son-of-a-bitch had no choice but to stand there and wait for his client.

As Steph and I were discovering her car battery dead, courtesy of a couple of power-sucking headlights, Ralph was escorting Harry to the prison's gate. They released him at 7am, just as the sun broke across the eastern horizon. A single photographer had managed to capture the embrace between lawyer and client, a young man by the name of Harry Bowden. He worked for the Daylesford Times, a small newspaper that was about to show the whole world Richard Lovett embracing his client as he emerged from the prison gates after being unjustly imprisoned for almost 20 years. The young reporter had awoken early, having had a suspicion that Harry Lightman may be released early, a suspicion that paid off in spades.

Young Harry nearly missed the entire thing. He had set off for Crab Apple at just after 3 that morning, as Steph and I were still enjoying our lightning-infused nap. He had pedalled for two and half hours, arriving at the prison a little after 6. He decided to park his bike next to a gum tree that sat on the edge of the carpark, then sat next to it, staring at the stars. He double checked his camera a couple of times, then rested it on his lap as he stared at Jupiter, burning brightly over the tree tops beside the prison walls. He had nodded off, tired from his early morning ride and almost slept through the whole thing. He slept through the car driving past him as the officer left to fetch Lovett. He slept through two cars returning a short time later.

What finally woke the young man from his slumber, was the eerie screeching of the massive iron gate as it opened up for Lightman to exit. He opened his eyes just in time, recognising Lovett instantly. He picked himself up, grasped his camera tightly and ran as close as he could. He stopped just in time to capture Lovett take a couple of steps forward and embrace Lightman tightly. The angle of the photo showed a beaming Lightman and the back of Lovett's head. Then he sat back and watched as both men climbed into Lovett's car. Harry wound his window down almost immediately. Young Harry watched old Harry as they drove past him, and as he did, a tune drifted to his ears, a smooth whistle that young Harry recognized immediately. It was the same song his mother would play on her piano. Fur Elise.

By the time the first reporter had arrived for the advertised time, young Harry was already pedaling hard to return to the office and develop the piece of history now contained within his camera. As Steph and I were asking another young reporter what was happening, young Harry was standing open-mouthed in his darkroom, holding the developed photograph in his hand. What made it even more special was that it was the first time that young Harry had used colour film. He had spent the extra money on the film only the day before, paying four times more than the normal black and white option.

He showed the photo to his editor, the man nearly falling off his chair. The photo was sold and resold, copies being sent across the world. The St. Petersburg Times in Florida, the first newspaper to use a colour photo in its pages earlier that year, offered the editor $10 000 for exclusive rights to use the photo. Harry's editor counter-offered them exclusivity for the colour part only, offering the black and white version to everybody else. The paper accepted and by the end of the week, young Harry Bowden was riding a shiny brand-spanking new Harley Davidson to his appointments. He had also been paid a $1500 bonus by the editor, a pretty poor sum considering the editor had managed to amass a total of just under $65 big ones from the sale of the photo alone, but you couldn't have wiped the smile off the lad's face. The kid had smashed one out of the park.

16.

Steph and I were sitting on the log fence as the reporters continued their anger-fueled tirade. They had begun chanting at one stage, one older man standing atop the steps that led to the front gate yelling and screaming for the governor to meet them. Thomas never made an appearance. There was a single guard standing on top of the wall, his rifle held up, cradled into his shoulder. We watched them yelling for Thomas, yelling for a statement, yelling for Lightman to be brought back.

We sat in silence, Steph smoking. There were no words needed for how we felt. He had gotten away with it. In some crazy way, the Daylesford Devil had beaten the system. He had help of course, but in the end, he had walked from the prison a free man.

The only way I can describe how I felt at that moment was that I was numb. I felt numb all over. My ribs hurt, my arm throbbed, my head felt heavy, but it was in my gut that I felt that heaviness, that low empty feeling of defeat.

"We have to get him, Steph. We have to speak to the Chief." She looked at me, her head nodding slowly as she butted her cigarette out on the log.

A car started just in front of us and I saw that the crowd was finally dispersing. Several other cars also fired up and began to leave the prison car park. We waited until they were all gone from the steps, had all walked back to their cars and were heading back to wherever they had come from. We stood as we watched the last of them leave, following slowly behind his brothers. I was about to ask Steph if we should call for a taxi when a very strong reflection caught my eye. It was the sun bouncing off the windscreen of one of the remaining cars. There were about a dozen or so and with all the other cars that had filled this lot a few moments before, hadn't noticed the one parked almost out of sight along the far edge of the park. It was a black Mercedes, and I knew instantly what I wanted to do next. I tapped Steph's shoulder, pointing at the car and I saw her face grow dim. She nodded, understanding what I meant to do.

Chapter 12: Secrets and Lies

1.

"Where's the Doc?" Steph asked the guard as he opened the smaller door that led into the prison. There were two guards standing on top of the inner wall, neither of them interested in us.

"He's in the med unit," he said, pointing at the only building that remained from the old Hancock farm, its tin roof glaring in the morning sunshine. Its thick bluestone walls looked ominous as we approached it, its small windows almost beckoning to us as we climbed the steps and walked through the door.

There was very little activity as we walked down the hallway, muffled voices coming from several of the cells that lined the corridor. At the end of the hall was the main medical unit, several beds set up like a normal hospital ward. Two of the six beds were occupied, a single guard sitting in one corner reading a book. A nurse was sitting behind a desk and looked at us as we walked in.

"Dr. Levinson?" Steph asked him and he pointed back down the corridor.

"Last door on the right," he said, looking back at the folder he was flicking through. Steph and I turned and left the room, making our way back down the corridor. When we reached the last door, we realized that it was the door we had been looking through when we watched Levinson have lunch with Lightman. I opened the door, expecting to find the doctor in the room but it sat empty. I also remembered how Lightman had disappeared into an adjoining room when the Doc had invited us in. We entered the room completely and closed the door behind us. It stood exactly like it had previously. I looked at the door that was set into the other wall and walked toward it. As I reached for the door handle, a slow low thudding came through it, sounding muffled and distant. I paused, waited, then when it stopped, turned the handle and opened the door.

2.

The room resembled more of a tiny kitchen than a medical room. I remembered that this room may have been the original kitchen that served the Hancock's back in the day. There was an old oven, the old timber box now empty, sitting beside it. It seemed a strange room to have Lightman wait while we were engaged in conversation with Levinson in the adjoining room, considering the facility. I had no doubt that there were a lot of questionable practices occurring here thanks to the good doc.

The low thudding began again, once, twice, three times then ceased. It sounded like it was coming through the walls. I looked at Steph but she shrugged her shoulders. I pointed to the exit and was about to head back out when I stopped and froze. The room only had the one door that led in, no windows and no visible ventilation. It had a small walk in pantry to the left, empty shelves lining both its walls. The far wall had a timber trellis wedged against it that had been used to hang fresh produce and jars of herbs from. The hooks, now a rusty brown, were still jutting out looking like greedy fingers. What stopped me in my tracks was a breeze that was coming from the pantry. I turned, walked towards the pantry door and stopped, closing my eyes.

"Jim?" Steph asked. I held up one finger, feeling the breeze on my face. I opened my eyes and waved for her to come to me. I pushed her into place and watched as she felt the breeze, her face peering into the darkness. She took a step into the pantry, feeling her way forward. The low light that lit the kitchen wasn't quite bright enough to light the pantry, its rays fading about halfway into the small room. Steph held out her hands and felt along the trellis. As she touched it, feeling the breeze come through from beyond it, we heard the low, slow thumping start again. Only this time, it wasn't coming through the walls. This time, the thudding came from directly ahead.

She looked at me over her shoulder, saw me point at the trellis and then watched as she slipped her fingers through it, grasping it tightly. The trellis acted like a door, old hinges creaking as it swung back into the pantry. Steph took a step back to allow it passage then looked at me, holding it open. My temples were throbbing so hard that for a moment, I thought that the thumping we heard had in fact been me.

3.

There were bluestone steps leading down into a dark passage. Steph and I waited for our eyes to adjust as much as possible before we slowly made our way down, each step taking a few seconds to navigate. When we finally reached the bottom, a dozen or so steps behind us, we were confronted with a low-roofed tunnel. I had to duck a little to prevent smacking my head on some of the rocks that were jutting out from the ceiling. The tunnel was pitch black, the light from the pantry all but faded out, and for a brief moment, Steph and I had to feel our way along the rocky wall. But after about 40 yards, a new light source was fading in from somewhere ahead of us. There was another bend a few yards ahead and as we edged our way forward, we could make out a larger cavity, something like an underground cave. The thumping began again, coming from somewhere directly in front of us now.

The cave resembled a small room, an electric light hanging from the ceiling. The tunnel continued on the other side of this opening, disappearing into more darkness further along. There were a couple of chairs, one lying on its side, and a small table against one wall. We heard groaning coming from somewhere on the other side of the table and could see movement. It was the doctor, lying face-up, the handle of a knife protruding from his chest. I ran over to him and lifted his head up a little, blood leaking from the left side of his mouth. He gargled something, then spat a large wad of blood to his right. There was a piece of timber in his hand with which he had been trying to raise the alarm.

"What happened?" I cried.

"Please, you have to find him," he whispered.

"I'll get help," Steph said from behind me but the doctor spoke up, begging her to wait.

"No, please, you have to hear me out first." His voice was quiet and laboured, his lungs gargling with every strained breath. I took off my jacket and folded it then placed it beneath his head. Steph tried to open his shirt to see his wound but his face contorted in pain and she stopped. She saw the piece of paper that had been pinned to the doctor's chest with the knife and pointed at it. I saw it, noticing writing on it, blood smeared across the five letters.

JAMES

I couldn't pull the paper free without tearing it apart and thought it better just to leave it be for the time being. The doctor took a couple of garbled breaths then began to speak, almost whispering most of his words.

"I'm so sorry. I was blinded by my own need for glory. My research took me to places I should never have gone," he coughed, more blood trickling down his chin, "but Harry was such a perfect specimen."

"Who is Loui?" I asked. He raised his eyes to mine, realising that I knew some or maybe even all of what he had been trying to hide.

"Loui is Harry's brother. Only, he IS Harry. You see, Harry has three distinct personalities. Harry is the oldest, the one you speak to most of the time. The second personality, the one born when he saw his mother killed, was Eddie. Eddie appeared on Harry's sixth birthday," he rasped, wheezed, then spat again," Eddie is the quiet one." His head suddenly turned to Steph, his eyes fixing on hers. Her head began to shake from side to side even before he began to speak, knowing of the words that were about to rise from his lips. "I'm sorry, my dear. Eddie is your father." Steph screamed; her worst fear finally confirmed. I tried to reach out to her but she pushed my hand away and turned from us, running down the tunnel, continuing to wherever it led. I called after her but she didn't slow. The doctor looked back at me and grasped my arm.

"What about Loui?" I asked again. He hesitated, then drew in another breath.

"Loui was born the moment that whore bit his penis off. Loui is the embodiment of every bit of anger, despair, rage and hatred Harry has ever experienced. Loui is the younger brother but also the most dangerous. He is the one I have been experimenting with. It's him I have been trying to control" He coughed again.

"Is he the one you've been using MD17471 on?" His eyes grew wide as he heard the name.

"How do you" he began, then realised, ", ah of course, Tami," he said, nodding a little, understanding that she must have left a message. "Do you know what that serum is for, Jim?" I shook my head. "It's designed to reduce the gaps between the personalities in someone suffering from multiple personality disorder. It's supposed to bring them together. Think about the millions of people that suffer from this condition. My work was going to help them all."

"Your work killed innocent people. Is that the price for helping people? To kill more?" It was too late to try and make this man see sense. Even if he did understand his crimes, he would never see the inside of a jail cell. His days had come to an end and he knew it. He would never pay for his crimes and the monster he had created was now out, back in the real world, free to wreak havoc.

"One of the side effects of MD17471 is the propensity for extreme rage. When Loui had too higher dose, his violence grew off the scale. He was uncontrollable. Jim, he's taken the vials."

"Vials?"

"He's taken the entire supply. He can turn himself into-" A coughing fit grabbed him, shaking him violently. I sat, waiting for it to subside

"Was it him that killed the Chief?" I asked when it finally did. The doctor nodded, looking away. I wanted to punch him then, right in the face, remembering what had happened to the chief and his wife. "What about Tami?" I asked, my own anger now growing, my fingers grasping his jacket tighter and tighter. "WHAT ABOUT TAMI?" I screamed into his face. I wanted to grasp the handle of the knife and plunge it deeper, pushing it down until the blade exited through his back, ending his life. But I took a deep breath, fighting my fury and relaxing my grip. I needed this man's information and needed to keep myself under control. Killing him now wouldn't bring Tami back, but his information would help me stop Lightman from killing another. His eyes drifted away from mine as he coughed again, a large chunk of congealed blood landing on my hand. I grimaced as I wiped it onto his jacket.

"I'm sorry about Tami, I really am. She threatened me, threatened to end my research. I didn't want to hurt her, I truly didn't. But Harry asked to finish what he had started the first time and threatened to expose me if I didn't help," he paused.

"And? If he did expose you?" I asked, but he either chose to ignore me or didn't hear my question.

"And he promised me it would be quick and painless. I'm sorry, I know I was blinded." He suddenly reached into one of his jacket pockets, feeling around. For a moment, I panicked, expecting to see a gun or something, but then saw him pull a small black book with a leather strap and metal clasp out of his pocket, instead. He held it out to me as he coughed again, the blood now thick and spraying almost fountain-like from his lips. I pulled away a little, shielding my face. He held the book up to me, holding it out. "I need you to have this, Jim."

"What is it?" I asked, taking it. I could hear footsteps coming back down the tunnel. I hoped it was Steph returning, her own shock under control. I turned and strained my eyes, a dark shadow slowly emerging. Her head was lowered, her face looking grave and angry, but I felt relief seeing her walking back. I needed her with me, needing her to hear and remember, to corroborate in case there were questions.

"It's his diary, well, their diary. All of Harry's personalities have written in it, but I think you will understand him a lot more once you've read it for yourself." I opened the clasp and flicked through the book, writing filling almost every page. There were blank ones towards the back, but for the most part, it was filled.

"When did he start this?" I asked, reading a couple of words here and there.

"Harry began that diary his first year in prison. But he writes a lot about the time before then, his childhood, his youth and yes, about the murders he committed back in the 30s."

"Why didn't you give this to anybody?" I said, anger building again, shocked that this piece of shit withheld such crucial evidence. He coughed again, long and bloody and I had to wait a few moments for him to catch his breath again. His eyes suddenly closed and for a moment I thought I'd lost him, that he had finally departed, but then he opened them again, looking directly at me.

"I will pay for my sins when I meet the almighty. But you, Jim. You have to find him. You have to find that monster and kill him, it's the only way to be sure." He gurgled again the colour now draining from his face, his time almost up. Steph knelt down beside us, her face cold with hatred.

"Does he know about me?" she asked in an almost snarl. He turned to her and for a moment watched as he considered the question. "DOES HE KNOW ABOUT ME?" she suddenly screamed, grabbing his scruff and shaking him up and down. He winced, then began coughing as she released her hold, his head dropping back into my lap. When the coughing fit subsided, he tried breathing but it sounded shallower now, the final moments now clear in his eyes. He looked at Steph again, and almost apologetically, began to nod. He tried to speak but the words were mostly just faint wisps of air, no sound accompanying the shapes being formed by his lips. His eyes suddenly opened wide, his fingers grasping mine as he tried his hardest to tell us something. We couldn't make it out and during his final seconds, it was Steph who suddenly grabbed him again. Her question sent chills through my veins, the gravity of the question becoming clearer with each passing second.

"Does he know about Judith?" He never answered, his eyes growing wider and wider until all the muscles in his face suddenly relaxed, then receded, his body becoming limp in my lap. His eyes remained fixed on Steph but now the pupils looked vacant, almost glazed over. She screamed, as only a mother would, the cold fear hitting me like an avalanche. Steph jumped to her feet, pulling me up as she went, her strength now impossibly strong, driven by her maternal instinct to protect her child. I jumped to my feet, then remembered the note, bent back down and with a mighty heave, pulled the blade from the dead man's chest. I slid the note off the blade, then into my pocket as I began running after Steph, her shadow already thirty or so yards down the tunnel. I saw a glimmer of shine on the table as I sprinted past it and saw a bunch of keys, the biggest with a distinctive star engraved on it. They were Levinson's car keys. I turned, snatched them up and continued running, never breaking my stride, continuing to follow the sounds of Steph's footfalls, now somewhere in the darkness ahead.

4.

The agony in my ribs seemed to grow with every step, then became secondary as my head painfully brushed against a rocky outcrop. I felt a warm trickle of blood run down the back of my neck as the stairs leading up to the kitchen finally came into view. Steph had already climbed them and was now pushing through the trellis. I had to steady myself as I began to climb, then felt her hand grab my arm as she helped me up. I tried as hard as I could, but still only managed one step at a time, Steph again shooting ahead when I finally pushed through into the ancient kitchen. We ran into the adjoining room and Steph ran out into the corridor, ripping the door open. It smacked the inside wall with a thud loud enough to draw comments from somewhere further up and I saw the guard standing at the end of the corridor looking at what the commotion was about.

"Call the station, ask for Chief Richards," I yelled at him, "Levinson is dead in the tunnel, look in the pantry." He nodded; his mouth now agape. He hesitated, then jumped when I screamed "GO, NOW!" at him. He finally bolted, as I turned and continued following Steph, already turning the corner at the other end of the hallway.

5.

"OPEN THE GATE! NOW!" She screamed at the guards as we ran across the grass. They stood there for a moment, like deer caught in headlights. She flashed her badge at them then repeated her command louder with more conviction. "OPEN IT, RIGHT NOW!" Her feet never lost momentum, her thin body squeezing through the opening gap of the huge gate. When she saw Pete standing at the small door on the other side of the wall, she only needed to yell once, the guard jumping to get the door open for her. I must have looked like a sorry sight, half limping, trying to keep up with her, blood seeping from my head, my right arm clutching my chest. To our relief, no one stopped us to ask questions, our way now clear to the car park before us.

"Take Levinson's car," I yelled at Steph, and she turned almost immediately towards the black Mercedes. It was unlocked and she climbed into the driver's seat, holding her hand out for me to throw her the keys. For a brief second I wished for June Trapnell to drive us, her lead foot needed now more than ever. I flung the keys at her, then ripped the passenger door open. Steph swung herself in and started the car in what seemed one motion. Then to my amazement, Stephanie Connor dropped the clutch and punched the accelerator with such force that I was thrown against my seat, the sound of the tyres grabbing at the gravel car park and spraying a jet of rocks and sand in a long arc behind us. The car lurched hard one way then flung the opposite way as she spun the wheel, steering the nose of the car into the driveway that led out onto the main road, never slowing, the tyres screaming in protest as she swung out onto the bitumen. We missed being turned into jam by a mere couple of yards, a truck ambling its way along the road as we blasted out directly in front of it. I screamed a little, then grinned comically as I saw Jacob in the truck's cabin, eyes wide and arm outstretched from the window, one fist shaking at us.

6.

Steph never took her eyes off the road, frozen concentration etched on her face, imagining the worst. I reached across and gave her forearm a squeeze. I'm not sure whether she felt it, or whether she was even aware that I was in the car.

"Steph," I tried to whisper, but she didn't respond, either not hearing me or ignoring me completely. "STEPH," I yelled at her, this time getting a short sideways glance.

"He's going after her, Jim. I know he is." The fear in her voice sent fear through my own mind. I was about to say something, but just as my lips opened, a patrol car came flying over the hill before us, its lights flashing and siren blaring. As it neared, the driver, an officer I hadn't seen before, pointed at us, his partner waving at us to pull over. Steph either didn't see them or chose to ignore them, never slowing. I turned to watch as the patrol car slowed, swung off the road, then turned in a sharp U-turn to pursue us. Steph continued to concentrate on the road ahead, rounding the next bend, leaving the patrol car far behind us.

7.

We had virtually no chance of avoiding the cow though, the beast standing almost in the middle of the road as we rounded a bend, hitting it virtually square in the back legs, the sickening crunch of bone and metal filling the car's cabin. Steph had just enough time let out a short "AH," before the tyres squealed for grip and the rear end of the driver's side clipped a small tree that skirted the road. The car spun in the opposite direction, lurching down the embankment, then skidding across the field. We finally came to a stop about 40 yards from the road, the rear of the car twisted sideways. The front driver's side of the car was a mess of broken headlights, bits of blood and torn metal, as well as two flat tyres.

I saw a small trickle of blood above Steph's left eyebrow, her head having connected hard with the steering wheel. I was relatively unscathed, although I couldn't confirm the state of my underwear. Thankfully, there was no immediate smell.

"You OK?" I asked her. She groaned, then hissed as she saw the bonnet hanging from one hinge.

"Bloody cow," was all she said, before climbing out of the wreck. Just as I was reaching for the handle, I heard the siren of the patrol car approach, then the tyres screeching to a halt beside the road. I could just make out the revolving red light on top of the patrol car's roof.

Two officers now came into view from the road, shouting something incomprehensible. I opened my door and fell out onto the grass, landing on my knees. When I stood, I felt Steph again, helping me to my feet.

"Thanks," I muttered to her, eyeing the cops off. We walked back towards the road, quickly trying to feel for any injuries we may have inflicted on ourselves, but I felt OK apart from the aches and pains that were present before. Steph also looked OK, the only injury seeming to be the blood on her brow, now leaving a thin trail down the side of her face.

"Boss wants to see you. Had a call from the Warden. He's pretty pissed, Steph," one of the officers said as we approached. He was about the same age as Steph, his partner maybe a bit younger.

"Not now, Nigel," Steph said to him.

"But the Chief said-"

"I SAID NOT NOW!" And that was when the young officer made the mistake of trying to grab her arm.

"He told us -" was all he could get out, before a right hook connected flush with his nose. I had heard of tomato punches before, but that was the first time I had actually witnessed one in person. And, one thrown by a girl. Let me tell you, it was fucking impressive. It wasn't the crunch of his nose that made it impressive. No. What made that punch so unbelievable was the blood that jettisoned from either side of his face. It sprayed both of his shoulders simultaneously, a warm funnel of red claret fountaining outwards. He screamed in pain, both hands coming up and holding his face as his knees buckled. Steph never slowed, stepping past him and continuing towards the car. The other cop just stood there, staring at his mate now kneeling on the ground.

"Stay or come, but decide right now," was all she said to the two officers, before climbing into the driver's seat, the engine still idling quietly. The cop that was standing took one final look at Steph then helped his friend to his feet, supporting his weight as they tried to run to us. Steph was already gunning the engine as they both slid into the rear seat, one almost diving in and sliding across to the other side.

"You broke my fucking nose," bleeding cop said as she spewed dirt into the trees, the tyres finding grip when they hit bitumen.

"It'll heal. I have to get to my baby," she said coldly.

"Your sister?" the other cop asked. Steph looked at me then turned enough to look the kid in the face.

"No, my daughter."

9.

The drive through Cider Hill was relatively quiet. There were a few more cars parked along the roads, thanks to the extra influx of reporters to cover the release of Harry Lightman, but our drive continued almost as swiftly as it did out on the open road. We could see quite a few extra cars parked out the front of the Railway hotel, as well as the Stanford, further up the street. Each of the open cafes had their share of customers as well, breakfast at the top of most people's agendas. We could see groups of men in suits congregating around tables, arms waving about as they all told of their travels. Most would be trying to find Lightman of course, to get that exclusive interview, but I knew that would never happen. Lightman had been too smart, knowing how to evade them all. He seemed to have a plan, but until that moment, I didn't know what it was.

Steph yanked the wheel left, the tyres instantly protesting. Her house sat at the far end of this street and as she raced toward it, I saw no other traffic or movement along its length. She slowed the cruiser just enough to swing its huge nose into her driveway, slamming the car to a halt. Tomato cop wasn't expecting such a sudden stop and his head snapped forward, his nose striking the back of her chair, then bouncing back as the car jolted to a halt.

"Aaahh, FUCK!" he screamed, grabbing his face with one hand, the other steadying himself, but Steph paid no attention. She had her door open even before the car had fully stopped, now already bounding up the stairs two at a time.

"STEPH?" I yelled, but she ignored me. I climbed out of the cruiser and scanned the front of the house. Nothing looked out of the ordinary, yet I had a growing feeling of dread, like I knew something was out of place but couldn't tell what. I looked across the fence at Mrs. Wong's house, standing silently on its elevated stumps. I was about to follow Steph up the stairs, but then froze as something held my gaze, looking strange in the old lady's front yard. She had a tall hedge that shielded her house from the street, one lone pine standing tall and thin in the centre of her front yard. A thick, round bush was growing to one side of it and it was there that I saw something that shouldn't have been there. A pair of men's brown leather shoes.

10.

I bolstered myself over the fence. I was lucky as it only stood as high as my waist, so swinging a leg over it didn't aggravate me too much. When I was over, I stole another glance at the house, now seeing the front door ajar and the window curtains drawn. I looked back at the shoes and saw that one lay empty, its sole flat on the grass. The other one had a foot in it, the leg only visible from the calf down, the top half disappearing into the bush. As I neared the bush, I could already see the blood dripping from its leaves, thick wads of it adorning the bush like Christmas tinsel.

"Who is that?" a voice asked from beside me. It was the young officer now standing behind me. As we neared the feet, he bent and grabbed the legs of the man, then began dragging him out. I recognized him instantly, his face setting off alarm bells in my head, alarm bells that exploded when I heard Steph.

"JUDE!" she cried from her porch. I turned to look and her eyes met mine. Even from the distance between us, I saw her face react to the sight of the man lying at my feet. She was running in an instant and hurdled the fence easily.

"STEPH, WAIT!" I yelled, but there was no stopping her. Richard Lovett was lying dead at my feet and that meant Lightman had been, or still was, inside this house. His throat had been bitten, a neat hole sitting where his Adam's apple should have been. And as if that hadn't been enough, Harry had also pushed his fingers into the man's eye sockets, popping both eyeballs like jellies, their oozy insides weeping down the dead man's cheeks. Ants had already begun to sample the eye nectar and were busy scurrying about his face as the young cop lost his breakfast.

I ran as fast as my legs would carry me to the stairs, already hearing the opening of doors from inside.

"Jude? Jude honey?" I heard Steph whisper. I ripped the front door open and ran inside as it thudded against the wall. I managed to take three steps, the living room door standing open on my left. And that was when I heard her scream. A long and painful shrill that sent gooseflesh all over my body, the hair on the back of my neck standing on end in an instant.

"Fuck," I muttered under my breath and followed the sound of the hysterical crying, preparing myself for the worst.

11.

It isn't often that you sigh relief when confronted by a dead body. They are all sad, confronting and tragic, when you realise that it means the end of a human life. But seeing Mrs. Wong at that moment and not a young 7-year-old girl, was such a relief.

Steph was standing over the dead woman, grabbing her hair and crying hysterically. I went to her, put my arms around her shoulders and pulled her away from Mrs. Wong, pulling her out of the room. She resisted, still frantically calling her daughter's name, with no answer in return. As I managed to persuade Steph into the living room, I heard the approaching ambulance. She was inconsolable, her words low and repeating, over and over.

"Jude, no, no baby. Jude, no." After the ambulance officers realised there was no helping the late Richard Lovett, or the very dead Mrs. Wong, they attended to Steph, first trying to calm her, then finally sedating her. They placed her on a stretcher and loaded her into the back of their van, her voice now almost inaudible as another patrol car arrived. It was Chief Richards, looking grim and confused. He gave Steph a once over before they closed the door, bent and whispered something into her ear then patted her shoulder. Then as the ambulance left with Steph now safe in the back, he turned to me.

"Jim, I need to know what the fuck is going on." When I didn't answer him immediately, my eyes still watching the ambulance driving away, he grabbed my shoulder and spoke into my face.

"JIM." I turned to him, myself not feeling the best. "Jim, can you come down to the station and give us a few minutes? Please?" I nodded and the young cop who lost his breakfast beckoned to me, putting me into a patrol car, then drove me to Cider Hill Police Station. Once there, he helped me from the car and led me inside.

12.

A lady brought me a hot cup of coffee a short time later and told me that the chief would be along shortly. He didn't disappoint, walking through the door before I finished half the beverage, carrying a cup of his own. Once seated in Rademeyer's chair, he lent forward and looked at me for a moment. I think he was contemplating *how* he was going to talk me, not so much as *what* he was going to say.

"Jim, I appreciate the help you have given this department in recent days," he began, and from experience, knew that this wasn't going to end well. He continued, still watching me intently, "and I understand you yourself have suffered some incredible personal loss as well."

"Here it comes," I thought, "the big BUT."

"But I need you to understand that you are no longer a police officer. This department is eternally grateful for the help you've given Officer Connor, and I hope she makes a speedy recovery. God knows we need all the help we can get. Jim, I need to know what happened. If you are going to be playing with our department, then I need to be kept in the loop ALL the time. Warden Thomas rang me and said that two very irate officers were harassing a prominent doctor in the prison." I wanted to scream at him, tell him just what a fine and upstanding doctor he really was. But I held back, still unsure of the man sitting before me. "Then come running from a building where a dead man is found in some secret tunnel, only to drive off in his car after flashing police badges and demanding to be let out. How did you know he was there in the first place?" I considered telling him everything, bringing him up to speed and having his men out looking for Lightman. But I didn't. I still don't know why, but I just didn't.

"We didn't know he was there, or that there was a secret tunnel. We knew that he had been seeing Lightman every single day thanks to the box of files they gave us. When we heard Lightman had been released and saw Levinson's car in the parking lot, we wanted to talk to him."

"Why?" I pondered the question, then figured I'd throw him a bone, a little one, wrapped in a little white lie.

"Because Lightman is Stephanie Connor's father." His eyes grew so wide that for a moment, I had an amusing image of them popping out and bouncing on the table like ping-pong balls. His jaw hung open as he put his cup down.

"Aaahh, but, what?" was all he could manage in total disbelief.

"And we needed to know if Lightman knew, because if he did, then there was a real possibility that he would go after her daughter."

"Not her sister?" he suddenly asked.

"No. Judith is Stephanie's child. So, as you see, once we found him and knew that Lightman wasn't as innocent as they were making him out to be, we had to go and find Judith, in case Lightman went after her, which he obviously did." He took this new information and tried to understand its implications, trying to make sense of it all. He didn't speak for a long time, finally taking a cigarette out and firing it up. He didn't offer me one.

"Did he say anything?" he finally asked.

"Who?"

"Levinson," he said. I shook my head, again wondering why I wasn't sharing the information.

"No. He had time to say one final, garbled word and then he died."

"How did you find him?"

"We had been in the adjoining room before, the day we first met him. Lightman had been in the room, but then when we came back in, he was gone. We figured there was a corridor or holding cell or something back there. When it turned out to be a dead-end kitchenette, we poked around a bit and felt a breeze coming from the pantry. After that, it wasn't long before we were climbing down the stairs. The rest you know." He took his time, filing the information into his mind. I was about to stand, to shake his hand, thank him for his concern and then head to the hospital. But just as I was getting ready, he opened his mouth and spoke, his words coming so unexpectantly, that it was my turn to be dumbfounded.

"Jim, I want to be straight with you. You understand what it's like to be an officer of the law. You know how important it is to be honest." I wondered whether he knew my story was bullshit, had seen right through it from the beginning. But then he continued. "To have secrets in this job is to play Russian roulette, because if you ever lose one, that secret can give someone the opportunity to hold something over you. And then, that secret becomes power for the other person, leaving you in a rather painful predicament. Secrets like Levinson had. I am not a man to hide secrets, never have. I'm sure by now you will have heard about certain ladies in this town providing services that, well, good Christian folk might see as a very big sin. I'm sure you know that this girl, Tami, was one of them. I'm sorry for your loss, by the way." He paused for a minute, sipped his coffee again, then continued. "I have indulged in their services on more than one occasion and I am not ashamed to admit it. I'm not married; have been living the single man's game all my life. I can tell you straight to your face that no man will ever hold a secret over my head. Never. I will be straight up with you, son. All I ask in return is that you are with me."

"Oh shit," I thought to myself, now feeling like I really did owe him something, and again, almost let him have the lot. But as before, I held back.

"I appreciate your honesty with me, Chief." He shook my hand, giving it an enthusiastic shake then stood. I understood my cue and bid him a good day.

The young cop was standing out in the station foyer as if waiting for me. As I neared him, I finally had a chance to ask him his name.

"Stanley Thornton, Sir," he said.

"Please, don't call me sir. Make it Jim." He shook eagerly then led me outside to his waiting patrol car, opening the door and waiting for me to climb in.

"Where to, Sir? I mean Jim?" he asked as he slid behind the wheel. I didn't need to think about where I wanted to go.

"Would you mind driving me to the hospital, Stan?" He nodded, then began driving with the air of someone who'd been tasked with an important mission, keeping two hands on the wheel and sitting tall and proud in his seat.

13.

We shook hands again as I climbed out of the car in front of the hospital doors, then hurried towards the entrance as Stan drove away. The desk was just inside the doors and I approached the lonely nurse sitting behind it.

"Steph Connor?" I asked her.

"Second floor, Sir. Right when you reach the top of the stairs." I followed her pointing finger and saw a stair well down a long hallway. When I reached the top of the stairs, I turned right as instructed and was again confronted by another desk. A stern looking woman was sitting behind the desk, her face looking as if set in stone.

"Yes? Can I help you?" she asked as I approached, her tone sounding as arrogant as her demeanour.

"James Lawson, ma'am. I'm here to see Stephanie Connor." Imagine my surprise, when her face softened almost immediately into that of a smiling admirer. Imagine my even further surprise, when she opened a drawer and pulled out a copy of Nightmares Unhinged, looked at the back cover and instantly matched the person standing before her.

"Oh, Mr. Lawson. Could I please have an autograph?" I was surprised to find that this lady, dressed in her nursing uniform, an oath sworn to protect and save life, was a fan of the horror that I had written in that book. I happily obliged then thanked her when she pointed me towards a doorway marked ROOM 4. There were two beds in the small room, marked A and B above them. Steph was lying on the bed marked B, her face peaceful and asleep. I could hear the faint snores escaping her nose and bent forward, lightly kissing her cheek. There was an easy chair with a big cushion sitting in one of the corners. I went to it and pushed it beside her bed. I sat down in it and watched for a while, hoping that her dreams were pleasant, far away from the terror she was now draped in with her baby missing. As if to confirm my hope, her lip arched up ever so slightly, a small grin forming on her mouth. I smiled back at her, hoping to have better news for her by the time she awoke.

I pulled out the diary, a thick, black leather-bound vessel which held the ramblings of a mad man. It was also the only lead I had to help me understand just what Lightman was planning. I opened it and began to read then paused, remembering another note that he had left for me. I unfolded the note and read the words, the single line that he had written there. It was more of an answer than a question and as I sank deeper into the chair I smiled, finally understanding that sometimes a killer's signature was so much more.

Hey James,
Do you like being watched when you eat?

Author's Note

I hope you have enjoyed The Final Alibi. The second novel, The Devil's Confession is available for pre-order right now. I cannot wait to share with you, just how far Harry will go to ensure his plan's success. I hope I haven't made the story too dark, too detailed with its often-gruesome reality. To me, Harry *is* the gruesome detail, a monster who doesn't care about the thoughts of others, only interested in fueling his hunger.

When I began this story, I had no idea where the characters were going to lead me. Imagine my surprise, when I discovered that this story would be told in 3 separate books, all a part of the greater tale, yet each with a distinct part to play.

If you enjoyed this book then please consider leaving a review for which I will be eternally grateful. I hope you will stick around and give The Devil's Confession a read. I promise that it will be far more graphic than this title, delving into the mind of the monster himself. You can subscribe to my website for the latest updates, news on upcoming releases as well as some free stuff.

From the bottom of my heart, I humbly thank you for reading my story.

Simon King

www.booksbysimonking.com

Made in the USA
Monee, IL
11 November 2020